# Gardner spotted the black-clad intruder and froze

Reaction came a heartbeat later and he was in motion, crouching, dodging toward the open doorway, snapping up the H&K P-7 pistol for a quick shot on the fly.

The intruder's Uzi stuttered, spewing bullets, gouging divots from the walls. His own shot didn't seem to score before a parabellum slug ripped through his shoulder and slammed him against the doorjamb.

Gardner dropped his side arm and had a vague impression of it bouncing on the carpet, then he lost a moment, while the pain and shock took over, shutting down his mind. When he came back in focus seconds later, he was lying on his back, the black-clad stranger looming over him. The muzzle of the Uzi, aimed directly at his face, looked like a storm drain from Gardner's position on the floor.

"Who are you?" the traitor managed to ask.

"I'm the guy who's taking you away from all this," Mack Bolan replied. "We need to have a little talk about the Farm."

# MACK BOLAN ®

## The Executioner

# DON PENDLETON'S
# EXECUTIONER®
## THE
## CRISIS POINT

## A GOLD EAGLE BOOK FROM
# WORLDWIDE®

TORONTO • NEW YORK • LONDON
AMSTERDAM • PARIS • SYDNEY • HAMBURG
STOCKHOLM • ATHENS • TOKYO • MILAN
MADRID • WARSAW • BUDAPEST • AUCKLAND

First edition August 1995
ISBN 0-373-61200-1

Special thanks and acknowledgment to
Mike Newton for his contribution to this work.

CRISIS POINT

They talk of a man betraying his country, his friends, his sweetheart. There must be a moral bond first. All a man can betray is his conscience.

—Joseph Conrad

Betrayal in the name of God and country is an old, tired story. Every traitor has a convenient excuse for his actions, but I'm not buying it. This time, we nip the problem in the bud, and those responsible are picking up the tab…in blood.

—Mack Bolan

To the memory of Charles Beckwith. God keep.

# PROLOGUE

*Hampton Roads, Virginia*

The cabin cruiser *Southern Belle* was making decent time. Not racing, which would certainly have called attention to the vessel and her temporary crew, but holding steady to her course and clocking the equivalent of thirty miles per hour. Seated in the stern, relaxing in a plastic lounge chair with his feet up on the rail, Ahmed Jazmil was satisfied.

It wouldn't be much longer now before he went to work.

Beside him on the deck, a heavy duffel bag contained his tools. When he was done with them, he would drop them overboard—a burial at sea that would leave no evidence for the police.

The area presented an embarrassment of targets. To the north, there were museums and war memorials, as well as the NASA Langley Research Center. On the southern flank, the U.S. Army Corps of Engineers disposal area, a naval hospital, the Norfolk Naval Base and the Little Creek Naval Amphibious Base.

So many targets, and so little time.

In fact, Jazmil didn't intend to strike at any of these so-inviting targets. Military bases were a risky proposition. Stiff security made them a job for suicide commandos. It was possible that he would be selected for a dead-end mission in the days or weeks ahead, but for the moment every soldier counted. Wasting lives wasn't an option with the task at hand.

It had been no great challenge slipping into the United States. Jazmil had flown from Paris to Jamaica, Kingston to Atlanta, using an Egyptian passport. His companions—

seventeen in all—had come by different routes: New York and Boston, Philadelphia, Chicago and Detroit, New Orleans. None of them was armed when they arrived in the United States. It would have been too risky, and weapons were the easiest commodity of all to come by in America.

Five weeks had passed since the last man had arrived in the States, and while Jazmil hadn't been briefed on all the targets—a security precaution to protect the several teams in case of an arrest—he could track their progress in the headlines: seven dead in a Manhattan bomb blast; three dead in Chicago, with a dozen badly injured; costly damage to a synagogue in Baltimore; a federal office building scarred by hand grenades and automatic weapons in Atlanta.

They had so far refrained from taking credit in the press, a hedge against providing the authorities with any leads that might assist them in their manhunt. There would be publicity to spare when they were finished with their mission and safely back on friendly ground, beyond the reach of FBI and CIA.

The cabin cruiser had begun its southward turn into the mouth of the Elizabeth River, approaching the Norfolk International Terminal. The vessels moored along this waterfront were merchant ships, unarmed, unguarded. Waiting. Ripe for the attack.

Americans were known to worship money. It explained their foreign policy—support for Israel and the Arab traitors who controlled the flow of Middle Eastern oil to the United States, suppression of the freedom fighters who were battling to depose tyrannical, reactionary governments around the world.

Jazmil was young, nineteen years old, but he had an old man's heart and soul. He had been steeped in history from birth, the details of his people's suffering drummed into him before he learned to read and write. At sixteen he had joined the movement, entered training as a Hezbollah commando, learning all the skills that he would need to kill—and stay alive—when he went off to war.

He had been lucky so far. Some of those who entered training with him were dead now, killed on border raids in

Israel, missions in Beirut, the Bekaa Valley, elsewhere. He didn't grieve their loss, though he would miss them. They had done their duty, sacrificed their lives for something greater than themselves.

Jazmil could do no less, but he didn't expect to die this day.

Not yet.

The *Southern Belle* was turning, heading back in the direction it had come from, toward the open strait. The cruiser would soon be passing the merchant ships, warehouses on the dock, vehicles, workmen bustling about their daily tasks.

Jazmil reached down, unzipped the canvas duffel bag and reached inside. The rocket launcher was a throwaway, constructed out of fiberglass, a tube that folded in upon itself. He pulled a safety pin and drew the launcher to full extension, then repeated the procedure with the other tubes, until four launchers lay beside him, lined up on the deck.

He felt the cabin cruiser slowing, the pilot giving him his shot. The terrorist picked up the launcher farthest from his chair and braced it on his shoulder, peering through the sights. His left hand cupped the forward tube, supporting it while the fingers of his right hand curled around the trigger and squeezed.

The armor-piercing rocket sped across the water, trailing brilliant flames. The target was a truck, backed up against a warehouse loading dock, but Jazmil didn't wait to see the missile strike.

At once he dropped the empty launcher and reached for the second tube in line. He shifted slightly, tracking with the second launcher, sighting on a warehouse where the giant doors stood open, crates of merchandise stacked up inside.

The shock wave from the first explosion rolled across the water like a thunderclap, and Jazmil fired the second missile from a range of eighty yards. A group of workmen on the warehouse loading dock had stopped to gape at the explosion, several of them pointing, but they didn't see the rocket coming for them on its wings of fire.

One stevedore glanced up just in time to see death looming and tried to dodge aside. Too late. The rocket clipped him, spun the tiny figure like a top and disappeared inside the warehouse. Flame and shrapnel spewed out across the loading dock as Jazmil cast the empty tube aside and reached for number three.

He picked out figures in the wheelhouse of a freighter moored against the pier, all staring down and pointing at the *Southern Belle*. Jazmil took aim at one of the unhappy faces, squeezing off his third shot at a greater elevation. Behind him, flames from the rocket's backblast scorched paint and varnish on the deck, but he wasn't concerned about the boat's long-term condition. At the moment he was interested in following the rocket's flight and watching it explode on impact with the freighter's bridge. A fiery mushroom sprouted there, and in a heartbeat it was raining glass and blackened, twisted scraps of steel.

One rocket left, and the terrorist raised the launcher with a mounting sense of urgency. The cabin cruiser's pilot had good nerves, but Jazmil felt the vessel straining, anxious to be off and running. He chose a mark at random—it appeared to be some kind of fast-food stand, a giant cup of coffee painted on the wall—and let his final rocket fly.

Before the high-explosive round was fairly gone, the *Southern Belle* lurched forward, digging at the water with its screws and throwing up a wake of churning foam. Jazmil was staggered, almost lost his balance, but he saved it with a firm grip on the rail.

Across the water, close to ninety yards away, the fast-food stand disintegrated, one explosion followed by another as the armor-piercing rocket touched off flammable materials inside. He wished the owners and their patrons painful death.

Two by two, Jazmil grabbed the empty launcher tubes and pitched them far across the rail into the swirling water. Hideously they appeared to float at first, but soon they filled with water, and the metal hardware of the sight and trigger mechanisms took them down.

All gone.

They still had weapons on the cruiser—a Colt Commando 5.56 mm carbine and an Uzi submachine gun, as well as a cache of semiautomatic pistols, just in case—but there would be no trace of the LAW rocket launchers. If investigators somehow found the tubes and managed to retrieve them from the bottom, Jazmil was convinced submersion would eradicate all fingerprints and other useful evidence.

They would have other ways, he realized. The rocket launchers would be numbered by their manufacturer, thus traceable to point of origin, but that would be no great help to the FBI. The rockets had been manufactured under military contract for the U.S. Army, later stolen from a base in Georgia. If the worst scenario came true and federal agents found the greedy soldier who had sold the weapons, they would only have the middleman. If *he* cracked under questioning, enough time should have elapsed for Jazmil and his comrades to complete their mission in the States.

The main event was coming. Not just yet, but they were making progress. Every blow he struck against America, the Great Satan, was a blow in favor of his people. Someday, when the holy war was won, Jazmil would be a hero to Islamic faithful everywhere. He might not live to see it, but that scarcely mattered. Paradise was waiting for him if he gave up his life for the cause, and what more could a righteous warrior ask?

The *Southern Belle* surged forward, knifing through the water, making for the mouth of the James River. The waterfront and urban sprawl of Newport News were on his right, churning under the causeway of Highway 17. On his left, the quaintly named town of Rescue marched down to the water, with sailboats and fishing craft moored at the docks.

So many people going about their daily lives, oblivious to what was happening around them. They would see it on the television news that evening, read it in the newspapers with breakfast. Would it shock them, or were the Americans so apathetic that they would take the sudden violence as one more incident on the chaotic local scene?

No matter.

Jazmil wasn't concerned with the reaction of America's man in the street. His target was the hated government in Washington, D.C., and its Zionist allies abroad. The men and women who were maimed or killed in a particular attack were simply pawns, set pieces in a game with global implications. Individual lives meant nothing in the grand scheme of things. Jazmil would gladly kill a thousand infidels if it would result in justice for his people.

It was fortunate, indeed, that Hezbollah had found an ally in the States, a man—or group of men—who could supply direction, weapons, guidance on such unfamiliar ground. Past efforts to conduct guerrilla warfare in America had always come to grief with barriers of language, understanding, cultural identity. It helped to have Americans on hand who, if they didn't sympathize with Hezbollah's campaign, at least were willing to accommodate the freedom fighters with supplies and information in their time of need.

Fort Eustis passed on his right, on the east bank of the James, and Jazmil half expected to see attack boats and helicopters swarming to intercept the *Southern Belle*. Instead the base was quiet—nothing to suggest that any general alarm had spread.

Beyond Fort Eustis the river curved west around a promontory, looping toward the town of Scotland on the western bank. Jazmil was braced and ready when the pilot steered toward the other shore, behind a peninsula bristling with trees. A wooden dock waited for them, as did a Jeep Cherokee parked on gravel with the engine idling and a friend behind the wheel. A fourth man crouched on the dock.

Jazmil tossed out the mooring line and waited while the cabin cruiser was maneuvered closer to the dock and tied up. The engines fell silent. He scrambled ashore, the pilot hanging back long enough to set incendiary charges in the wheelhouse. They would have ten minutes to clear the scene before the vessel went up in flames.

They piled into the Cherokee, their weapons in another duffel bag behind the driver's seat. The county road ran into Highway 60, five miles to the east, then they were northbound, hurrying toward Richmond. From the capital, they would catch Highway 95, through Fredericksburg, Woodbridge and Alexandria, to Washington, D.C.

Another step toward victory, the main event.

Jazmil hadn't yet been trusted with the information on his final target, but it was coming. He could wait. Each blow he struck against the enemy would bring his people that much closer to the day of final triumph. He could feel it coming.

That day of fire and blood would make his life worthwhile.

**1**

*McLean, Virginia*

Rolling through the night on Old Dominion Drive, Mack Bolan checked his rearview mirror once again to make sure that he wasn't being followed. There were headlights, two miles or so back, but nothing that concerned him. Nonetheless, he pulled into the next rest stop and killed his lights, but kept the rental car's engine running, waiting with the Desert Eagle automatic in his lap.

The vehicle came into view, a station wagon with an older couple in the front seat, what appeared to be an Irish setter in the back. They didn't glance at Bolan as they passed, but he was still inclined to wait and watch their taillights fade before he laid the gun aside, switched on his own lights and resumed his journey.

He wasn't embarrassed by the small precaution, nor did he feel paranoid. Survival for a man in his position—living on the razor's edge—came down to his capacity for taking pains with details, managing his own security. This close to Washington, with the CIA's Langley headquarters less than five miles distant, a warrior couldn't tell who might be trolling on the highways, watching for suspicious vehicles. Aside from county sheriff's officers and spotters for the Company, there were the FBI and ATF, the Secret Service, countless military types . . . The list went on and on.

And, Bolan told himself, there were the strangers he had come to kill.

There were admittedly some gaps in Bolan's battlefield Intel this time around. He had a fix on his intended targets, knew their business in the States, but there had been no breakdown on their numbers, firm identities, the kind of armament he could expect to face. It could be three men or a dozen, maybe more. For all he knew, they might be packing field artillery and pocket nukes.

It made no difference to his mission, though. The die was cast, and the Executioner had accepted the assignment. It had been critical enough, by all accounts, to make it worth the risk.

The past three months had witnessed seven terrorist attacks on U.S. soil, with a substantial loss of life. No one was claiming credit for the raids, but Hal Brognola's sources blamed Hezbollah, a group of Muslim fundamentalist guerrillas who had brought their action to the States as far back as the World Trade Center bombing in New York in February 1993. Before that they were better known for taking hostages in Lebanon or launching raids from Syria against Israeli settlements.

It was a new war these days, and the Executioner was keeping pace.

The target was approaching on his left, down a narrow access road with hard-packed earth in place of pavement. Bolan killed his lights, turned onto the road and drove by moonlight, creeping, knowing he had time. It wasn't midnight yet, and he was running early, but the warrior reckoned he could use the extra time to polish off his strategy.

A half mile down the narrow road he passed a turnoff, someone's private driveway, and continued on another thousand yards before he found a likely place to leave his car. He didn't want the vehicle to block traffic, if another vehicle passed by that way, and Bolan also had concealment on his mind. When he was finished he would need wheels to get away.

The night was silent as the warrior stepped out of the car. He shed his slacks and jacket to reveal the jet-black skinsuit underneath, the sleek Beretta 93-R in a shoulder rig. He walked back to open the trunk, where a large Adidas gym bag gave up combat webbing hung with combat gear and ammo pouches. With the .44 Magnum Desert Eagle on his hip, he reached into the bag once more and found an Uzi submachine gun, silencer equipped, with folding stock. A stick of camouflage war paint darkened Bolan's face and hands to match the night.

All ready.

The Executioner used a compass and his combat instinct to direct him through the trees and shadows, taking time to keep his progress quiet, knowing well enough that no man ever did a perfect job of moving silently through woods at night. The trick wasn't so much to pass without a sound as to approximate the noises that a native forest dweller would expect to hear in any given situation. Stumbling progress, snapping twigs and cursing, wheezing with exertion, mumbling curses—any of that could be the kiss of death.

The final target was a private home, four bedrooms, tucked away from prying eyes, but still convenient to McLean, a short drive into Arlington or Washington, D.C. It would have been a nice home for an overworked commuter, but background research told him that the owner had retired to Florida in 1989, preserving the Virginia house as rental-income property.

The latest tenant was a certain Elroy Jaeckels, who, although he paid his rent three days ahead of schedule every month and could produce a list of heavy references upon demand, appeared to have no history before the day he signed his lease.

It wasn't that unusual to find a pseudonym employed on rental contracts in the neighborhood of Washington. Bureaucratic headliners liked their privacy as much as anyone else—sometimes complete with sexy mistresses—but this, from all appearances, was something else. The men who came and went from Elroy Jaeckels's house these days, according to a nosy neighbor down the road, were Arabs. *Looked* like Arabs, anyway. They seemed to change cars frequently, and on the one occasion when the neighbor jotted down a license number, it had come back stolen.

Bolan didn't know or care how the report had made its way from Loudon County to the Feds, from there to Hal Brognola and the team at Stony Man. It was enough for him to know that close surveillance had been mounted, photographs obtained, and files on terrorism had revealed two Hezbollah associates.

The FBI was ready to descend in force, but Brognola had flexed his bureaucratic muscle, claimed the job for Stony Man and passed it on from there to Bolan. Mere arrests weren't enough. In fact, aside from immigration charges and a single count of auto theft, there was nothing to use against the terrorists in court.

He saw the house now, pale lights showing through the trees. No sentries were on post to intercept him as he closed the gap and began his circuit of the property, investigating angles of attack. Three cars stood in front of the house.

Whatever else these strangers had in mind, they didn't plan on being caught without a set of wheels.

He marked the back door opening onto the patio and started counting down the doomsday numbers, moving closer.

The warrior had covered half the distance from the tree line to the house when the back door opened and a gunner stepped out in a spill of yellow light.

ALI JARASH WAS always nervous when it seemed that things were going well. A lifetime of adversity had taught him that the good times never lasted and that each forward step was purchased with the blood of friends and enemies.

So far their mission in the States had run like clockwork, with no mistakes that Jarash was aware of. It was time for something bad to happen—overdue, in fact—and he couldn't help feeling restless as the hours ticked away.

His six comrades seemed perfectly at ease with their accomplishments so far, imbued with every young man's personal conviction of his own invincibility. They all knew freedom fighters who had fallen in the cause, and each had enlisted with the understanding that he might be called upon to sacrifice his life. But no one truly harbored thoughts of death when every move seemed blessed by God, and his enemies were on the run.

It was Jarash's duty, as a strike-force leader, to anticipate disaster and prepare his men accordingly. He couldn't rest when things went well, but rather racked his brain for plans to compensate when luck ran out and they were forced to hide like vermin in the sewers. That was *real* life for

guerrilla warriors, making do with marginal supplies an
shortages of personnel, continuing a hopeless war against a
odds.

They had substantial allies this time, but Jarash woul
never fully trust Americans. Their generosity was alwa
grounded on self-interest, and they took pains not to gi
their private games away.

His contact in Virginia was a young man who had intro
duced himself as Mickey Drood. The name was false, c
course, as if that mattered. The American's identity mea
nothing to Jarash, as long as he produced the weapons an
intelligence they needed, on demand. So far their strang
collaboration had gone off without a hitch, but there wa
still the nagging question of a motive.

"What's shaking, Ali?"

Mickey Drood smiled as he entered the room, a smile tha
made Jarash suspect the young man's brains were scran
bled. He had seen that smile before, on other faces, in th
killing grounds of Lebanon and Syria. The men who wor
it didn't value human life, and they killed without remorse
sometimes for pleasure.

It wasn't a smile to trust, in any case.

"I'm looking forward to our next adventure," Jarash re
plied.

"Adventure, right." The crazy smile grew wider, oper
ing Drood's young-old face from ear to ear. "I like your at
titude."

Jarash didn't return the compliment. Instead he asked
"You have the information and material we need?"

"It's coming," Drood assured him. "Take another cou
ple days, I wouldn't be surprised. We're getting there."

"The special target we were promised?"

"Never fear. It takes some work, is all. A little pa
tience."

"Time is of the essence."

"Sure. Thing is—"

He never had a chance to finish the remark. A warnin
cry came from somewhere in the back part of the house, cu
off as though a blade had fallen from the sky. The gunsho
was muffled by the intervening walls. Jarash was movin

toward the sound, past Drood, when an explosion rocked the house. Now everyone was shouting, startled voices erupting from several rooms.

Jarash reached for his pistol with one hand, grabbing Drood with the other before he had a chance to slip away.

"Safehouse, you said!" His voice was stainless steel.

"I'm on it, man. No sweat." Drood drew a submachine gun from beneath his denim jacket and cocked it. "Just get your boys together, okay."

Still smiling, he turned and walked away.

THE GUY WAS GOOD, you had to give him that. Flat-footed, taken by surprise at the sight of Bolan in his blacksuit, the young Arab took a backward step and drew his pistol with a speed that testified to constant practice. As he pulled the automatic, he was calling out a warning to his comrades in the house.

And he was almost good enough to pull it off.

The Uzi stuttered through its silencer, a short burst ripping into Bolan's target, slamming him against the doorjamb at his back. A single shot exploded from the pistol, high and wide. The slug missed the Executioner by at least a yard, but there could be no question of surprise, from that point on.

He palmed a fragmentation grenade, removed the safety pin and pitched the bomb through the open doorway, sidestepping to avoid the storm of shrapnel as it blew. The windows facing Bolan shattered, spewing glass into the yard, and smoke wafted outside as the warrior entered, moving in a combat crouch. He heard excited voices in the aftermath of the explosion, speaking in Arabic.

Bolan moved in that direction, through a kitchen where the frag grenade had wreaked its havoc on the walls, appliances and cabinets. No one challenged him, but he kept his finger on the Uzi's trigger, stalking his intended prey with all deliberate speed.

The next guy up was nothing but a shadow, striding through the pall of smoke, when Bolan saw him coming—average height, athletic looking, with some kind of stubby automatic weapon in his hands. One step across the thresh-

old, and he seemed to feel the danger waiting for him,
dropping to a crouch and diving to his left as Bolan
squeezed the Uzi's trigger.

A half dozen parabellum rounds gouged divots in the wall
as Bolan's target went to ground. The mark responded with
a short burst of his own, and spent brass rattled on the tiled
floor, the bullets swarming over Bolan's head.

Too close for comfort.

The Executioner dropped into a prone position, digging
with his elbows, going for cover. At the same time his adversary was retreating, reaching out to snag a table leg and
flip the table over. It would afford little protection, but was
better than nothing.

Bolan held down the Uzi's trigger and stitched a line of
holes across the table, tracking left to right. His target
bolted, scrambling for his life, unloading a burst that flew
six or seven feet too high. Another blast from the Uzi caught
the guy in midstride, and he went down on hands and knees,
his weapon skittering across the floor.

That should have finished it, but the hardman was tough,
not giving up, regardless of the pain and mortal wounds. He
rocked back on his haunches, reaching underneath his jacket
for what had to be a backup weapon.

No time to hesitate.

The Uzi felt like an extension of the warrior, its power
rippling through his arm and shoulder as he emptied the
magazine. There was no way to count those final rounds
before the bolt locked open, but they did the job. He saw the
gunner's shirt and jacket ripple as the bullets struck him,
crimson spouting from the wounds. Impact punched the
target over on his back, his legs folding awkwardly beneath
him as he fell.

The Executioner had a glimpse of his opponent as the guy
went down. No Arab, this one. He was a professional, but
strictly homegrown by the look of him. Another mystery for
Bolan to decipher, if and when he had the time to spare.

The firefight had consumed mere seconds, but it seemed
to take forever. Bolan ditched the empty magazine and fed
his SMG a fresh one as he rose. From beyond the kitchen

doorway, silence had replaced the sound of angry, frightened voices.

They were learning.

The warrior hesitated for a precious moment on the threshold leading to a hallway and the rooms beyond. There were no neighbors close enough to raise immediate alarms, and Bolan's quarry weren't about to call for outside help. Time was on his mind, regardless. Any strike could fall apart if it went on too long, and this was the beginning of his journey, not the end.

No time to waste.

Footsteps scurried away from Bolan, toward the front part of the house. He followed, picking up the pace, and ducked as someone sprayed a burst of automatic fire from the direction of the living room.

Outside, he heard an engine come to life, immediately followed by another. Was he too late?

He burst from cover, following the footsteps of his enemies.

ALI JARASH HAD TEN or fifteen seconds to decide if they should run or stand and fight. It was an easy choice, all things considered: unknown enemies, a midnight raid against their "safehouse," with explosives being used. For all he knew, the FBI might have a SWAT team in the woods outside, and standing firm would only jeopardize his men, his mission.

It was time to go.

He didn't give a second thought to Mickey Drood. The wild ex-soldier could face the enemy alone, if he were so inclined. Security was his responsibility, and if the lapse cost Drood his life, so be it. What was one death, more or less, when holy war had been declared?

He brought his men together—five of them, at least—while gunfire echoed from the kitchen. There was no sign of Mahmud Arish, and that could only mean one thing. The warning cry and pistol shot, preceding the explosion.

Two lives, then.

And he was right. It had been time for something to go wrong.

His men were dressed and armed, but there was no tim
to gather all of their equipment. They would take what the
could carry in a rush, and leave the rest, replace it later
when he devised a way to reach their Yankee allies.

Everyone had questions, but he silenced them and le
them toward the only exit that remained. It was a risk. I
federal agents were outside, the front door would be cov
ered. But there seemed to be no choice.

"You first!" he told Ahmed Jazmil.

The young man didn't hesitate, but took a firm grip on hi
AK-47, reached for the doorknob and rushed out into th
night. Jarash expected gunfire, screams, but there wa
nothing. Only silence in the outer darkness.

"Go!"

He waved a second soldier forward and fell in close be
hind him, trusting in the other three to follow. The vehicle
were waiting in their proper places, no floodlights o
shouted orders, nothing to suggest they were surrounded b
the enemy.

But Jarash would take no chances. Waving three men to
ward the nearest car, he led two others to the second vehi
cle in line. It crossed his mind that he should somehow mak
an effort to destroy the third, but he had no explosives wit
him, and he didn't feel that he could spare the time re
quired to place a burning wick inside the fuel tank.

Never mind.

The car was stolen, and aside from fingerprints—whic
were no use to anyone, since none of his commandos had ￼
set of prints on file—there would be nothing helpful to th
FBI or any other law-enforcement agency. Inside the house
they would recover stolen military weapons, but the trail le
back from there to Hezbollah's American contact. Again
Jarash and his surviving men shouldn't be jeopardized.

They piled into the car, with Jazmil behind the steerin
wheel. He was a decent driver, and he knew the road
around McLean, the best ways to evacuate their so-called
haven.

Still no gunshots rang out from the darkness of the tree
around their hideout. How could the police have made suc
a grave mistake and failed to cut off his retreat? Jarash sti

clutched his pistol, waiting for the night around him to explode at any moment, bullets pouring down upon them from the tree line.

But the bullets didn't come. No hand was raised against them.

As the engine roared to life and they began to move along the gravel drive, Jarash thought of his comrades in the other strike teams. He assumed that Mahmud Arish was dead. The young man knew enough to keep himself from being taken prisoner. But what about the other teams?

Were they in danger even now? Was the assault confined to one strike team, or had they been betrayed somehow, perhaps by their purported native allies?

Security prohibited Jarash from reaching out to warn the other teams of their potential jeopardy. He had no way to get in touch with them directly and understood the need for separation, which would keep one strike team's failure from disabling the other two. But there was still a number he could call to leave a message, and, perhaps, request assistance.

First, though, they would have to give their enemies the slip and find a new place to hide.

In front of them, the point car reached the county highway and turned left on Old Dominion Drive, heading toward Chesterbrook and Arlington. Jazmil did likewise, cranking on the wheel and goosing the accelerator, grinning as the tires found traction. Jarash was pushed back in his seat by the momentum of acceleration, both hands wrapped around his automatic pistol ready, with the hammer cocked.

A roadblock could be waiting for them up ahead. Would that explain the startling lapse his enemies had shown in covering the house? Perhaps they thought it would be easier to kill his soldiers on the highway, pouring bullets into loaded, speeding cars, than to pursue them through the woods at night.

No roadblock.

After a half mile Jarash began to think that he had pulled it off. He didn't understand how such a thing could happen, how the mighty FBI and CIA could be so clumsy, but he knew that they wouldn't have let him run this far if they had any means in place to bring him down.

"Behind us!" Jazmil snapped.

A quick glance in the mirror showed another pair of headlights, just emerging from the access road to their safehouse. Mickey Drood? The notion died as soon as it took shape in Jarash's mind. He knew the wild American was dead, just as he knew the fate of Mahmud Arish.

Which meant that it was someone else.

"What shall I do?" the driver asked.

There could only be one answer in the circumstances.

"Drive on."

**2**

As Bolan moved through the house, the prospect of an ambush weighed on his mind. His enemies were clearly anxious to put space between themselves and their assailant, but he wouldn't put it past them to assign a rear guard, sacrifice another of their men, if necessary, to buy time for their escape. Hezbollah was known worldwide for mounting suicide attacks on targets that were unassailable by any other means, and there appeared to be no dearth of volunteers when human sacrifice was deemed essential.

There was nothing in the bedrooms as he passed. Outside, the cars were rolling. More than one, according to the different engine sounds, and Bolan's heart sank at the thought of having to retrace his steps, retrieve his vehicle and thereby give his prey a greater lead.

But, no. Two cars were moving along the driveway, one remaining where he had seen it parked on his approach.

He had a chance.

At first he was concerned about the possibility of booby traps. The Ford Fiesta, so conveniently abandoned, was a natural. It beckoned him to slide behind the wheel, pursue the taillights winking out of sight around the long curve of the driveway. The keys were in the ignition, Bolan saw, to make it even more inviting. All he had to do was sit in the driver's seat and give the key a twist.

A small bomb would be adequate to do the job. A hand grenade would do it easily, but it was time that made him take the chance. His enemies were running for their lives, uncertain who was chasing them, or how many adversaries were involved in the attack. He guessed that they wouldn't take precious time to tamper with the car, but rather seize the moment and make good on their escape.

He checked the driver's door regardless, and slid behind the wheel. A heartbeat of hesitation passed, then he gave the key a twist and heard the engine come alive. He released the parking brake and dragged the gearshift into drive.

He stood on the accelerator, powering along the driveway and out to the access road. The two cars were out of sight, but there were only two directions they could follow once they left the narrow road—north or south.

A last glance at the house revealed no signs of life. It was a disappointment to him, dropping only two of the elusive enemy so far, but he could make that up if he was quick enough to overtake the others, find a way to force them off the road.

He reached the county highway and pulled out far enough to glance in both directions. There were taillights on his left—one car that he could see—and nothing but darkness on his right. Go south, then, trust that they hadn't split up, one carload heading north, the driver smart enough to douse his lights and navigate by moonlight.

Bolan made the left-hand turn, accelerating on the straightaway. A curve loomed ahead of him, and he spotted two sets of taillights. In the Executioner's estimation there was no chance at all that one carload of his enemies would somehow overtake a civilian vehicle just here, just now.

The Fiesta hadn't been constructed with pursuit in mind, but it was doing fairly well. He cranked down the driver's window and listened to the wind rush, felt the perspiration drying on his face and underneath his nightsuit. Bolan thought about his headlights and left them on, deciding that the enemy would have already seen him, if the drivers were awake and on the job.

Three miles to Arlington, but it would work against the gunners if they led him there. The urban traffic meant police patrols, and they couldn't afford a traffic stop at this stage of the game. He flashed back to the local road map he had studied while preparing for the strike, and recalled that Kirby Road was a mile or so ahead. It ran east-west, from the Potomac River, south of Pimmit Hills, to intersect with Cedar Lane below Dunn Loring. From that point, it would be an easy two-mile run to pick up Highway 66 due west, or southbound Highway 495.

The sooner he could overtake his prey the better, before they met civilian traffic and the whole thing fell apart.

He picked up the Uzi and put it in his lap, the safety off. The taillights of the lead car were three hundred yards ahead and running at a steady sixty-five. The Fiesta's headlights had to be clearly visible by now. The driver in his sights had started weaving, drifting back and forth across the faded yellow line, both lanes, as if to stop the Ford from pulling into range.

Soft shoulders lined both sides of the road, with ditches harrowed out to channel rain. Bolan knew that he couldn't run off the pavement and attempt to pass his quarry. They were playing smart, both enemy vehicles weaving like a pair of Indy cars before the green flag dropped. It was a fair defensive strategy, but it detracted from their speed and kept the drivers focused on their rearview mirrors. If they met oncoming traffic, it would have to fall apart to avoid a catastrophic head-on crash.

The only way to get it right, Bolan knew, was to go ahead and get it done. Delays increased the risk to the warrior, to his mission and to any innocent civilians they encountered on the way.

Bolan held the pedal to the floor, his right hand frozen on the wheel, his left gripping the Uzi. He stuck his gun arm out the window, bracing it against the molding of his door. A submachine gun had its drawbacks—the extravagant expenditure of ammo when the shooter lacked experience, a tendency to "lose" rounds in extended fire—but it had compensations, too. In Bolan's present situation, he wasn't required to take precision aim and nail his moving target with a single shot.

He held the Ford Fiesta steady, straddling the yellow line, and waited for the nearer vehicle to drift across his line of fire before he squeezed the trigger, getting off five or six rounds, the spent brass bouncing off his hood and windshield like a swarm of shiny insects. He had two hits on the vehicle in front of him, both punching through the trunk.

It didn't slow them down. If anything, it urged the Hezbollah commando on to greater speed, his vehicle surging ahead like a horse reacting to a hornet's sting.

The Ford was giving all it had, the engine whining. If the enemy cars had more power, they could simply pull away from him.

He fired a second burst, and this time Bolan was rewarded with a hit on the rear window, chips of safety glass imploding from the strike. The car immediately swerved again, with less control this time. It was too much to hope that he had winged the driver, but at least he knew the guy was getting nervous.

He twisted the Fiesta's steering wheel a fraction of an inch and drifted to the right, just as the car in front of him shied to the left. The Executioner loosed another burst, then saw a gunner leaning from a window on the right-hand side, a weapon glinting in his hands.

The muzzle-flashes started winking back at Bolan like a baleful eye from hell.

ALI JARASH FELT TENSION mounting as the headlights of his faceless adversary bore down on him in the rearview mirror.

"Take evasive action," he instructed, and Ahmed Jazmil responded instantly. The narrow strip of road restricted the maneuvers they could try, but Jazmil started swerving back and forth across the center stripe to block their enemy and spoil his aim if he began to fire at them.

The driver of the lead car noticed their maneuver and began to swerve accordingly, the two cars weaving back and forth as if engaged in some weird game of tag. A casual observer might have thought that he was watching drunks, but the picture changed abruptly when their adversary opened fire.

The first two hits reverberated through the car like hammer blows. Behind Jazmil, Rani Zarka recoiled and searched the vinyl-covered cushions with his fingertips to see if either of the bullets had penetrated. It seemed to mollify him for a moment, but Ali Jarash felt no sense of security. Their vehicle was far from bullet proof, and any small advantage that accrued from speed would swiftly disappear if one round struck a tire or pierced the fuel tank.

Instantly, as if in answer to his silent fears, another muzzle-flash erupted from the chase car, and a bullet drilled the wide back window, whistling between the driver and Jarash to snap the driver's rearview mirror off its stalk. The broken mirror bounced once off the dashboard, landing in Jarash's lap.

"Rani! Wake up!"

The gunner muttered something beneath his breath, but he responded to the order, turned in his seat and kneeled on the cushion, edging toward the window on the left side of the car. He wound down the window and leaned out to get a shot at their pursuer with his submachine gun.

"Slow down, Ahmed!"

The driver blinked. "He'll catch us!"

"Do as you are told!"

The car began to lose momentum as Jazmil lifted his foot off the pedal, and he tried to hold it steady, even though his hands were trembling on the wheel. Another burst of automatic fire erupted from the chase car, knocking divots in the trunk and opening another blowhole in the window. Hunched across the steering wheel, Jazmil rasped out a curse but held it steady, focused on the swerving car in front of them.

Zarka got off a burst, his MP-5 K submachine gun spitting fire, spent casings blown into their wake and bouncing on the asphalt. The chase car weaved to dodge the bullets, and the terrorist's awkward posture likewise worked against an easy kill.

It had become a running duel, Jarash reduced to the status of a captive bystander stuck in the line of fire. He felt a mix of fear and anger churning in his stomach, like the remnants of a poisoned stew. He wasn't afraid of death per se, but it enraged and frightened him to think of dying in the present circumstances, veering off the road and going up in flames without a chance to stand and face his enemy.

He swiveled in his seat, watching Zarka firing at the Ford Fiesta as it swerved across the two-lane blacktop. The MP-5 K had a cyclic rate of some 800 rounds per minute. Even with ideal control, a 30-round box magazine was gone in seconds flat, and any hits on moving targets owed nearly as much to luck as skill.

As if on cue, Zarka ducked back inside the car and started fumbling with his weapon, drawing out the empty magazine and digging in his pocket for another. He found it, snapped it into place, then hesitated, slapping at his pockets.

"It's all I have," he told Jarash.

"So make it count!"

He cursed the haste that had compelled them to evacuate the house without collecting their supplies. It would be bitter irony indeed if they were doomed now, for a simple lack of ammunition, when they had left several thousand rounds behind.

Zarka hunched across the seat and poked his head back through the window, angling for another shot. He started milking short bursts from the subgun, aware that he was on the verge of running out of ammo.

Their nemesis was driving like a madman, veering back and forth from berm to berm and fighting back with automatic fire. He had the easy part of it, all things considered, since Jazmil was holding steady, trying to let Zarka get a better shot.

The burst that nailed Zarka came as he lifted off the trigger, waiting for the Ford to drift across his sights once more. One bullet struck the window, then another, drilling through and ripping into the terrorist's side. Number three glanced off the vehicle's bodywork, then a fourth round burrowed into Zarka's skull. His head snapped back, and lifeless fingers lost the submachine gun as he slumped across the windowsill.

Jarash cursed bitterly, reaching back to grab the dead man's blood-wet shoulder and draw him back inside to clear the field of fire. It would be up to him now, and he only had the pistol to defend himself.

He cranked down the window, his anger lending force enough to nearly rip the handle from its mooring. Cold wind roared into Jarash's ears and stung his eyes as he leaned out the window, making certain that his door was locked before he put his weight against it.

This was bad. He had to fire left-handed, with a semiautomatic weapon, which possessed little in the way of stopping power when matched against a motor vehicle. He would require a miracle to get it right, but even that wasn't possible.

If God truly took the cause to heart, as he believed, then anything could happen.

He waited, sighting down the automatic's slide as the Fiesta came back into range. Another second. Just one more.

He saw his moment and squeezed the trigger, firing for effect.

THE FIRST WILD BURST of automatic gunfire missed the Fiesta altogether, screaming past as Bolan whipped the steering wheel hard left. The maneuver spoiled his own aim for the moment, but he drifted back in line a heartbeat later, tracking on his target with the Uzi.

There!

He saw the muzzle-flash and pressed the trigger on his SMG, spraying a half dozen rounds. Two or three of them struck home on painted steel, the rest were gone. It was a rough trick to control both his weapon and the unfamiliar vehicle while under hostile fire.

He saw the gunner aiming and flicked on his high beams to try to blind the guy, but glaring lights wouldn't deter his trigger finger. Muzzle-flashes issued from the stubby weapon, nothing in the way of tracer rounds, but Bolan fancied he could see the bullets rushing at him like a swarm of killer bees. The Uzi answered round for round as the warrior swerved his vehicle across the line of fire and back again.

More bullets struck the Fiesta's hood, the window frame, a glancing hit on Bolan's door below his elbow. Too damned close for comfort. He couldn't suppress a curse as he swung out of line and reeled in the Uzi, running empty now.

Reloading the weapon one-handed was a challenge, but he got it done. He released the empty magazine and dropped it with a sharp jerk of his wrist, then replaced it with another, while the weapon lay inverted in his lap. Bolan took both hands off the wheel to cock it, then resumed his firing posture, with his left arm out the driver's window.

Ironically the Hezbollah commando was apparently reloading, too—or maybe reaching for another weapon in the car's back seat. The gunner's head and shoulders lunged back into view a heartbeat later, angling with his buzz gun for a better shot.

Too late.

This time the Executioner was waiting for him. Firing as he held the Ford Fiesta steady, he could see the bullets striking home. The broad back window shattered, caving in, and Bolan made a small correction to his right. The gunner lurched erratically, perhaps a body hit, then there was no doubt about it, blood exploding from his face and scalp as Bolan nailed him with a solid head shot.

He went limp, the submachine gun tumbling from his hands and bouncing on the pavement, gone as the Fiesta straddled it and kept on going. Someone from inside the car grabbed the dead man and yanked him back.

Bolan took a chance and tried to swerve around, catch up and pass his quarry on the driver's side. No go. The wheelman saw him coming, drifted to his left and blocked the road. The warrior swung sharply to the right, and while he had no room to come abreast, he was in time to see another gunman poke his head and shoulders through a window on the front passenger's side.

The Executioner felt a sudden rush of optimism. If the gunners in the nearer car were down to side arms, it should be no problem. He could drop back several yards, go for the tires and gas tank with his Uzi. Sweep them off the road and overtake the point car before it had a chance to get away.

All he needed was a little time and lots of luck.

But neither was forthcoming.

Bolan saw the bullet strike his hood, chip paint away and drill a hole the size of a half-dollar in his windshield. He was already recoiling, flinching to his left, when the projectile struck the steering wheel and shattered, peppering his face with superheated metal, one shard opening a two-inch gash below his eye.

Simple reflex made the warrior raise a hand in self-defense, losing control of the wheel, and by the time he caught himself a moment later, the Fiesta had already veered dramatically away to the left. The right front tire exploded, and he knew immediately that he had no chance to save it from the skid.

An open meadow spread before him, waist-high weeds and grasses, but he never got that far. The roadside ditch was waiting for him, stopping the Fiesta with sufficient force to slam the Executioner's chest against the padded steering wheel. The wind rushed out of him, and then he was entirely conscious of the fact that he was a sitting duck.

He found the door latch, ripped it open and spilled out into the ditch. It was a five-foot drop, and Bolan wound up sprawling on his face, tasting dirt and blood. He forced himself to check the Uzi to make sure its chamber wasn't fouled. From what he felt and saw, the weapon seemed all right.

He poked his head above ground level, ready to duck back again if bullets started flying. It made sense to Bolan that his enemies might double back and try to finish him, or maybe capture him alive for subsequent interrogation at their leisure. They'd want to find out what was going on and who was chasing them.

In fact, the second of the two cars did slow down, the brake lights flaring, but a judgment call was made, and after several seconds it accelerated out of sight. He came erect and started dusting off.

Goddamn it!

There was no point in wasting time with the Fiesta. It was done, a write-off. Someone would be getting bad news from the sheriff's office or the state police that morning on their stolen car. If they were wise, insurance ought to cover it.

The thought of squad cars gave new urgency. He had to clear the scene before a crowd of uniforms arrived, and there was no time like the present to begin his trek.

Where to?

His rental car, with hardware in it, would be waiting fo him in the woods, not far from the terrorist safehouse. Bo lan made it close to four miles as the buzzard flew, say fiv and change if he was forced to follow the established roads Three-quarters of an hour if he alternately walked and ran The night would give him cover, and he guessed that h could gain some time by cutting overland through ope fields.

How long before police turned up to check the highwa accident or the abandoned house? The running fight ha carried them past several dwellings, with gunfire from th Hezbollah commandos loud and clear. But waking up an reaching for the phone, to get involved in someone else' grief, was something else. Were locals close enough to Ar lington and Washington, D.C., that they would share th city dweller's apathy, the strong aversion to involvement?

Bolan hoped so.

He climbed out of the ditch and crossed the road, strik ing off across the open meadow on the other side. His pat† would take him north and east, past the dwellings he ha noticed, and maybe get him to the rental car without en countering police, watchdogs or any of a hundred differen hazards that could turn the present inconvenience into ¹ disaster.

As he walked through darkness, Bolan added up the scor and ranked himself a loser in the first round of his ne\ campaign. He had eliminated three men—one of then American, with no ID—but the majority of his intende targets had escaped unscathed. Worse yet, he had had n opportunity to question them or pick through their belong ings for a clue that would have pushed him on, directing th warrior to the next stop on his hit parade.

His enemies were spooked and running. Where the would end up from here was anybody's guess. The laps meant wasted time, since he could do no more than wait fo them to strike again, reveal themselves to Bolan with a trai of bodies.

It galled him, but he seemed to have no choice.

The Executioner would have to bide his time.

**3**

*Stony Man Farm*

"He's running late," Barbara Price stated, still pacing, glancing from the wall clock to her watch and back again.

"It's been only an hour and a quarter," Aaron Kurtzman said. "He had to cover fifty miles and watch for cops along the way. He'll be here."

"Right."

She didn't sound convinced, but Kurtzman sympathized. The call from Bolan had been logged at 2:19 a.m., from a pay phone off the Leesburg Pike in Falls Church, west of Arlington. The message had been cryptic, of necessity, with Bolan calling on an open line. They knew the probe had somehow gone to hell, but they would have to wait for Bolan to explain in person. He was driving down, presumably on Highway 66 from Falls Church into Gainesville, to pick up Highway 211 from there into the mountains, and on to the link with scenic Skyline Drive.

"What's doing with the Bureau?" Price asked.

"Hal's on top of it. They got the squeal from Loudon County homicide, the sheriff's detail. Two dead at the safehouse, but we're waiting on the details. It could take awhile."

In fact, as Kurtzman knew, they would be lucky if they ever got ID on any soldiers of the Hezbollah. They would be in the States illegally, perhaps on phony passports, maybe none at all. In either case, it was extremely rare for Palestinian guerrillas to have fingerprints on file, unless they had been jailed in Israel or some Western nation. Even so, with a mission of this magnitude—whatever the invaders ultimately had in mind—it was unlikely that the shock troops would be drawn from prison veterans.

"Hal's still coming?" Price queried.

"Pretty soon. He has some bases left to touch in Wonderland."

She knew that, but it helped to hear the words, thought Kurtzman. Part of working for Brognola was tapping into his strength, his many connections, and drawing silent encouragement from the man in charge. There were times when Kurtzman wondered who Brognola leaned on when the going got rough, but he had never found the nerve to ask.

Price poured herself a mug of coffee, then sat at the far end of the table. They were in the mess hall, killing time and waiting for Mack Bolan to arrive. The strain wasn't as great on Kurtzman, he imagined, since he didn't have the same extremely personal connection the mission controller nurtured with the hellfire warrior, but he still felt anxious, knowing the campaign had started off on shaky legs.

It could be worse, of course. They knew that Bolan was unharmed, and he had managed to retrieve his gear before the uniforms came swarming in. The downside was that Bolan's targets would be driven deeper underground, alerted to the fact that someone had them spotted, marked them for termination.

Would the warning put them off their game, perhaps encourage them to flee the country altogether? And if so, how would they go about locating the remainder of the strike force?

Questions, always questions. But the answers had to wait.

Kurtzman heard the door open behind him and turned in time to see Akira Tokaido cross the threshold. He was wearing his customized uniform of the day: blue jeans and a T-shirt, with a cutoff denim jacket. A small CD player was clipped to his belt. When he slipped the earphones off to speak, the slamming riff from the heavy-metal band of the day charged at Kurtzman from across the room.

"What's up?" Kurtzman asked, feeling the familiar urge to shout. He was convinced, despite all contradictory evidence, that Akira's music had to have left him more than slightly deaf.

"He's past the gate. Just got word. Two minutes on the ETA."

Price was on her feet and halfway to the door before Kurtzman could turn his wheelchair around and push off in the same direction. Muscles bulged in Kurtzman's arms as he propelled himself across the polished floor, dodged chairs and tables like a pro.

He reached the porch a moment after Price and took his place beside her, staring north across the darkened acreage of the Farm. A pair of headlights was approaching, following the road. He couldn't see the guards or various security devices from his present vantage point, but they were out there. Bolan would have cleared at least two checkpoints—one of them unseen—before he got this far.

A guard came out of nowhere as the car got closer. There was nothing obvious about his hardware, but Kurtzman knew he would be carrying an automatic weapon, sporting lightweight body armor underneath the flannel shirt and sheepskin jacket.

Bolan killed the lights and engine, then stepped out of the car, unfolding with a kind of weariness that Kurtzman recognized. The feeling wasn't strictly physical. A part of it was knowing he had done his best, and still had fallen short of victory. Two king-size Band-Aids had been plastered to his cheek.

The guard took Bolan's car, to stash it out of sight, while the warrior climbed the steps to stand with Price and Kurtzman on the porch.

"It looks like you could use some coffee," Kurtzman observed.

"You got that right."

"What happened to your face?" Price asked, reaching out with fingers that were slowly, almost painfully withdrawn.

"I caught a graze," Bolan said. "Nothing major."

"I'll wake up the medic."

"That's not—"

"Don't argue! I'm calling him."

"Looks like I blew it." There was resignation in his voice.

"Shit happens," Kurtzman said. "We're not done yet."

"We'll make it up," Price added, putting more confidence into her voice than she felt.

"Maybe."

"Let's get that coffee," Kurtzman put in. "Are you hungry?"

"I could eat."

"One Stony special coming up."

"Hal's coming down," Price said. "He should be here in a little while. With any luck, he might have something on the marks you tagged."

With any luck, Kurtzman thought, wheeling back into the mess hall. If it all came down to luck, they were in trouble. Deep and dark.

"I hope so," Bolan replied, but there was nothing hopeful in his voice.

He knew a setback when he saw one. Now the only question left was whether it would slow them a bit or put them on the bench for the remainder of the deadly game.

*Glengary, West Virginia*

ALI JARASH WASN'T EXACTLY captivated by their latest hideout, but he told himself that it was only temporary, for a night or two, until he got directions from control. Before they made another move, he had to know if they were still on schedule, if the targets had been changed.

By now he reckoned the police would have their hands on Mahmud Arish and Mickey Drood. They would learn nothing from Mahmud. He wasn't as sure about the Yankee mercenary.

There was a great deal still remaining to be done. They weren't finished with their mission yet. Not even close. To come this far and have the triumph snatched away would be disastrous. Worse, he would be subject to a personal humiliation that would ruin him, make life unbearable.

To die was one thing. But to fail . . .

Enough!

They had escaped the trap, and nothing else mattered at the moment. Assuming that the other strike teams were intact, their allies still at liberty, he saw no reason why the mission couldn't go ahead on schedule.

Ironically, he told himself, the raid against their safehouse at McLean might work in his favor. If the enemy—whoever he might be—believed that Hezbollah was on the run, it was possible that certain aspects of security would be relaxed. The manhunters would concentrate on searching out their prey, instead of standing fast and guarding certain targets that Jarash and his compatriots had marked for destruction.

And, he told himself, the more secretive the target, the more likely that his enemies would think it safe.

The prospect made him smile, but any stranger would have taken the expression for a grimace. There was no warmth in Jarash's eyes, no vestige of humanity in his demeanor. Those who knew him realized that he was all the more dangerous when he smiled. It was a kind of warning signal, like the flaring of a desert cobra's hood.

The first call to their contact, after checking out the safehouse, had been intercepted by an answering machine. Jarash didn't expect an answer. He would call back in an hour, and at sixty-minute intervals from there, until a living human voice came on the line. At that point he would speak in code, request instructions, find out how he was expected to proceed.

Nothing short of an absolute stand-down order would stop Jarash from carrying out his mission, to punish the Americans for their allegiance to Israel. Even then he would think twice about retreating with the job unfinished. If he saw a way to go ahead, at any cost, his men would never have to know the difference. They would take his word, unquestioning, and sacrifice themselves to see the mission through.

It was a rather thrilling notion for Ali Jarash to see himself as the ranking leader of a strike force, rather than the go-between who carried messages and put the soldiers through their paces like a drill instructor. What might he be able to accomplish if it weren't for the timid men above him, mixing courage up with caution?

Not so fast.

He had a duty to his people and the great *jihad*. It would be a grave mistake for him to place his personal desires ahead of the blood oath that he had sworn when he enlisted with Hezbollah.

The cause was everything; the individual nothing. Any man who placed himself before the greater good was both a traitor and a fool. The punishment for such disgraceful conduct was inevitable death.

He was anxious for the hour to strike so he could make another call. They needed weapons, ammunition and explosives to replace the precious items they had lost. They also needed battlefield intelligence, a fresh assessment of the chosen targets, backup sites, in case the A-list was discarded by the men in charge for safety's sake.

Jarash still hoped it wouldn't come to that. He liked the plan exactly as it was, a chance to strike at the American political machine on different levels, all at once. The outings that had gone before were warm-up exercises, bee stings to distract the enemy and make him overlook the lethal scorpion that had been creeping up his leg.

Six men remained in Jarash's group, and while he still expected reinforcements for the final strike, he would be willing to proceed with what he had. Of course, they would require more weapons. One rifle, two machine pistols and a half dozen side arms would hardly suffice for the job he had in mind. Some rocket launchers would be helpful. At the very least they would require more automatic weapons, hand grenades and surplus ammunition.

Waiting galled Jarash, but there appeared to be no choice. Whatever he decided in the long run, he was bound to notify his contact of the risk he had encountered. He was still a soldier, acting under orders. He had spent the whole of his adult life waging war against the Zionists, and he had never broken faith with his superiors.

So far.

Five minutes were left until the hour. It had crossed Jarash's mind that his team might not be the only one in difficulty. What if the entire strike force was under fire. Could he still trust his contact, having never met the man, or even seen him? To be sure, the disembodied voice had so far guided him without a hitch—had even forged the link with Mickey Drood, may God keep his soul—but what if someone tapped the line or traced the call?

His first call had been brief enough, but there were new machines, Jarash had heard, that traced and printed out a caller's number instantly, before the telephone was even answered. From the number, federal agents could proceed to throw a ring of steel around the house, and then—

He caught himself before his imagination could run wild. Outside, the night was dark and silent, no strange lights or noises to betray a lurking enemy.

And if they came, well, Jarash and his soldiers would deal with that problem when it arrived. Whatever happened, they wouldn't go quietly. The infidels would have to pay a heavy price for peace and quiet on their native soil.

They were already paying, even now, but worse still lay ahead.

The cost of harmony was going up.

## Stony Man Farm

BROGNOLA'S FLIGHT CAME on the radar screen at 5:09 a.m. Forty-seven minutes remained until daybreak, but the Farm was up and running, with workmen circulating on the grounds, some others tucked securely out of sight, but no less ready to respond with action if a threat was recognized.

The airstrip had been cleared for Hal's arrival, a tractor removing the shabby mobile home that concealed a battery of miniguns behind hinged walls. The landing lights came on just long enough to guide the Cessna in, then they were extinguished. Wheels were waiting for Brognola as he stepped down from the plane, no luggage for the driver to retrieve. The man from Justice had a job to do, but he wouldn't be sleeping over.

Moments later he was on the porch, where Aaron Kurtzman waited.

"Bear."

"I'm glad you made it," Kurtzman said.

"Was there a doubt?"

"Not really."

"Striker's in?"

"A while ago. Barb's with him in the War Room."

"Well, we might as well get to it."

"Right."

The elevator took them down to basement level, where Brognola's friend was waiting, seated beside the honey-blond mission controller of Stony Man Farm. Bolan looked tired, with dark circles under his eyes, but he was wide awake and leaned across the conference table to shake hands as the big Fed sat. There was a fresh wound on his right cheek, underneath the eye, the sutures bristling like insect legs.

"We caught a break with one of those guys at McLean," Brognola said, by way of introduction.

"Oh?"

"You noticed he was native?"

Bolan nodded. "Yes. I didn't recognize him, but he obviously wasn't Palestinian."

"Okay. We washed out on the Arab. That's to be expected. But the other guy..."

He hesitated long enough for Barbara Price to take the bait.

"Who was he?"

"Michael Francis Drummond," Brognola replied. "We got a print match through the Bureau. Their source was the Pentagon—specifically, the Army. Drummond put in six years with the Rangers, squeaky clean until the day he pulled the pin."

"And afterward?" Kurtzman asked.

"That's another story, and I got the details only half an hour ago. Looks like our boy went private for a while, some business with the Contras, free-lance mercenary work. The last two years or so, he's been a troubleshooter for the National Redemption Party."

"Well, now." Kurtzman's frown was almost audible.

"That rings a bell," Price said.

"It should," Brognola told her. "Organized in 1990 by Lieutenant Colonel Wallace Schroder. As the name implies, he thinks the country needs redemption—more specifically, deliverance from leaders he refers to as 'November criminals.'"

"What's that supposed to mean?" Price queried.

"A reference to election day," Brognola said. "In Schroder's view, there hasn't been a decent President since Roosevelt—and I mean Teddy. You've got Congress full of thieves and traitors, the Supreme Court staffed by Communists and 'femi-Nazis.' Put it all together, they've been selling out the country—and the military, in particular—for fifty, sixty years. The answer is a 'new line of defense.' That's Schroder's private army, just in case you couldn't guess."

"How many members?" Bolan asked.

"According to the FBI and ATF, between five hundred and a thousand. Membership is theoretically restricted to honorably discharged veterans. Schroder doesn't want them confused by 'serving two masters,' as he puts it in his interviews."

"Five hundred or a thousand's not much of an army," Price stated.

"How many brownshirts stood with Hitler in the beer hall?" Kurtzman asked.

"This isn't Germany," she said. "It's not the 1920s, either."

"Right on both counts," Brognola agreed, "but the Bureau has a hunch that Schroder might have shifted to recruiting active-duty troops. They can't be sure, but it would take only a few men, burrowed into sensitive positions. They could raise all kinds of hell. And if the party is now collaborating with outside terrorists . . . You work it out."

"This Schroder," Kurtzman said. "He was some kind of hero, right?"

"Affirmative." Brognola spoke without referring to the file in front of him. "He won the Congressional Medal of Honor his last week in Nam. Threw himself on a grenade to save his men, and it turned out to be a dud. Go figure. He came out of it with skinned knees and a white streak in his hair, some kind of nervous thing. Retired eighteen months later and took a stab at politics, but it was the wrong year for Republican hawks. He's been hanging around private industry since then, managing executive security. He banked enough by 1990 to retire again and run full-time with the Redemption Party."

"He goes out of pocket?" Bolan asked.

Brognola shook his head. "The party takes donations, some of them from sources that might come as a surprise. They get the old John Birch society contingent, naturally, but we've traced major corporate donations, too. It's not unknown for certain churches to support the cause. A fair percentage of the payments are anonymous."

"They pay their taxes?" Kurtzman asked.

"As far as we can tell," Brognola said. "The IRS has a perpetual watch on the party, based on Schroder's tax-resistance spiel, but so far they've got nothing."

"Do as we say, not as we do," Price cracked.

"That sums it up. The ATF's had better luck. They've intercepted two or three shipments of illegal weapons, but only the small fry go down with the goods. They wouldn't dump on Schroder if their lives depended on it, which, in fact, they do."

"Loyal troops," Kurtzman commented.

"Loyal or scared, it all works out the same," Brognola said.

"And now they're branching out," Bolan stated.

"Looks that way."

"I don't see Schroder rubbing shoulders with the Hezbollah," Kurtzman said. "He's always pushed a hard line in the Middle East. 'No crude, no food.' Word is, he advocated taking out the Ayatollah three, four months before the hostage situation in Tehran."

"Could be an angle, anyway," Price said.

"Such as?"

It was Bolan who replied. "Such as a cover. Who does Schroder hate the most?"

"The government," Brognola answered without a second thought.

"*Our* government," Bolan said. "Who was it who said, 'The enemy of my enemy is my friend'?"

"I don't remember," Kurtzman interjected, "but you've got a point."

"It fits, all right," Brognola said, "but we still need a line on the hit team."

"Maybe we should take it backward," Bolan said.

"Start with the party?" Price asked.

"Why not?"

Brognola thought about it for a moment.

"Why not?"

## 4

## Cincinnati, Ohio

Great rivers never failed to make Tarik Hassan recall his childhood in the desert that had once been Palestine. He marveled at the water, countless gallons flowing under bridges, rising to flood tide after a rain, sweeping along with power enough to crush man, his machines and his dwellings.

It seemed ironic, to a stranger, that Greater Cincinnati International Airport should be situated in Kentucky, on the wrong side of the great Ohio River from the city for which it was named. He didn't understand the foibles of Americans, their penchant for absurdity. The logic of the airport's situation—close by Turfway Park, to serve the wealthy gamblers—made perfect sense, but why not choose a name for it from among the nearby towns of Hebron, Springton, even Constance?

Never mind.

His flight from Baltimore arrived ten minutes early, one more circumstance Hassan would not encounter in the Middle East. He left Musa Kmeid to rent the car, try out the bogus driver's license and bank card. It went without a hitch, and a half hour after touchdown they were driving east on River road, toward Covington. They crossed the river on Highway 75 and motored five miles north to Mount Storm Park.

The meeting site had been a compromise. His contact had requested something farther west, while Hassan suggested a location close to Washington. In light of the Virginia incident, however, he hadn't protested when the compromise in Ohio was offered.

Compromise was part of life, despite his chosen avocation as a terrorist. Hassan didn't avoid the term, as some of his compatriots were prone to do. It was politically correct, back home, to call himself a freedom fighter or a liberation warrior. Either term was accurate enough, of course, but terror was the weapon he employed. Why not admit it?

Killing had come easily since childhood, when the Jews assassinated his two brothers, left his father crippled and deranged with grief. His first time, at the tender age of thirteen years, he merely acted as a decoy for a sniping team, enjoying the sight of three Zionists ambushed and riddled while dismounting from their jeep. It was pleasurable, but not the same as killing with his own two hands.

He had that experience six months later, in Jerusalem. The Jew wasn't a soldier. He was old, stoop shouldered, and he ran a store that carried everything from guns to garden tools for the Israeli kibbutzim. Each Friday afternoon, before the Jewish sabbath, he packed his weekly earnings in a leather bag and walked the money six blocks to his bank. The old man's route had never varied. On the last day of his life, Hassan was waiting for him in an alley, with a knife. The old man fought, but he was weak, helpless as the six-inch blade slid in between his ribs.

The money bought Hassan two guns, a semiautomatic pistol and an AK-47. Both weren't new, and that had pleased him, knowing that his weapons had been used on Zionists before. Tarik Hassan was certain it would bring him luck.

And so it had.

He had five murders to his credit when he joined the PLO, and he soon earned a reputation for ferocity in border skirmishes. His life was charmed, or so it seemed. When comrades fell on either side of him, Hassan came home without a scratch. He killed more Jews than anyone else in Arafat's private army, but the old man had betrayed their cause. When Arafat began to speak of peace, negotiating with the Zionists, Hassan knew it was time to find another army, switch allegiance.

So it was that he had found Hezbollah.

The movement and the man had served each other well, so far. Hassan had risen through the ranks, commanding troops instead of merely taking orders, and his score had blossomed into triple digits. Jews weren't the only targets now. He killed Americans and Englishmen, a Greek—even Palestinians, when they turned traitor to the cause.

He was prepared to try for Arafat himself, looked forward to the challenge, but his orders brought him to America instead. He had a chance to punish the Americans for decades of their meddling and support for Israel. It would be a foolish terrorist who passed up such a chance, no matter what the risk involved.

So here he was in Cincinnati, waiting for a stranger—an American—whom he would happily have executed under any other circumstances. It wasn't precisely true to say that he and the American were strangers, though. Two meetings and perhaps a dozen conversations on the telephone made them acquaintances, at least.

They never would be friends.

Hassan knew the American despised him, though he made an unsuccessful effort to disguise his bigotry, but it was immaterial. A warrior of Hezbollah would work with anyone if it would help advance the cause.

This mission, if he managed to succeed, would be the pinnacle of his career. He might live on another fifty years and never have an opportunity like this again.

He checked his watch and frowned. Five minutes remained before his contact was expected. Being early gave him time to scout the field and check for traps. He didn't think that the American would try to sell him out this early in the game, but something had gone wrong back in Virginia. He would take no chances at this stage of the game, when they had come so far and still had so much farther yet to go.

The submachine guns had come through in his suitcase unchallenged. The team wouldn't be staying overnight, and so the luggage was superfluous, but he was put off by the thought of traveling unarmed. The crossing to America from Europe had been bad enough—no way to sneak the weapons through on transatlantic flights—but the Americans were children when it came to airline safety on their own home ground. They scanned each passenger, of course, and x-rayed carryons, but no one gave a second thought to checked luggage.

It sometimes amazed Hassan that every aircraft in the country wasn't hijacked or blasted from the sky. Dumb luck, perhaps. Or were the people of this country somehow more pacific than they seemed on television news reports?

No matter.

War had come in search of them this time, and there was nothing they could do to save themselves. Hassan would see to that.

He checked his watch again, and didn't frown this time.

Two minutes left.

The war could wait that long.

"I CAN'T BELIEVE the ragheads fucked it up," Eulon Trask said.

"We don't know what went wrong. It might not be their fault."

Projecting tolerance wasn't his strong suit, but it was a talent cultivated with command. To Wallace Schroder, understanding people was the same as understanding movements, governments, whole nations. If you knew what motivated people—what they hated, loved and feared—you could predict how they would act in any given situation, whether they would stand and fight or break and run away.

The Arabs were fighters, but they had a tendency toward histrionic gestures, dying for a cause when it would serve them better to retreat, survive and fight again another day. Sometimes it seemed to Schroder that the whole Third World had a martyr complex, children reared from infancy with the idea of being victims, one way or another.

"You think the FBI's involved?" Trask asked.

"No way. They wouldn't kill two men and let the others skip like that without some kind of air play. We'd be seeing Drummond on 'America's Most Wanted' if the feebs were on it."

"Who, then?"

"That's the question," Schroder said.

He had selected Cincinnati almost on a whim. Kentucky was close by, and he had people there—a handful now, but growing. Rather than expose them to his visitors, he had suggested Cincinnati. Meet the Arabs in a crowd, and nobody would notice. It would be the Arabs' job to make sure no one followed them from Baltimore. Security around the site itself was Schroder's game, and he had stationed a half dozen men to cover Mount Storm Park.

That jogger, over there, was one of them; the young man lounging on a bench, brown-bagging it; two more parked in a stolen car, where they could watch the eastern flank; another couple staked out at the burger stand on Hamilton.

There would be hell to pay if anyone came snooping at the meet, with all those guns around. They wouldn't stop a SWAT team, necessarily, but they could do some righteous damage, cover his escape while Schroder got away.

No martyr syndrome here, thanks very much.

"They made it," Trask told him. "Blue Toyota."

Schroder spotted it, the Palestinians just sitting there, as if they belonged in Cincinnati, rather than some smelly tent behind a sand dune. Still, they had their uses. Schroder couldn't ask for any better bogeymen, the way things were in the United States today.

"Pull in beside them," Schroder said. The park was clean, as far as he could tell. No matter who had jumped the Arabs back in Virginia, it would take a miracle for anyone to trace them here. If someone pulled a gun, or flashed a badge and started asking questions, he would simply have to die.

Hassan looked calm enough as Schroder's vehicle pulled in beside the blue Toyota. Schroder didn't know the driver's name, but he had seen him once before, the first time that he met Hassan. Some kind of bodyguard or aide-de-camp, whatever. Two of them against eight guns ruled out a double cross.

Besides, they needed Schroder now more than ever. They were trying to conduct a war on foreign soil, without supplies or friendly contacts. If he cut them loose today, they would be forced to fall back on the Arab immigrant community for shelter. Even strangers to the country realized that cops and federal agents would be covering that angle.

He left the car and stretched, your average tourist soaking up the sunshine. Trask sat behind the wheel and kept the Arabs covered, one eye on the rearview mirror, watching for anyone who showed a trifle too much interest in the meeting.

Nothing obvious so far.

Hassan left the Toyota, and his driver stayed behind, observing Trask and checking out the park.

"Shall we take a walk?" Schroder asked.

"If you like." Hassan didn't sound nervous, but a sheen of perspiration glistened on his forehead.

They started walking aimlessly, with Schroder keeping one eye on the cars. He knew where each one of his soldiers was at every moment, didn't have to track them with his eyes. They would be ready, if and when he needed them.

"You had some trouble."

"Two men lost."

"Three, counting one of mine," Schroder said.

"You know the men responsible?"

"Not yet. I'm working on it."

"In the meantime?"

"We proceed. That is, if your team's up to it."

Hassan took no offense at the remark, nor did he smile. In fact, he gave no visible reaction whatsoever.

"We are ready," he replied, "but you will understand if I have certain doubts about your preparation."

"What, you mean the safehouse?" Schroder frowned and shook his head. "It wasn't our leak, I can promise you."

"What, then?"

"We have to wait until the Feds get finished picking over the remains. A few more days and I'll know what they know."

"Days? Are we abandoning the schedule?"

"I didn't say that, did I? Don't get nervous."

"It is not my nature," Hassan said.

"We need some time to set the final target, anyway. You know that."

"How much time?"

"If all goes well, we should be ready by the weekend. Can you get your men together in four days?"

"I can . . . on one condition."

"Oh?" It rankled Schroder, but he didn't try to put the man in his place. He needed him for the moment. It would all be settled when the smoke cleared. "Go ahead. I'm listening."

"To gather all my soldiers means a risk, you understand. I do not wish another repeat of the trouble in Virginia."

"Nor do I."

"You will not take offense, then, if I choose the safehouse for myself."

"You think that's wise?"

"We are not children, Mr. Schroder."

"By no means. As long as we can keep in touch, of course, the choice is yours."

"I have the contact number," Hassan stated.

"Yes, indeed."

"May we discuss the final target now?"

"It may be premature."

"I think about last night's unpleasantness," Hassan replied. "If some new problem should occur, and we lose contact, I would hope to have some means of going on."

"I can't afford to let you jump the gun," Schroder said.

"What does this mean, to jump a gun?"

"Commit yourself too early. A deal like this, the timing's everything."

"I understand these things."

Schroder wondered how much he could say without enabling the Hezbollah commandos to go off half-cocked and blow it. Still, the more he thought about it, Schroder wasn't certain that he needed a conclusive victory. The raid itself could be enough, if he was lucky—the media exposure, the resulting storm in Washington. Hassan would take the rap for all of it, with no fallout for the National Redemption Party, if he played his cards well from this moment on.

He made his choice, felt good about it as he stopped and turned to face Hassan.

"You have a team in West Virginia at this moment?"

"That's correct."

"Okay," Schroder said, putting on a smile. "They won't have far to travel."

*Glengary, West Virginia*

IT TOOK FIVE CALLS—five hours—for Ali Jarash to raise a living person at the contact number. Finally, when the delay was grating badly on his nerves, he got past the recorded message and heard a new, familiar voice come on the line. He knew the owner of the voice as Cobra, while Jarash himself was Viper Three, the leader of the third strike team on U.S. soil.

"Good morning, Viper Three."

"You have received my messages?"

"We are aware of your predicament," Cobra said. "Steps are being taken to replace the critical supplies."

"I am concerned about the schedule," Jarash said. It was a classic understatement, barely hinting at the turmoil that had left his stomach tied in knots since the Virginia firefight.

"Ah." If Cobra was concerned, it didn't affect the timbre of his voice. "A brief delay is forced upon us, but we still anticipate proceeding with the plan."

Jarash felt something loosen in his chest, as if a fist, once clenched around his heart, had suddenly relaxed. If Cobra planned to move ahead, it meant the leadership had faith in him, his soldiers, that they could succeed against the odds.

"And the delay?" he asked.

"We have decided you should find another residential property."

"The new house seems adequate."

"A new selection has been made," Cobra said in a tone that left no room for argument. "I will supply you with directions when we speak again."

"Again?"

"In a half hour," Cobra said. "Collect your men and find a public telephone. Leave nothing in the house where you are now. In thirty minutes you will call again and leave your contact number on the tape. I will call back immediately."

"What if something should go wrong?"

"It will not," Cobra told him, stating it as fact. "We cannot take a chance with any more diversions."

"And the new equipment?"

"Matériel is being gathered as we speak," Cobra replied. "It shall be delivered by your comrades to the new address."

Jarash was instantly alert. "Comrades?"

"We are consolidating forces in preparation for—how do you say?—the main event. Your new house will have ample room for everyone, and its location will facilitate your final task."

So that was it! Aside from the considerations of security, Cobra was calling in the troops, preparing for the push against their final target. While Jarash still had some doubts about the wisdom of another move this soon, he wouldn't argue with a plan that placed him closer to his goal.

"I shall speak to you again in a half hour," he informed Cobra, signing off.

"Till then," his contact said, and severed the connection.

There was little to be done in terms of preparation for departure, since the great majority of their belongings had been lost. They had disposed of Zarka's corpse by weighting it with stones and dropping it into the Opequon River, en route to Glengary. They would have to check the house of course, make certain nothing had been left behind by accident. From there it should be easy for Jarash to find a gas station with a public telephone, fill up the cars while he made one more call and, hopefully, received directions to their latest sanctuary.

There were still concerns about security, he realized, or Cobra wouldn't have insisted that he make the next call from a pay phone. He didn't believe that anyone knew where they were, or that their present telephone was tapped, but he was still a soldier, trained to follow orders. It was always possible—no, make that probable—that Cobra had some private information he had held back.

It was enough to know that his superiors still trusted him, that they were giving him another chance to join his comrades for the grand finale.

He would do as he was told.

His men had questions when he gave the order, but Jarash was quick to silence them. Obedience was the priority on any mission of this nature, and they didn't argue when their leader laid down the law. He had no doubt these young men would perform upon command, for God's sake and for the holy cause they served.

No word from Cobra on the nature of the threat they faced, or the identity of the assailants in Virginia, but there was no reason to expect that his superiors would solve the mystery so quickly, if at all. The key wasn't so much to name his enemies and seek them out for battle, but to wriggle through the net, avoiding contact and distractions while proceeding toward the goal. If they were forced to fight again along the way, Jarash would cope with that problem when it arose. Meanwhile, it was enough for him to watch his back, keep both eyes open and do everything within his power to complete the job at hand.

They took both cars and kept their weapons handy as they left the safehouse, carefully observing posted limits on speed as they wound through the residential streets, making their way toward Highway 81. It had been thirty-two minutes when Jarash stepped into the phone booth at a Chevron station, dropped his coin and tapped out seven numbers, waiting for the answering machine to pick up on the other end. He read the number from the pay phone, cradled the receiver and had ticked off forty-seven seconds when the phone rang.

"Identify yourself," Cobra said.

"This is Viper Three."

"Directions are as follows."

He didn't take notes, committing routes, directions, numbers to his memory, repeating them verbatim when his contact finished.

"It should take about one hour, if you do not stop along the way," Cobra said. "You will find a telephone connected at the house. Your comrades will arrive within the next two days. I recommend no further contact with this number until all are present."

"As you say," Jarash replied. "God be with you."

"And with you."

The link was broken once again, and Jarash walked back to his car. When he had settled in his seat, he took a road map from the glove compartment, following with his index finger the route he had been given. It was strange, but who was he to question his superiors?

"Where are we going?" Jazmil asked.

"Back to Virginia. A cabin in the Blue Ridge Mountains."

**5**

*Owyhee County, Idaho*

"Ten minutes," Jack Grimaldi said. His voice was thin, metallic sounding through the earphones both men wore to compensate for the noise of the helicopter engine and the rotors spinning overhead.

"I'm set," the Executioner replied.

Below them, almost close enough to touch, he saw the Battle River snaking south toward its convergence with the Owyhee. The terrain was hilly, sparsely populated, in a corner of the state that bordered Oregon due west, Nevada on the south. The nearest town was Grasmere, thirty miles behind them, but they weren't alone.

Not quite.

"Ass end of nowhere," Grimaldi said. "This is where the Fourth Reich starts, I guess."

"Some people think so."

Racial politics was part of it, although the National Redemption Party periodically denied the charge of ethnic prejudice. Still, they had joined the ten-year exodus of paramilitary groups to the Northwestern states, drifting toward the never-never goal of a separate "white bastion" in that corner of the country. Unwanted and reviled by their unwilling neighbors—ranchers, businessmen, homesteaders—the assorted skinheads and brownshirts still hung on in isolated compounds and stockades, where violent fantasies and automatic weapons flourished in a brooding atmosphere of hate.

The National Redemption Party's compound had been chosen with geography in mind. The proximity of two state borders made it easy for potential fugitives to reach the compound—or escape, at need—while members of the rank and file were free to carry out their war games, safe from prying eyes. Beyond convenience, there were also two nearby Indian reservations—Fort McDermitt on the Nevada-Oregon border, and Duck Valley, sprawling across the line from Nevada into Idaho—which gave the NRP commandos a focus for their hatred in an area where blacks and Jews were few and far between.

There had been rumbles in the past of skirmish parties straying onto reservation land "by accident," exchanging shots with residents of Indian communities. No charges had been filed since there had been no casualties and no conclusive evidence, but it was clear that members of the National Redemption Party loved to play at being soldiers.

They would have their chance this afternoon.

The news of NRP involvement with Hezbollah commandos had disturbed Mack Bolan, but at least it offered him another starting place, a fresh take on the problem, once his early targets had eluded him. If he couldn't immediately trace the Muslim gunmen, he would damn well light the candle's other end and see what happened as it burned from both directions toward the detonation point. If he learned nothing from the exercise, at least his enemies would be on notice that their time was running out.

And that could be enough.

"I still think you should let me take the first wave," said Grimaldi. "Use the Hellfires. Light 'em up a little."

"Negative," Bolan said, smiling at his friend. "I want to see if I can shake a little information loose before we wrap it up. I can't ask questions from the chopper."

"Do you really think they'll talk?"

"One way to check it out."

"Your call," Grimaldi said. "Don't say I didn't warn you."

"Not a chance."

"Okay. We're getting there."

The National Redemption Party owned two thousand acres in the county, purchased with donations from the faithful and a list of corporate sponsors who endeavored to remain anonymous. The bulk of that expanse was forest land, the compound proper occupying fifty acres near the middle of the tract, with access on a narrow, unpaved logging road. There could be sentries in the woods—in fact, he thought it probable—but Bolan had no option. If he didn't want to set down in the middle of a fortress, he would have to come in through the trees.

Grimaldi chose his route accordingly, stayed well north of the NRP encampment, hoping their advance would go unnoticed. Even if the chopper was observed, however, the terrain would militate against a swift reaction from the compound.

"Got a clearing up ahead," Grimaldi announced. "Two o'clock."

"One pass," Bolan said. "If it's clear, we'll make the drop."

The Stony Man pilot still had reservations, but he kept them to himself. He made a treetop-level circuit of the clearing. No one was visible from the bird's-eye view. Bolan had the simple harness fastened at his hips and chest as Grimaldi manipulated the controls to hover sixty feet or so above the ground.

"Stay frosty, brother," Grimaldi said.

"Glacial," Bolan replied with a brief smile as he stepped out of the chopper, one foot on the landing strut, then swung into empty air. The cable played out smoothly, as if from a fishing reel, with the Executioner on the hook.

This was the vulnerable time, with Bolan dangling in midair. If anyone cut loose on him, there would be little he could do to help himself. It could be finished by the time Grimaldi reeled him in.

His weapon was an M-16 A-2, complete with an M-203 grenade launcher mounted below the barrel, and he kept his finger on the rifle's trigger, with the safety off, as he descended toward the clearing in the forest. He might not be able to control what happened in the next few moments, but at least he could defend himself if sentries opened fire.

Touchdown.

His free hand found the quick-release latches on the harness and snapped them open. He stepped clear of the tether, moving toward the trees without a backward glance as Grimaldi reeled in the line and banked away, the chopper's rotors whipping at the air.

The compound lay southeast from where he stood, around two klicks. His compass told him where to go, and Bolan struck off through the trees at an easy double time, before patrols could fix the aircraft's sound and move in that direction.

There were time constraints, as always. Grimaldi was on the clock, with fuel considerations, and the more time Bolan spent on hostile ground, the greater were his risks of being cut off, cornered, overrun.

The FBI and ATF agreed that there were forty-odd enlisted members of the National Redemption Party dwelling in the compound on a year-round basis, some three-quarters of them male and all proficient with the weapons they collected almost as religious icons. Thinking of the women gave him pause, but Bolan knew that he couldn't discriminate by gender when the lead began to fly.

Whatever came to pass, from this point on he had to keep the mission foremost in his thoughts. If members of the NRP had closed ranks with Hezbollah against their native country and world peace, then they could take their chances with the foreign enemy.

The Executioner was blitzing on, and God help any human predators he met along the way.

EDDIE PAGE AND A FEW of the boys were in Silhouette City when Bolan touched down and began the long march toward their camp. The setup was a practice range the NRP had copied from an old Clint Eastwood movie. It had phony storefronts made of plywood, painted up to look authentic, covering the distance of about two city blocks. All kinds of pop-up targets in the open doors and window—selected and manipulated by the range commander, well behind the firing line—made it interesting. A cable overhead was rigged to pass a simulated helicopter back and forth, the half-size dummy labeled with police insignia. The FBI had something similar—if more elaborate and costly—at their training school in Quantico. It kept the soldiers sharp, and every tenant of the compound was required to shoot the range three times a month.

A former first lieutenant in the U.S. Army Special Forces, Eddie Page was thirty-one years old. He had an anniversary coming up: three years next month since he had joined the National Redemption Party. At the time he had been young and unemployed, considering a run at college on the GI Bill. It angered him to see how blacks, Chicanos, Asians and a laundry list of immigrants were bumped ahead of him in line for scholarships and jobs. One speech by Colonel Wallace Schroder, and he knew exactly what was going on.

The colonel readily confirmed what Page had long suspected: there was someone out to get him, working overtime to make a mockery of his ambitions and defile his dreams. The Jews were part of it, and various mud people, but the worst offenders, those truly responsible, were the November criminals. The two-faced, lying bastards had a way of charming voters, using any lie that would persuade and hoodwink voters long enough to work a little magic at the polls. Once they were settled into office, they could kick back, take their time, start raking in the graft, while they were screwing every decent citizen of the United States.

His first three weeks at Camp Redemption had been rigorous, but no great challenge to a recent Green Beret. His discipline and military bearing led to swift advancement through the ranks, and for the past six months he had been serving as the base commander, managing the show whenever Schroder and his number two weren't in residence.

Like now.

He stood before Silhouette City with a Heckler & Koch MP-5 submachine gun braced against his hip, the safety off, his index finger on the trigger. As with the vast majority of combat ranges, lifelike targets were employed, depicting enemies: black muggers, hook-nosed Jews complete with yarmulkes and automatic weapons, Oriental immigrants and agents of the IRS. It also depicted some "good guys" representing innocent civilians, but their purpose on this range was very different from their use at Quantico and other law-enforcement combat ranges.

Soldiers of the NRP were taught to take down anyone who jeopardized their mission of the moment: old folks, women, children—nothing mattered but the job at hand, and most of them were probably deserving of a bullet, anyway—race traitors, Communists and scum with muddled blood lines. Only those who wore the party emblem were immune.

Page waited, felt the others watching him, and he was ready when a target popped up in a window ten yards to his left—a cop in uniform, his service pistol drawn. Page spun in that direction, stroked the SMG's hair trigger lightly, five rounds ripping through the piglet's chest and shoulder.

Another target snapped up, this one on his right, and Page swung back to face a black man with an Uzi in his hands, a blue bandanna wrapped around his head. Another short burst from the hip ripped through the target's head, his hair rag fluttering away and out of sight.

The third mark, when it came, was dead ahead. Page almost fired, but then he recognized the stately crimson lightning-bolt arm band, the glossy photograph of Colonel Schroder's face stapled onto the silhouette's head.

He held his fire and drifted to the left, no guarantee that future marks would pop in that direction. Every target on the course was theoretically in range from any point on the firing line, though distance obviously worked against a shooter when he had no time to stop and aim.

In fact, the next one sprang up on the far right, threatening the camp commander with an AK-47 and a yellow Star of David bright on its lapel. Page smiled and stitched a 4-round burst across the cutout's chest. The target didn't fall, of course, but shivered with the impact of his parabellum rounds.

Stay sharp!

The silhouette of Colonel Schroder had retreated. In its place another target filled the doorway, this one a young woman with a baby cradled in her arms. Page shot them both without a second thought, and he felt good about it, knowing he had done his duty. No distractions. There were no such things as innocent bystanders in a war of national redemption.

For a moment Page mistook the sound of gunfire for an echo of his own. He recognized the error instantly—wrong sound, the wrong direction for an echo. Was a forest combat exercise in progress? War games in the woods? Page thought about it, but he knew he had approved no exercise that afternoon.

What, then?

It angered him when members took it on themselves to throw a war game, shooting up the woods and raising hell. He didn't care about the neighbors, for there were none, but impromptu parties were a lame excuse for wasting ammunition, pegging shots at anything that moved. Without the proper strategy laid out in advance, the troops learned nothing, and their discipline was compromised.

He was about to ask somebody, when the first explosion rocked the compound. Christ, it sounded close! Somebody playing with grenades? There would be hell to pay for breaking discipline, if that turned out to be the case.

Page shot a stony glance at his companions, stepping out in the direction of the sound.

"Let's go."

The sound of angry, frightened voices set alarm bells ringing in the back of Page's mind. They had been taught that there might come a day when their satanic enemies would descend on the compound, trying to wipe it out. Page was inclined to treat the rap as slightly paranoid, but what if he were wrong?

He kept a firm grip on the MP-5, prepared for anything.

It someone tried to storm the camp, it wouldn't only be the worst mistake they ever made.

It would also be the last.

BOLAN STARED at the compound proper from the shelter of the tree line, crouched in shadow, checking out the buildings that included barracks, an assembly hall and mess, latrines, storehouses and an open shed for vehicles. The CP was a smallish prefab structure on his right, with a radio antenna and a TV satellite dish on the side. From Bolan's left, outside the closed ring of the camp, short bursts of automatic gunfire echoed from a practice range, perhaps two hundred yards away.

He holstered the Beretta, slid the M-16 A-2/M-203 off its shoulder sling and double-checked the safety. Live rounds were chambered in both weapons, with a 40 mm high-explosive kicker on tap in the M-203.

And there was no time like the present to begin.

The warrior left the cover of the trees, moving cautiously across the open ground to reach the shadow of a barracks. Men were moving here and there around the compound, all of them in olive drab or camouflage fatigues, but it surprised him that they didn't have more guards in evidence. Perhaps, he thought, the years of being left alone by the police and FBI had bred complacency. If so, he meant to take advantage of the fact.

Bolan headed toward the CP. He was barely halfway there when two men suddenly emerged and turned in his direction, one guy grinning while the other dropped the punch line to a joke. Both lost their sense of humor when they caught a glimpse of the Executioner, stopping short and reaching for the side arms that were standard items of apparel in the camp.

They never made it.

The warrior dropped them with a stream of 5.56 mm tumblers, tracking right to left, and both men went down squirming on the grass. Bolan heard a warning shout from someone on the far side of the camp, in the direction of the mess hall. Turning that way, he saw three soldiers gaping at him, two with rifles in their hands. He reacted in the only way that seemed appropriate.

His M-203 launcher, with an effective range of some 375 yards, was well under one-third of maximum distance from the present targets. He fired from the hip, saw the men try to scatter before the 40 mm projectile fell among them, but they were too late off the mark as it detonated in a smoky thunderclap.

Two of the gunners went down instantly. The third was wounded, staggering away before a short burst from the M-16 reached out to drop him in his tracks.

So far, so good, but it began to fall apart from there.

Instead of a confused reaction, slow and lackadaisical, the compound dwellers came to life as if they had been standing by in readiness for an assault. They seemed to come from everywhere at once, exploding from the barracks and the storage buildings, even the latrine. All were armed, responding by the numbers, fanning out to cover their respective beats.

He was exposed, not quite surrounded, but the situation had potential for degenerating in a hurry. Bolan moved toward the command post, hearing shouts behind him as the NRP commandos spotted him and started closing in. He made the threshold, ducked inside and kicked the door shut after him.

A burly crew-cut youth with sergeant's stripes on his fatigues stood gaping at him, reaching for the automatic on his hip. A short burst from the M-16 ripped through the man's chest and punched him backward, sprawled across an Army-surplus desk.

Outside, the rising sound of voices told Bolan he was cornered. He crouched below the line of sight from windows to the front, and no one took the risk of firing at him yet, but it wouldn't be long. If he couldn't find some way out, they had an opportunity to riddle him at leisure, pouring bullets through the windows, wooden walls and door.

The CP was a two-room structure, with a small reception area in front and a private office in the back. There was no exit at the rear. He could summon Jack Grimaldi now, but airborne cannon fire and rockets didn't differentiate between one building and another. First, before he made the call, it was essential that he buy himself some time, a little combat stretch, to give himself at least an even chance against the storm of friendly fire.

He risked a glance through the nearest window, and a bullet drilled the glass a foot above his head. He ducked out of range and raised the M-16 to fire a burst in answer.

Instantly all hell broke loose.

The troops outside began unloading like a firing squad, but most of them were firing high, as if they thought he would be standing upright, waiting for a bullet. Bolan hugged the floor and made his way behind the desk, his late and unlamented adversary taking more hits where he lay.

What Bolan needed was an exit from the CP hut, and soon, before his enemies got lucky and he found himself disabled, maybe dead. There was no question of escaping through the front door, pocked with bullet holes already.

The Executioner fed the M-203 launcher with another HE round and picked his mark, a corner of the private office that would leave him partly screened from shrapnel, with the main bulk of the structure still between him and his enemies. He braced the weapon tight against his hip, squeezed off and dodged back under cover as the high-explosive can went off.

There was no hesitation on Bolan's part in the wake of the explosion. He was on his feet and running while his adversaries gaped in shock, uncertain whether their incoming fire had caused the blast. He charged through gagging smoke and ducked his head, feeling grass beneath his feet before the view was clear.

And he was out.

The only question now was whether he could stay alive.

## 6

It took awhile for Eddie Page to find out what was going on. A prowler was in the camp, from what his people told him, with some righteous hardware. He had five or six men dead already, and the mess hall had been trashed by an explosive charge. Now they were telling Page that they had the intruder holed up in the CP hut with no way out.

"How many guys?" Page asked the nearest man with any kind of rank.

"We just saw one."

That boosted Page's confidence a bit. He couldn't picture any kind of strike force leaving one man on the hook this way, and if the guy was on his own, they should have no great difficulty handling him.

"I want him out of there," he said to no one in particular. It was an order, but he didn't have to say so. Everybody in the compound knew that when the other brass was gone, his word was law.

"Let's do it." That was Big Joe Bertolucci, one of Schroder's small-arms experts at the compound. He was carrying a SPAS-12 riot shotgun, and the bulky weapon still looked like a toy in Big Joe's massive hands. He started toward the CP hut, and then somebody pointed toward the nearest window, shouting, "There he is!"

At once a shot rang out, punched through the window with a brittle cracking sound. The stranger's face ducked out of sight before Page caught a glimpse, and then a burst of automatic fire crashed through the window from the inside, making everybody duck for cover.

Everyone, that is, except Big Joe.

Size didn't mean a thing to bullets. He was just a bigger target, standing there, when three or four rounds ripped into his chest. The impact pitched him over backward, index finger clenching the shotgun's trigger as he died, the muzzle blast a foot or less from Page's face as he lay huddled on the grass.

His ears were ringing, and it felt like several rounds of cotton had been stuffed inside his skull, but he could hear the other weapons when they opened up. At least two dozen soldiers unloaded on the CP hut at once, and never mind that one or more of their own people might still be inside.

It figured that the prowler—whoever he was—had taken care of anybody in the office when he got there. That was basic. Now he had some cover, but it wouldn't stand for long against the massed fire of so many weapons pouring bullets through the windows, walls and door.

Page wished that Colonel Schroder was around to take responsibility. It looked bad, having shit like this come down on Page's watch, and never mind that he couldn't predict a sneak attack. The colonel would have some opinion— maybe that he should have had more sentries in the woods, or stationed at the camp itself—and what could Page offer in his own defense?

Jack shit.

Hot brass was spilling over his head and shoulders from an AK-47 on his left. One of the casings stuck between his neck and collar, burning him. He reached back, cursing as he missed the shell and felt it wriggle farther down his back, still hot.

"Goddamn it!"

Page let it go, worming backward to a point where he could safely rise on hands and knees, no risk of being shot by his own. He hadn't fired the MP-5 as yet, and didn't do so now. It was superfluous, he told himself, with so much lead already pouring in. The CP was a wooden structure, and it didn't stand a chance against the present storm of automatic fire.

He looked around and saw two men sprawled out on the ground a few yards to his left. Neither one had drawn his side arm, indicating they were taken by surprise, no opportunity to fight. Across the compound, several of his men were wielding fire extinguishers to save the mess hall, stepping over bodies that had fallen to the blast of a grenade or bomb.

One man?

Entirely possible, Page thought. With training and the proper weapons, dropping a half dozen men would certainly be no problem. The greater trick was getting this close to the target in the first place, when he had sentries orbiting around the compound, theoretically on guard. If Page found out that someone had been dozing on the job, there would be hell to pay.

Before he started kicking ass among the home team, though, Page had to find out who the creeper was and what he wanted at Camp Redemption. Not a cop, for sure. They came in by the dozen, wearing snappy uniforms and shoving warrants in your face.

A private shooter, then. But why?

Before he could suggest an answer to himself, a new explosion shook the compound, this one close at hand. Page saw a cloud of smoke boil up behind the CP, spreading rapidly.

Now what?

"Is anybody back there?" Page shouted. "No? So *move* already! Check it out!"

But something told him he was already too late.

BOLAN HIT THE GROUND running, smoke trailing behind him like gossamer wings. He cleared the smoke in time to hear his adversaries coming, several runners from the sound of it, at least a couple of them shouting back and forth. The noises came from both directions, men enveloping the CP in a hasty pincers movement, which they should have done before he had blown himself an exit at the back. They still might overtake him, but at least he had some combat stretch, a fighting chance.

He stopped and turned to face enemies, aware that he was in the open now, his would-be targets covered by the drifting smoke. He glanced around, saw no one in position for a lucky shot and waited, ticking off the numbers in his mind.

The point men came in sight on either side, within a heartbeat of each other. Both were armed with automatic weapons, each intent on using his. Bolan took the gunner on his right because the man was somewhat closer, thus a slightly greater threat. A rising burst of 5.56 mm tumblers met the hardman, spinning him and dropping him before he had a chance to fire. If any bullets missed the mark, they had a fifty-fifty chance of striking someone else, one of the troopers bringing up the rear.

He swiveled to his left and found the second shooter lurching to a halt, his weapon braced to fire. The guns went off together, bullets swarming close to Bolan before his own slugs found the target, staggered him and knocked him backward in the dirt.

Bolan saw no shame in running for his life. There was a time to stand and fight, lay down your life if necessary, but a savvy warrior had to weigh the cost against rewards, decide which sacrifice was worth it, which would be a waste. Grand gestures held no appeal for Bolan, unless they produced grand results.

He ran, palming the compact walkie-talkie as his long legs carried him in the direction of the nearest barracks. Thumb on the transmitter button, the warrior brought the handset to his lips and spoke to Grimaldi.

"Mayday, Wings! Let's do it!"

How long until the chopper made it? Grimaldi would be within a klick or two of Camp Redemption, circling, waiting for the signal. Any minute now the giant dragonfly would swoop down to the rescue.

He reached the barracks and used a corner of the building as a screen. The first incoming rounds smacked wood, and splinters flew. He took a moment to reload the M-203 launcher, checked the rifle's magazine and snapped a fresh one into place on finding it was low. He needed time while waiting for Grimaldi, and he couldn't think of any better way to spend it than in raising hell among his enemies.

He had no realistic hope of gaining any useful information now, but there was still an opportunity to put a dent in chroder's personal militia, shave the odds in any future lash, perhaps.

Assuming Bolan lived that long.

He ran along the back wall of the barracks, circling round to come out in front. He met a group of six or seven ien advancing on the point where they had seen him disppear from view, a couple of them firing as they came to over the approach and keep his head down. By the time a anker noticed Bolan sighting on them with the M-16, he ad the range and was prepared to answer them in kind.

He hit them with an HE round and followed up with short ursts from the rifle, tracking individuals as they recoiled rom the explosion. Two or three went down immediately, ppled by the blast, their comrades reeling awkwardly un-l his bullets sought them out and dropped them on the turf.

The other hardmen from the CP had him spotted now, nd Bolan ducked back out of sight as they began unload-ng, a half dozen streams of automatic fire converging on he corner of the barracks. He crouched against the wall and ed another high-explosive round into the launcher.

It was thirty feet or so between his present shaky haven nd the next real cover, an apparent storehouse to the east. Jot far, perhaps, but it was open ground and every step of : was covered by his enemies. If he stayed where he was, .owever, they would certainly surround him, catch him in cross fire, and the end result would be identical.

If Bolan had a choice, he would prefer to meet the enemy n his terms, standing up and fighting back.

A new sound came to Bolan, audible despite the steady lrumbeat of staccato fire, a heavy chopping sound from omewhere overhead.

The copper.

Jack.

GRIMALDI'S HELICOPTER WAS a HueyCobra, the Bell AH-1G that had served so well from Vietnam to Iraq. The ingle engine was a 1,400 shp Avco Lycoming T53-13 urboshaft, propelling the chopper at a maximum speed of .72 miles per hour, with a cruising range of some 357 miles. The nose turret mounted an M-197 20 mm cannon, the

three-barrel Gatling design that could fire up to six thou
sand rounds per minute. The Cobra's stubby wings sup
ported twin quad launchers for the Hellfire laser-guided
missile.

He was cruising at an altitude of eighteen hundred feet
three klicks due north of Camp Redemption, when the voice
he had been waiting for came to him through the padded
earphones.

"Mayday, Wings! Let's do it!"

He was on the case and banking to the south at once, the
throttle open, coming down to treetop level in his haste. It
made no difference if they had patrols out and someone
heard him coming. There was no way men on foot—or even
in a jeep—could match his speed, nor would a radio alert
accomplish anything, since battle had been joined inside the
compound proper.

He was on the scene within five minutes, closing on a
northeast-southwest axis, scanning Camp Redemption as it
came in view. The action was seemingly concentrated at the
south end of the camp, where smoke was rising from at least
two buildings, bodies scattered on the ground. There was a
general movement of the troops in that direction, many of
them firing on the run. No view of Bolan from the air, but
Grimaldi could guess approximately where he was from the
directed fire of his assailants.

The Stony Man pilot came in behind them, from their
blind side, swooping low and squeezing off a long burst
from the 20 mm Gatling gun. The M-197 made a sound like
King Kong strumming on a huge bass fiddle, armor-piercing
bullets whipping up a dust storm on the ground below. Stick
figures lurched and spun, going down like shattered man-
nequins.

It took him all of fifteen seconds on the first pass, circling to the west and coming back again before the stunned
survivors had a chance to mount an organized defense. This
time he spotted Bolan, dodging from behind a bullet-riddled
barracks toward the next building in line, well off to the
right of Grimaldi's glide path.

He switched on the laser tracking system and armed the
Hellfires, fixing his sights on the camp motor pool. The

issiles operated by homing on a laser beam directed from
e Cobra, then bouncing back from the target to receptors
the Hellfire's nose. It was a no-risk, no-miss system, bar-
ng critical malfunctions, and the armor-piercing rockets
ere designed to stop a heavy tank dead in its tracks.

A truck or plywood building would be no sweat at all.

He sent one of the Hellfires on its way, holding true to fix
e flight path, then veered off a heartbeat prior to deto-
ation. From the smoke and flame, he knew it was a solid
t. A portion of the roof peeled back as if a giant hand had
renched it free. A lake of burning fuel spread out beneath
e other vehicles in line, flames leaping in the shade, as
rimaldi swung back to make another pass.

A number of the riflemen downstairs were sniping at him,
e fire disorganized and random. He picked out a group of
ree and homed in on them with the M-197, strafing, heavy
ullets ripping turf and flesh together, pinning them to
arth. He kept on firing as he swept above the barracks just
hind them, raising spouts of dust and knocking shingles
om the roof.

Again.

He came in from the south this time, and loosed twin
ellfires on a run across the compound, slamming into an
pparent storehouse that held arms and ammunition, from
e way it blew. The detonation of the Hellfires merged into
condary blasts, a rising mushroom cloud of smoke and
ame almost enveloping the Cobra as he hauled back on the
ick.

Too close for comfort, shrapnel pinging off the under-
arriage, but he wasn't finished yet.

A pair of automatic weapons opened up from some-
here on his left, and the pilot swung instantly in that di-
ction, lining up his sights, the drifting pall of smoke
adequate to screen his enemies. He lined up on the muz-
e-flashes, put the laser sight to work and launched an-
her Hellfire toward the gunners. Riding on a tail of fire,
went to ground a yard or so in front of them and bur-
wed in, erupting in a burst of stone, sod and shrapnel. If
s adversaries weren't buried by the fallout, it was close
ough, their weapons falling silent in a flash.

Returning from the west, he still saw movement in the camp and went after one quartet of stragglers with the M-197. One of them turned to make a stand and cover the retreat of his companions, firing from the hip with an assault rifle. He was vaporized where he stood by the armor-piercing 20 mm rounds, pitched over backward, while the others tried in vain to beat the doomsday clock. Grimaldi left them scattered in his wake, unmoving, draining crimson life into the sod.

How many left?

Grimaldi saw no point in taking rockets home when he could use them here to good effect. Scorched earth? Why not.

If Camp Redemption rose again, it would be rising from the ashes. Try "Camp Phoenix" on for size, if there was anyone around to care. Right now he wasn't betting on a second coming, but he knew that stranger things had happened.

And he brought the Cobra back for more. Scorched earth, damn right.

And then some.

GRIMALDI TOOK the heat off, giving Bolan time and room to move. The Executioner broke from cover as the M-197 opened up—Grimaldi's first pass at the compound—dodging swiftly toward the cover of a nearby structure.

Would the pilot see him? And if not, how long could Bolan last before a rocket or a stream of 20 mm armor-piercing bullets cut him down?

Forget about it.

There was all the difference in the world between anticipating trouble and surrendering to fear. Defeatist thinking killed more fighting men than snipers on the other side could ever claim. He took a moment, listened to the Cobra ripping up the compound with its cannon fire and rockets, screams and scattered gunfire. When he moved, he clung to the perimeter, a strip of open ground between the buildings and the trees, still clear of what had turned into a killing pen inside the compound.

On the way he met two tattered hardmen just emerging
from the space between their barracks and the mess hall.
Both were dirty and disheveled, one man bleeding from a
gash along his hairline, so that half his face was streaked
with crimson. For perhaps a heartbeat, there was hope in
both their faces when they first caught sights of Bolan, then
they saw his warpaint, recognized the enemy by type.

They had a choice of doubling back into the Cobra's field
of fire or of standing where they were, which came down to
no real choice at all.

The taller of them, Mr. Blood, was carrying an Uzi submachine gun, but it seemed to have no magazine in place.
His sidekick had a Ruger Mini-14 rifle with a folding stock,
and he stood ready to defend the both of them, while his
companion fumbled with the ammo pouches on his web
belt.

Bolan wasted no time on the fair-fight principle. The hero
in a movie always gave his evil adversary one free shot to
prove himself a gentleman, but art and life parted company
when it came down to do or die. Without a script or helping hand from Hollywood, he had no reason to believe the
gunner facing him would miss, and Bolan didn't feel like
stopping bullets, maybe dying where he stood, to demon-
strate some code of honor from a West that never was.

Instead, he stitched the young man with a rising burst of
5.56 mm tumblers, opening his body up from crotch to col-
larbone and blowing him away. The dead man had no
chance to fire, or even aim his weapon, as the impact
punched him over backward in a lifeless sprawl.

His friend was just about to get the Uzi loaded, but he
plainly realized that he was out of time. Instead of standing
fast, he dropped his SMG and turned to run.

Too late.

The second burst from Bolan's M-16 A-2 went home between his shoulder blades, with force enough to pluck the
young man off his feet and slam his face into the nearest
plywood wall. Recoiling from that contact in a boneless
slump, he wound up on his back, sky-gazing, stretched out
head-to-toe with his companion of the moment.

Bolan moved along the breezeway his most recent adversaries had emerged from, with the damaged mess hall on his right, and scanned the central compound as Grimaldi made another pass. He heard one of the Hellfire rockets taking flight and ducked from force of habit, just in case. The detonation, when it came, was from the far side of the camp, but it was close enough for him to feel the shock wave reaching out to shove him, like a giant hand.

In other circumstances, the Executioner could have pitied Schroder's army, but he knew what they were up to—had a fair idea, at any rate—and he had zero sympathy to spare. The troops at Camp Redemption might not have a clue about their leader's tie-in with Hezbollah, but they were still part of the problem, operating as a law unto themselves and scheming overtime to bring down the elected government of the United States.

It took a moment for the Executioner to realize that Grimaldi was hovering at center stage now, taking no return fire from the compound. If he still had enemies alive in Camp Redemption, they were lying low and keeping to themselves, afraid of calling hellfire down upon their heads.

With some misgivings Bolan stepped from cover, edging into view. He held his weapon ready to respond if he met any opposition. None appeared as he was striding toward the chopper, and Grimaldi brought the Cobra down to earth, the rotor wash flattening grass on all sides. The hatch was open, waiting for him when he got there, and he went aboard without a backward glance.

"All done?" Grimaldi asked him.

"Looks that way."

"So what's the word?"

"We didn't have a lot of time to chat."

The Cobra lifted off and spiraled out of there, treetops below them in another moment.

"Next?" Grimaldi asked.

"It wouldn't hurt to have a talk with Schroder," Bolan said.

"You want a word with Santa, while you're at it?"

The warrior smiled. "It couldn't hurt."

While he was at it, Bolan thought, he just might take a leaf from Santa's book. He was making a list, and checking it twice.

**7**

*Savannah, Georgia*

It was a far cry from the old days, Wallace Schroder thought, when he would land at Hunter Army Airfield and receive full honors, everybody snapping to attention, firing off salutes and stumbling over one another in a rush to satisfy his every wish. RHIP, he told himself—rank has its privileges—but he preferred his present life-style for its freedom and the progress he was making on his personal crusade.

The summons came as no surprise, all things considered, but the choice of meeting place had raised some eyebrows back in Idaho. No problem. Schroder was a veteran traveler, accustomed to life on the road...or in the air. He had spent several years in Georgia, most of it around Fort Benning, and he knew Savannah well.

This afternoon, driving west on Bourne Avenue from Savannah International Airport, picking up Augusta Road southbound through Garden City to Savannah proper, Schroder knew that he would have to do some fancy talking if he meant to put the general's mind at ease. The firefight in Virginia was a tempest in a teapot, but there were problems, even so. It troubled him that enemies—and unknown enemies, at that—could run the strike team down that way and catch them by surprise. It was embarrassing that one of Schroder's men had wound up on a slab in Arlington, with all kinds of niggling questions from the FBI, and he sure as hell didn't need the extra scrutiny just now, when they were on the brink of changing everything.

The plan was damn near perfect, but it had the same drawback as any other piece of strategy: its execution still relied on human beings. Men—and women, too, God bless them—were the weakest link in any chain, forever subject to emotion, illness, all the frailties humankind was heir to. He would have the perfect army, Schroder thought, if he could only work with robots, maybe aliens, like in the movies.

Screw it.

He would do with what he had, as always, and the job would still get done. If Schroder had to bend some rules along the way, well, that was the advantage of civilian life. He made his own rules now—subject to oversight and ultimate approval from the general, of course—and there was no one second-guessing him along the way, demanding paperwork in triplicate or pulling the financial plug if they got nervous.

They were on the verge of something great—if not a total victory, at least a major breakthrough after years of struggle, propaganda and determined organizing efforts. Too bad they had needed Arabs to achieve their goal, but that was life. You took the tools at hand and did your best with what you had.

He glanced at Eulon Trask and found his driver frowning.

"What's the trouble, Eulon?"

"Sir? Oh, nothing."

"Straight talk, please."

"Yes, sir. I can't help wondering about the scramble in Virginia. We've got nothing from our eyes at Justice so far, and it worries me."

"You know what worry is," Schroder said.

"Yes, sir."

He went ahead regardless. "Worry," Schroder told his driver, "is a dividend paid on disaster before it's due."

"Yes, sir. It's on my mind, though."

"Understandable."

It preyed on Schroder's mind, as well. A strike from nowhere, three men dead, and the elusive enemy was out there somewhere, gearing up—he had no doubt at all—for some new mischief that would jeopardize his master plan. He hated the idea of anything intruding on his dream, but they would cope, make do.

As if they had a choice.

They picked up Bay Street eastbound, following the river past the Great Savannah Exposition and Visitor's Center, Riverfront Plaza and the U.S. customs house, into Savannah's historical district. How many battles had been fought within a few miles of the ancient neighborhood? It had begun with Spanish troops and Indians at one another's throats, then Spaniards versus British colonists. The Revolution, War of 1812 and Civil War had all been centered on the crucial port. Small wonder that a military presence lingered in the area, where jobs and patriotic fervor came together in an atmosphere that welcomed Army personnel and federal dollars.

"Coming up, sir." Trask's voice was tight, and Schroder saw him checking out the sidewalks, storefronts, the pedestrians and traffic. There were mostly tourists, which made it easier to pass unnoticed.

The meeting point had been selected with security in mind, and while his faith in the old man was absolute, approaching adoration, Schroder still took time to check his mirror, watching for a tail. If they—whoever "they" were—had the smarts to track the Arabs to Virginia, he couldn't assume that any place was safe.

A squad car passed them, heading in the opposite direction, but the blue suits didn't even glance at Schroder. No good reason why they should, a clean-cut white American with ramrod posture, riding in a Cadillac. If he was being tailed, the shadows knew their business and he couldn't pick them out. It was the general's ultimate responsibility, in any case, since he had picked the rendezvous.

Small consolation if they walked into a trap.

"Here goes."

He followed Trask's gaze and saw the general's batman leaning up against a nondescript sedan. The car was decked out with civilian plates, no uniforms in evidence. The old man's driver was a captain, Special Forces, but he could have been a model—finely chiseled features, auburn hair, with sky blue eyes concealed, on this occasion, by a pair of mirrored aviator's shades. The bulge beneath his left arm would be a Beretta Model 92, the standard military side arm since replacement of the old Colt .45.

"Let's do it," Schroder said, and Trask nosed the Cadillac into the parking lot. They found a space beyond the general's car, three places down, and Trask killed the engine. He released his seat belt and was reaching for the inside handle of the door when Schroder stopped him.

"You wait here."

"Yes, sir... if you think it's safe."

"I'm covered."

Schroder left the Caddy, closed the door behind him and straightened his jacket as he walked back toward the general's car. The captain nodded to him, opened the sedan's back door and ushered him inside. The old man waited for him with a dour expression on his face.

"So, tell me, Wallace," the general began as Schroder settled in the seat, "exactly what the hell is going on?"

MAJOR GENERAL Arthur Coltrane was a lifer of the old school, battle tested, with the scars to prove it. He wore custom-tailored uniforms—a suit on this occasion—and his iron gray hair was buzz cut, close enough to show his scalp. The face beneath that crew cut had been molded out of supple leather, tanned beyond all fading by the heat of battle and the glare of tropic suns.

The Old Man always seemed much larger than he was. At five foot nine he was no more than average height, with 160 pounds distributed proportionately on his wiry frame. It was unlikely any stranger would have guessed that he was ambidextrous with small arms, that he held a black belt in tae kwon do or that he could lift two hundred pounds in free weight from a standing start. In fact he could have been the guy next door, somebody's doting grandfather.

Until you looked into his eyes.

If eyes were the windows of the soul, then Coltrane's had been painted over. They were black—not charcoal or dark brown, but pure jet black—like twin gun barrels aiming from beneath the salt-and-pepper brows. They seemed incapable of showing warmth, or any other human feeling, for that matter. When he smiled with his expensive dentures, none of the expression reached his eyes.

Those black gun-barrel eyes were aimed at Wallace Schroder now, as Coltrane skipped past the amenities.

"So, tell me, Wallace," Coltrane said, "exactly what the hell is going on?"

"Sir?"

"Have you listened to the radio the past two hours or so?"

"No, sir. What is it?"

"Jesus H." The old man shook his head. "You've got a problem, Wallace. Out in Idaho."

He watched the color drain from Schroder's face. "A problem, sir?"

"Somebody hit your compound. Went through your people like a dose of salts, from what I heard. It's been on CNN, for Christ's sake."

"I don't— The compound?"

"Gone," Coltrane said, "or the next best thing. You've got all kinds of badges scrambling around out there. They have a couple of survivors, last I heard, but neither one of them is in great shape."

"How many dead?" Schroder asked, sounding slightly dazed.

"I don't know if they've finished counting yet. You don't have many left out there, from what I gather."

"Jesus. When was this?"

"Three hours, give or take. Some kind of forest ranger ran into a straggler, wounded, and he figured out that there was something going on. It took awhile for deputies to reach the camp and contact the Feds. I don't have all the details yet, but it appears there was an air strike."

"*Air* strike?" Schroder shook his head, bewildered. "What the hell—"

"That's what I'm asking you," the old man said.

"I haven't got a clue, sir. This is news to me, I swear to God."

"Well, that's unfortunate. One soldier in Virginia was unfortunate, but this . . ." It was the general's turn to shake his head. "We could have trouble up the ass, you know."

"No, sir. I mean, I'll handle it."

"I hope so, Wallace. If we let this get away from us, it all goes up in smoke. We're done."

"They won't find anything in Idaho to jeopardize our operation, sir."

"You're sure of that?"

"Damn right, sir."

"I hope you're right." He hesitated for a moment, shifting gears. "And what about our friends?"

"I've got them relocated, closer to the target site. They're covered."

"Really?"

"I assure you, sir."

"Be careful, Wallace."

"Sir?"

"Before you promise anything, make sure you can deliver."

"Yes, sir. I'm on top of it."

"I trust your inside man wasn't at Camp Redemption," Coltrane said.

"No, sir. He's up in Maryland. I've got him under guard."

"He doesn't mind that?" Coltrane's tone showed less concern about the soldier's feelings than for Schroder's plan.

"He's with the program, sir. Committed, down the line."

"And he's been paid."

"I gave him half up front, yes, sir. The rest of it's contingent on our ultimate success."

"Good thinking. How did he respond to that?"

"What could he say? I told him it was my way or the highway."

"Risky business."

"He wasn't going far, sir."

Meaning six feet down, into a hole, unless he played along. All right, then. They had that much squared away, at least.

"The preparations?"

"Right on schedule, sir." A bit of color had returned to Schroder's face. Instead of looking dead now, he was simply pale. "We've got the aerial surveillance photos and a working model. I'll be briefing them first thing tomorrow morning, and we start the drills tomorrow night. I'm optimistic."

"Confident?"

"Yes, sir."

"That's better. Something comes to mind, about the problem in Virginia."

"Sir?"

"Have you considered that the target may be conscious of our interest? They're equipped for striking back in force, I understand."

Schroder blinked, appeared to think about it for a moment. Finally he shook his head. "I don't believe so, sir. How could they know?"

"I'm asking you," Coltrane replied.

Another hesitation, then, "I don't see any way at all. If we had leaks, I'd know about it. I'd have federal agents coming out my ears."

"You do, in Arlington and Idaho."

"We're still on track," Schroder protested. "Nothing's happened that would change our plans. I stand by that."

"It strikes you as coincidental that we have these incidents two days apart?"

"I think our colleagues in Virginia had some bad luck, sir. They came expecting losses. Their commander didn't seem especially upset."

"And Camp Redemption?" Coltrane prodded.

"I don't have an answer for you, sir. I'll have to check that out when we get finished here."

"Your last surveillance of the target site was when?"

"Last Friday, sir."

"Let's bring that up to date." It was an order, couched as a suggestion. "It would be a shame to send our colleagues in and find out the defenses had been changed."

"No, sir."

In fact, no one expected the commandos to survive, as long as they could raise sufficient hell on earth before they bought the farm. Ends justified the means. Hell, in this case means *were* the end.

"I'll get right on it, sir."

"The layout won't be altered," Coltrane said, almost talking to himself, "but if they pull in reinforcements, it could be bad news."

"Yes, sir."

"We're in agreement then?"

"Of course, sir."

"Good. As for this trouble out in Idaho…"

"I'm on it, sir."

"I leave it in your hands."

"Sir."

"That's all."

"Yes, sir."

It tickled Coltrane, watching Schroder pause and think about the wisdom of saluting, finally restrain himself and step out of the car. He hoped his colleague wasn't losing it at this late date. The inconvenience of replacing him would be significant, to say the very least.

Relax.

He trusted Schroder, to a point. The man had proved himself in combat situations, handling men, and it was premature to think of ditching him. There was an outside possibility that the attack in Idaho was unrelated to the firefight at McLean, Virginia, but it stretched the envelope of credibility. They had an enemy—or enemies—out there, and Schroder's team had suffered major losses. The publicity was even worse, but they could still proceed on schedule if the target wasn't on alert.

He would consider it a challenge. They had come too far to turn back now. There wouldn't be another chance like this to strike at the November criminals and make them pay for decades of subversion and betrayal of the Founding Fathers.

Coltrane had been treated to a glimpse of their Achilles' heel, and he would be a fool to let the golden opportunity slip through his fingers. If he had to sacrifice a few men on the way to his objective, so be it.

Acceptable losses.

It was the name of the game.

## Baltimore, Maryland

THE TELEPHONE began to ring at 5:09 p.m. Joe Gardner waited for his bodyguard to pick it up, but Tom was in the bathroom with a magazine, and Gardner answered in between the sixth and seventh rings.

"Hello?"

"Who's this?"

He had no trouble recognizing Schroder's voice, long distance, sounding pretty tense.

"It's Joe."

"Where's Tom?"

"He's in the crapper. Wanna talk to him?"

"No, that's all right." There was hesitation, Schroder thinking. Then, "Have you been watching television?"

Gardner knew what he was getting at right off the bat. "We saw the news, yeah. What went wrong?"

"I'm looking into that. Is everything okay where you are?"

Gardner took his time and looked around the Spartan living room. Let Schroder sweat a little. What the hell.

"No problems here," he said at last. And then it hit him. "Should there be?"

"No way." It came too quickly, setting Gardner's nerves on edge, but Schroder tried to reassure him. "I just got the news myself and wanted to make sure that everything was cool with you."

"So far, so good."

"Okay, that's fine. Another day or so, I'll have you meet those people that we talked about and take them through a couple practice runs, okay?"

"Sounds good."

"I'll be in touch with Tom tomorrow night sometime to set it up."

"Okay."

"Make sure he's off the toilet, will you?"

"Right."

When the dial tone started buzzing in his ear, Gardner cradled the receiver, frowning to himself. "Those people that we talked about" would be the Arabs. Gardner hadn't seen them yet, and that was fine. He had been hoping they could get along with aerial surveillance photographs and simulations, but their time was running short, and now the colonel wanted him to do his part.

Okay.

For what the NRP was paying him, why not? A quarter million dollars wasn't chicken feed. With that much money in his pocket, he could disappear forever, start from scratch. Whatever happened afterward, no matter which way it went down, Joe Gardner would be home and dry.

It would have put a torque in Schroder's shorts to know what he was thinking. Well, tough shit. It was a fact that he had joined the National Redemption Party and believed in what the party stood for, but he had some major problems with the notion of a coup d'état. The plot that Colonel Schroder had in mind would raise some hell in Washington, no doubt about it, but there was a world of difference between that kind of shitstorm and a crisis that would overthrow the government.

No matter.

Joe Gardner was twenty-six years old. His six years in the Special Forces had opened Gardner's eyes to certain facts of life that he had never recognized in childhood, on through high school. He had seen how grafting politicians used the military, skimming money off the top and putting lives at risk to shore up foreign policies designed with the next election year in mind. The current White House occupants were no exception to the rule—a little worse, if anything, than those who went before. A warrior couldn't really do his job without the Monday-morning quarterbacks demanding explanations, second-guessing every move from Washington.

The National Redemption Party seemed to offer a solution—or at least a sympathetic ear—and Gardner had enlisted six months after turning in his uniform. He liked the rallies, speeches advocating a return to basic values and support for military personnel as guardians of the American ideal. It was a few months later on when he had raised the subject of his special duty with the Green Berets, and you could almost see the lights go on when Colonel Schroder heard the news. The plan had taken root right then and there, although the details took some time to figure out.

The Arabs were a twist, of course, and Gardner had his doubts when that part of it was suggested, but he saw the logic of it, once the details were explained. By that time, though, he also had the money on his mind, and that would settle any doubts that lingered in his mind, except when it came down to personal survival.

If the plan went on schedule, there would be no problem. That was being optimistic, though, and life had taught Joe Gardner to expect the worst. If things went sour, he would still have cash enough to make a run for daylight. Let them try to catch him, if it felt like payback time. He still knew how to fight, and he would match his skill against his fellow soldiers any day.

Besides, if things went sour, Colonel Schroder and his men would have more pressing matters on their minds than chasing Joe Gardner around the world.

In fact, where worry was concerned, he felt more qualms about the possible reactions from the people Schroder and his Arabs planned to target for their raid. He knew the way these people operated—some of it, at least—and rumor had it that their reach was long, indeed. How long would it be, once Schroder played his hand, before they started checking back, examining old personnel files, looking for a ringer.

For a moment, there and gone, he felt like bailing out, but it passed. A soldier didn't cut and run the first time things got hairy. Only when the case was plainly hopeless, going down in flames, would Gardner pull the pin and save himself.

Besides, he couldn't reach the money this time of day, and by nine o'clock tomorrow morning Schroder would have found a way to freeze the bank account. And where would Gardner be without his cash?

Nowhere.

It was simple when he stopped to think about it. He would play along with Schroder's plan and keep his eyes wide open, watch for any sign that he was being set up for a fall. Look out for number one, but in an unobtrusive way. No waves. Don't rock the boat.

And when the first cracks started showing in the plan, bail out as if his life itself depended on it.

Which it would.

Gardner heard the toilet flush and walked back to the couch. He sat down and switched on the television. A talk show, with transvestites babbling on about their whacked-out life-style. Jesus wept.

The more he saw of "normal" life, the more Gardner thought they ought to tear the whole thing down and try again. Well, he had done his part, and if it didn't work, too bad. Let someone else sift through the rubble when the smoke cleared.

Joey would be gone by then.

Long gone.

## 8

**Stony Man Farm**

At least, Barbara Price thought, it wasn't all bad news. Returns from Idaho were hit-or-miss on the official wavelength, but they knew from Bolan's early report that he had emerged undamaged from the probe at Camp Redemption. As for useful information, that was something else, but it had been a long shot from the start.

She thought about it, sipping coffee, staring hard at the computer screen, as if sheer focus could produce some kind of news flash from the hinterlands.

Good luck.

It could go either way from Idaho, she realized. On one hand, it was possible the sudden strike at Schroder's base camp would produce a ripple in the National Redemption Party, throw the master plan—whatever that might be—off track and leave the Hezbollah hit team exposed. The flip side, though, was something else. The Owyhee County raid could also warn their enemies and drive the targets further underground, perhaps abort the plan entirely. They could lose it, Price realized . . . but did they have a choice?

The door was quiet, but she heard the wheelchair coming up behind her, turned to smile at Kurtzman as he closed the gap.

"What's new?" he asked her.

"Nothing, damn it."

"Are they finished with the head count out west?"

"Um . . . thirty-one, the Bureau says. I guess that's final."

"Anyone we know?" Kurtzman asked.

"I don't have all the names yet. Some of them will have to wait on dental records, I suppose." She felt a shiver starting and suppressed it. "Anyway, no Schroder, but we weren't expecting him. The rest are rank and file. The NRP is strictly veterans, right?"

"That's what they say."

"Goddamn it, what a waste."

"I hear you." Kurtzman had a knack for reading moods and tapping into feelings, empathizing with the team. He didn't always know exactly what to say, but he could listen with the best of them.

"Still working on the outfit from McLean?" he asked.

"Still praying, would be closer to the truth. We don't have any more to go on than we did last night."

"They've gone to ground," Kurtzman said.

"Looks that way."

"No reason to believe they're finished, though."

"You're asking whether I'm an optimist?"

He almost laughed at that. "I wouldn't dare. Has anybody talked to Hal about informants?"

"Not since breakfast. If he had a lead, he'd pass it on."

A swarm of letters started filling up the screen of her computer monitor, scrolled downward from the top, and Price keyed the printer instantly, to save a copy of the text.

"What is it?" Kurtzman asked.

"We've got a line on Schroder. Two lines, really. He flew into Cincinnati yesterday, around this time. Today he had a booking to Savannah, out and back. Both flights originated out of Dulles, in D.C."

"Terrific," Kurtzman groused. "We're looking for him everywhere, and the slug's right under our collective nose."

"We don't have any line on Schroder or the NRP in Washington," she said. "I've checked that every which way."

"So, we're overlooking something," Kurtzman countered.

"Or the guy likes Dulles."

"Think he's playing with us?"

"It's a possibility," she said. "Not us specifically, but Feds in general."

"Maybe." Kurtzman didn't sound convinced.

"You think he's got a crib in Wonderland?"

"He wouldn't be the first."

"God knows. He isn't on the books, though. Telephone, utilities, we checked it all."

"He's hinky," Kurtzman said. "I have to figure that he'd use a cover."

"Granted. There's no way for us to check out every rental pad in town, much less the suburbs."

"So, we wait," Kurtzman said. "It's what we do. We'll catch a break."

"I tapped some Bureau sources on the NRP, to see if there was any better place to look."

"And what you got was . . . ?"

"Zip," she said. "Across the board."

"We can't work miracles. Cut yourself some slack."

"It tells you something, doesn't it? I mean, if they can take it underground that quickly, no loose ends."

"We knew they were professionals. You're watching tax dollars at work, once removed."

"It scares me sometimes."

"As it should. You train a million men, and some of them go bad. Your basic law of averages."

"What's Schroder's selling point?"

"Dissatisfaction with the system," Kurtzman answered. "Anger, unemployment and frustration. Take your pick. He'd call it patriotic fervor, I suppose."

"We need to take him out," she said.

"You'll have to find him first."

"I will." It sounded like a promise. "Bet your ass, I will."

*Paradise Valley, Nevada*

THE PUBLIC TELEPHONE wasn't secure, but Bolan had a compact scrambler unit with him as he stepped inside the booth and closed the folding door behind him. Half the size of a cigarette pack, it clipped directly to the telephone and—theoretically, at least—ruled out the danger of electronic eavesdropping. A descrambler at the other end would make sense of his words, and there would be no risk of strangers listening in, if the receiving station was secure.

And Stony Man, in Bolan's estimation, had the most secure land lines available.

The tiny crossroads village in Nevada was a pit stop, nothing more. The heat in Idaho was too intense for Bolan and Grimaldi to remain, and there was nothing left for them to do there, even if they chose to stay.

Survivors out of Camp Redemption would be scattered to the winds and running for their lives from the police, the FBI and ATF, from enemies unknown. They would be small-fry, not worth chasing, probably impossible to find in any case.

He glanced back through the smudged glass of the phone booth and saw Grimaldi waiting in the car. No one was looking for them here, but anything could happen, and it always paid to keep your guard up. Trouble showed up when you least expected it, and there was nothing to be done except stand firm and be prepared.

For anything.

He clipped the scrambler to the telephone and dropped a quarter in the slot, tapped out eleven digits, waiting while the link went through. The call was made collect and automatically accepted. Anyone who had that number was a trusted friend, and knew that it was used only in cases of emergency.

"Hello?"

He didn't recognize the voice, and that was fine. No reason why he should.

"It's Striker," Bolan said. "I'm scrambling ... now."

He punched the scrambler button, tried to put a face on the technician who was doing likewise in the War Room, some two thousand miles away. There was a fleeting crackle on the line, and when the unfamiliar voice came back at Bolan, it was crystal clear. A stranger tapping in somewhere along the line, however, would be treated to a medley of peculiar squawks and squeals, no more intelligible to the human ear than birdsong in the forest.

"Scrambled," said the tech at Stony Man. "Recording."

"We're all done in Idaho," Bolan said.

"Copy, Striker. It's been on the air. Well done."

"Have there been any stats?"

"The count's ongoing. Can I get your twenty?"

"Passing through Nevada. I could use a pointer."

"We've been scanning, Striker. Nothing in the way of useful information, I'm afraid."

"No word on Schroder?"

"He was spotted twice in the past two days, in Cincinnati and Savannah. Airline records going in, but nothing coming out. We don't have anything on his group or the visitors in either town."

It was the kind of news he had expected. Without a lead, they didn't have a prayer. No targets, no direction.

"We'll be coming in," he said at last.

"Back here?"

"Affirmative."

"I'll pass it on. That's it?"

"Should do."

He cradled the receiver and removed the scrambler, walked back to the waiting car and settled in the shotgun seat.

"What's new?" Grimaldi asked.

"They haven't heard a thing."

"What, nothing?"

"Zip."

"Well, damn it. Where are we supposed to go from here?"

"I told them we were coming in."

Grimaldi thought about it for a moment, then he shrugged. "Okay. Suits me."

"Whatever's going down," Bolan said, "I can't shake the feeling that we should be looking to the east. There hasn't been a strike west of the Mississippi yet, and I don't think there will be."

"What was this about, then?" He nodded in a general northerly direction as he asked the question.

"Think of it as Schroder's wake-up call. I don't want anybody from the opposition getting too relaxed."

"I think we've taken care of that," Grimaldi said.

"We might have lost them in the process, though."

Grimaldi turned the key, released the brake and put the rental car in gear. "It's not like that," he said. "You had to figure that he'd go to ground."

And that was true, of course. It simply didn't make the taste of failure any sweeter. If the National Redemption Party was prepared to wait a while—or even scrub its current plan—he knew there was a chance that they would never see the end of it. Their raid against the base in Idaho would be a poor rejoinder for the acts of terrorism that had rocked America in recent weeks. He might be leading on the body count, so far, but he hadn't reeled in a single fish of any consequence. Foot soldiers were expendable. The serpent's body could regenerate itself, if Bolan left the brain intact.

The problem was, he had to find the head before he could remove it. And so far the leads were slim to none.

"If you want to call ahead and grease the wheels, we've got a naval air base at Stillwater, about a hundred miles south. We can pick up some wings."

"Sounds right," Bolan said.

"Next stop, Stony Man."

"Let's make it Washington instead."

Grimaldi blinked, then flashed a crooked smile. "Your wish is my command."

*Washington, D.C.*

"YOU MIGHT AS WELL take off," Brognola told his secretary.

"Are you sure, sir?"

"Positive."

"I'll see you in the morning then."

"Sure thing, Kelly."

When he was fretting, Brognola preferred to have the office to himself. It helped him think, without Kelly hovering in the background, keying data, fielding calls. The quiet didn't ease his mind exactly, but at least it freed him of distractions while he thought about his problems.

At the moment, number one was Striker and this business with Hezbollah and Wallace Schroder's National Redemption Party. The big Fed was ready to accept the link between those groups as having been conclusively established, but the knowledge didn't help him solve his problem.

It might even make things worse.

For weeks now, every law-enforcement agency in the United States had been alert for some lead on the Muslim fundamentalist commandos who were raising hell across the countryside. When news of the connection to a group of native neo-Fascists and survivalists leaked out, the headlines would be lurid. Questions would be asked in Washington—not only at the *Post*, but on the Hill.

Someone should have seen the bad news coming, and in Hal Brognola's world, that someone typically meant Justice. The U.S. Attorney General's office, FBI and DEA, you name it—all of them were paid to monitor the crazies, drop a net on those who broke the law and keep the others on a short leash, just in case. In practice, though, the Bill of Rights and several hundred state or federal laws, backed up by court decisions and interpretation, left the crazies more or less at liberty to do their thing—at least until they started throwing bombs and pulling triggers.

By the time it went that far, of course, the good guys were a lap or two behind the pack and sweating to catch up. They managed, sometimes, but they also ate a lot of dust.

For Brognola's part, he had never grown accustomed to the taste of failure. It still gagged him, each and every time.

The blitz out west, in Idaho, had gone like clockwork. Bolan and Grimaldi were okay, and they had dealt the NRP a solid blow, for all the good it did. Unfortunately no one from the party's brass—and none of the elusive Hezbollah guerrillas—had been present when the raid went down. To Brognola, that meant the game could still go either one of two ways: Schroder and his playmates could get wise, slip off somewhere without a trace, or they could push ahead, against the odds.

Brognola had a sneaking hunch his adversaries weren't about to quit the game, at least before they had a chance to play for all the marbles.

"Jesus."

Talking to yourself, Brognola thought, and shook his head. A Section Eight was one way out, but who would haul the garbage if he split? Young agents coming up just didn't have the same knack for it these days. He couldn't fault them on their education, anything like that, but they lacked the old familiar fire.

It came from growing up in modern times, Brognola told himself, where black and white had blurred to countless shades of gray. There had been plenty of corruption in the good old days, of course, but this was different. Politicians started bailing out on campaign promises before they took the oath of office, and nobody seemed to care or even notice. Hell, you couldn't turn the television on or read a newspaper without discovering some item on police accepting bribes, protecting pushers, pulling burglaries, committing murder in their free time.

They were still a sad minority, the bad ones, but the temper of the times said otherwise. Subversion of authority was widely touted as the rule, instead of the exception. "Common knowledge" had it that the bad guys always won, or broke even, anyway.

Stony Man had been established to reverse that trend, and it had done the trick wherever Hal Brognola's warriors had applied themselves. A fact of life in covert operations, though, prevented Bolan and the others from receiving credit for their deeds. Instead of lining up for medals, they were tucked away from prying eyes, their most spectacular successes credited to other agencies, or written off as internecine war between contending terrorists, crime syndicates, what have you.

Such was life, Brognola thought. The up side of clandestine ops was that a failure didn't make the headlines, either. No one got to see Dan Rather roasting Bolan on a spit, but most of that was smoke and mirrors, anyway. If anything went seriously wrong, Brognola knew about it, and the Man would have to know, as well.

"Forget it."

Talking to himself again.

They weren't done yet, regardless of the setback. It was strictly temporary—or so Brognola hoped. If they could find a way to turn the game around, snoop out the heavies somewhere in the next few hours or days, before they struck again, there was a chance the team could come out smelling like a rose.

But how?

"I'll think of something, damn it!"

No one contradicted him, and Brognola took that as a positive sign.

All things considered, it was the best that he could do.


"I HATE THIS TOWN," Eulon Trask said.

"It sucks, I know," Bobby Elliott agreed.

He had the wheel, westbound on Pennsylvania Avenue. The FBI building was coming up on their right, with Justice followed by the IRS immediately on the left.

"They ought to drop the bomb right here," Trask told his driver, scowling at the stately buildings housing everything he hated.

"Make it easier on us, at least. How come this couldn't wait?"

"I don't ask questions, Bobby. You should take a lesson."

"Hey, I like to have some vague idea of why I'm doing things, okay."

"It's need-to-know."

"Whatever."

"If you want to know what I think," Trask went on, "it's somehow tied in with what happened at the compound."

"Schroder told you that?"

Trask shook his head and pointed as they came up on Eleventh Street. "Turn here. I want to go around the block once more and check it out."

"Okay."

"He didn't spell it out," Trask said, continuing, "but what else could it be? Check out the timing, will you?"

"Even so, the TV didn't say the Feds were involved."

"So, you believe the networks now?"

"Hey, Eulon—"

"Hey, yourself. If they're not part of the solution, they're part of the problem. Who's been pushing this liberal-socialist crap down our throats for the past thirty years?"

"Yeah, I hear you."

"Besides, it's an order, all right? You remember that much from your training, I hope."

"I'm on your side, okay."

"Yeah, I know. It's just I hate this town."

The target was coming up again.

"They all park underground," Elliott said. "Security and that. We'll never reach the car."

"Don't have to," Trask told him. "We'll do it on the street."

"That's dicey."

"That's the only way to go, unless you'd rather go inside the building."

"Right. Or we could just stay home and shoot ourselves. Eliminate the middleman."

"It's doable," Trask said. "Don't sweat it."

"Does this guy have a driver or a bodyguard?"

"What difference does it make?"

"Details," Elliott said. "We're gonna do it, we should do it right."

"That's why we're here," Trask said. "It doesn't matter if there's one guy or a dozen in a car. They bleed the same."

"They might shoot back, you know."

"He's not the fucking President. I'm counting on surprise."

"Well, here we are."

The car turned right on E Street, traveled three blocks east, then turned right again on Ninth.

"See there," Elliott said. "That leads to the garage below."

"Okay."

"You want him going in or coming out?"

"I'll think about it," Trask replied.

"We should have brought the others, maybe."

"I don't need three navigators, Bobby. All they have to do is aim and keep their powder dry."

"There's gonna be some heat on this one, Eulon."

"Never mind the heat. We've got our orders."

"Even so—"

"Ours not to reason why," Trask said.

"Is that some kind of poem, or an old wives' tale?"

"Who gives a flying fuck? We carry out our orders, and we don't ask stupid questions. Right?"

"Amen to that."

"This time tomorrow," Trask said, "we'll have it done. No hassles, if we play it right."

"We need to think about the traffic," Elliott reminded him. "I ain't no fucking kamikaze."

"You don't have to be. If necessary, we can trail the target home to Arlington. I'd rather do it here, though. We can use the traffic for a cover."

"Maybe so."

"If it's a problem, Bobby, I can ask for someone else. You tell the colonel all about your difficulty when he calls you in."

"I didn't say that, Eulon." Elliott's voice was troubled now, a sharp edge of panic underlying his words. "The colonel doesn't have to be involved in this."

"You're sure?"

"Damn right."

"Okay, then. We've got three shooters, counting me. If you can keep up with the car, we got it made."

"Keep up." The driver's voice was scornful. "Are you kidding me?"

It never failed, Trask thought. You zap them in the ego, and they kick in with the preprogrammed response. Psychology 1A, and Trask had never even gone beyond his senior year of high school.

"Well, then, if you're positive..."

"Hell yes. I mean, he's driving normal wheels, right? Not some kind of weird Ferrari testosterone or something?"

Trask had to smile at that. "Forget about it. He'll be driving federal four door all the way. The government is trying to economize, remember?"

"Yeah? I thought all their cuts were coming out of military budgets and Social Security."

"Things are rough all over," Trask told his driver. "Time for a change."

"Fucking ay," Elliott answered.

Lesson number two: When the specifics of a mission got too hairy, fade back for a long shot, concentrate on ideology and the big picture. Soldiers who were running short on nerve before a battle could be turned around, sometimes, by an appeal to God and country, even simple hatred of their enemies. What was it that kept Japanese soldiers hiding in the jungle, sniping total strangers, twenty years after the bomb dropped on Nagasaki?

Commitment and determination, sure.

Raw guts.

It was enough to get the job done, anyway. Let Schroder do the thinking for the NRP. All Eulon Trask had to know, for the moment, was the name of his next target. Anything to smooth the path toward Judgment Day.

And it was coming.

It wouldn't be long now.

**9**

*Blue Ridge Mountains, Virginia*

The exercise began at dawn. In fact, Ahmed Jazmil had been informed that they would strike by night, when it was time, but he could see the sense in practicing by daylight, running through the course at different times to make sure every member of the strike team knew his job, exactly where to go and what to do.

There would be no room for mistakes once they were all committed to the main event.

It was a treat to have the whole team reassembled. Nineteen men, with two killed in the field, all known to one another from the early days of training, scattered on their passage to America, but reunited now to do the job they have been chosen to perform.

They all wore camouflage fatigues and combat boots, their hands and faces painted. Jazmil's weapon was an MP-5 SD-3 submachine gun, manufactured in Germany by Heckler & Koch, with a telescoping butt and built-on silencer. He also had a double-action Browning semiautomatic pistol, plus a fighting knife, garrote and hand grenades. They couldn't know exactly where the guards would be when they began their raid, and silence was essential in the early stages.

Later, once the battle had been joined, well, noise would be no problem.

The basic plan had called for seven three-man teams to strike the target from all sides at once, but they were down to six teams now, and one of those with four men. Jazmil's team still had the basic three, and he had been selected as its leader, serving with Mohammed Duabi and Jian Assad. Duabi was armed identically to Jazmil, while Assad was carrying a CAR-15 with greater range, no silencer.

They came in through the trees, with nothing but the photographs they had memorized to guide them. There had also been a small-scale model, tiny trees and all, with which to plot their movements, but it felt like playing with a toy.

Today was real.

Almost.

The guns were all loaded with blanks, of course, and the grenades were dummies. There was no point wasting precious ammunition or calling attention to themselves with explosives when they could practice the moves just as well with play-acting equipment. The guns were real enough, and when the time came, their magazines would hold live rounds.

The sentries in this morning's exercise were American, as they would be when Jazmil and his comrades stormed the final target. Each was under orders to remain alert, do everything within his power to detect and kill the Hezbollah commandos, wipe them out—with blanks, of course—before they had a chance to reach their destination.

Crouching in the shadow of a giant oak, Jazmil was ready when the sentry showed himself, a young man, moving cautiously, dressed much as they were and armed with an M-16 rifle. He was clearly alert and well trained, prepared for anything.

Except, perhaps, to die.

Jazmil sighted down the barrel of his submachine gun, index finger lightly curled around the trigger. Let him come a little closer, just a few more steps.

He fired a 3-round burst, the SMG's report suppressed until it sounded like a muffled sneeze. The sentry didn't fall or even stagger, but his shoulders slumped a little, and he shook his head, disgusted with himself.

"Well, shit."

At first it had been planned for them to run the exercise with paint-ball weapons, but on second thought it was decided that they ought to use the very guns they would be carrying in battle, to provide familiarity and weed out any problems in advance.

They broke from cover, silently, with Jazmil in the lead, moved past the sentry who had slung his rifle in preparation for the hike back to the staging area. He didn't speak to them, nor they to him. It was enough to know that they had killed him, and without sustaining any friendly casualties.

Three hundred yards remained before they reached the buildings. Distances weren't as great here as they would be on the battleground, but it hadn't been possible to fabricate a perfect simulation. They were lucky, Jazmil realized, to have such similar terrain available. At least it wasn't like the camps in Palestine, where they were forced to practice in a desert wasteland prior to striking at a modern town.

He could feel his men behind him, moving through the trees. He didn't have to look and satisfy himself that they were there. They were committed to the mission, even as he was. Each man would do his part, regardless of the cost.

It was their destiny.

ALI JARASH CAME IN behind the sentry, moving silently on tiptoe. He didn't unsheathe his knife—this tall American wasn't supposed to die—but rather moved in close enough to loop one arm around the young man's neck, his free hand curled into a fist and thumping home below the sentry's ribs.

"You're dead."

The young man shrugged him off, appeared as if he might start swinging with his fists, then slowly broke into a smile.

"Not bad," he said. "Not bad at all."

Jarash didn't remain to watch the dead man leave. He had a mission to perform, and never mind that it was merely practice. Urgently he beckoned to the other members of his team, Afif Hussein and Hamil Ismah.

"This way."

They followed him, unquestioning, obedient. A narrow trail wound through the forest, north to south. It might have once been a streambed, but it was dry now, overgrown with ferns and weeds that whispered every time he took a step.

Jarash wasn't accustomed to the forest, but a soldier could adapt himself to any climate or terrain, with courage and determination. This would be a change, at any rate, from planting bombs and drive-by shootings, more like all-out warfare than the hit-and-run guerrilla tactics he was used to.

All or nothing in a single fight.

They spent a quarter of an hour creeping through the trees before they saw the first of several buildings. Walking past was another sentry with an M-16.

The guards knew they were coming. Not precisely when or where, but they were obviously conscious of an exercise in progress. This gave them an edge, he realized, which—hopefully, at least—their real-life enemies wouldn't possess. Therefore, the war game should, in some respects, be harder than the real thing.

If nothing else, the thought was comforting.

The sentry had to go before they could proceed, but there was too much open ground between Jarash and his intended target for a duplication of his last attack. Instead, he took a firm grip on the MP-5 SD-3 submachine gun, creeping forward, inch by inch, until he had a clear shot at the young man on patrol. He pegged the range at thirty feet, no challenge for an automatic weapon with 9 mm rounds.

He waited until the sentry's back was turned, then whistled softly, saw him start to turn. The M-16 was in his hands, but he would have no chance to use it. Three rounds stuttered from the SMG, immediately followed by another burst of three from Ismah. Certain death at that range, and the sentry shrugged expressively, a slow smile on his face. He didn't speak, but simply sat down where he was to let them pass.

The buildings weren't perfect, understandably. It would have meant preparing an identical tract of land, complete in every detail, and the risk of prior discovery had been too great. They had a choice of working near the target or conducting dress rehearsals far away, and all concerned had opted for proximity. They had floor plans, drawn by one of their collaborators, to make up for any deficiency in the models, but for now the team would work with what they had.

Jarash flattened himself against the wall, his soldiers doing likewise. Cautiously he crept around the corner, taking care with every step. A door stood just ahead of him, unlocked, of course, but he went through the motions of fixing a clay plastic charge to the lock, inserting the make-believe detonator and scuttling back under cover to wait for the explosion.

Ten seconds, and then they rushed forward, Hussein and Ismah close behind him. The imaginary blast removed all need for caution. Once the enemy had been alerted to their presence, only speed would matter—that, and accuracy when they found a target.

There was no one waiting for them as they cleared the threshold, but the lights were on inside, and voices carried to Jarash's ears from somewhere farther down the corridor. Motioning for his teammates to follow him, he led the way, his submachine gun tracking ceaselessly, like the antennae of some lethal insect.

Up ahead, on Jarash's left, a door stood open, spilling light and sound into the corridor. He didn't hesitate, stepping through and dodging immediately to his left to clear the field of fire for those behind. His finger tightened on the trigger of his SMG, and he began to sweep the room with phantom bullets.

Crowding in behind him, Hussein opened fire with his own submachine gun, Ismah adding racket with his CAR-15. Their targets tried to scramble out of canvas camp chairs, but the effort was too little and too late. If Jarash and his men hadn't been firing blanks, the floor would have been slick with blood by now, instead of scattered cotton wadding.

"Jesus Christ!" The nearest of the young Americans was gaping at Jarash, amazed by what he saw. "I think I shit myself!"

"No way," another man said. "You always smell like that."

Jarash ignored them, lowering his weapon and unclipping the compact radio transmitter from his belt. He brought it to his lips and pressed the button with his thumb.

"Team One," he told whoever might be listening. "Mission accomplished."

FIVE HUNDRED FEET above the treetops, riding in an observation helicopter, Tarik Hassan received the message from his pilot.

"Team One's home and dry," the pilot told him, flashing teeth that testified to years of dental care no refugee from Palestine could ever have afforded.

"So. Acknowledge, please."

The pilot did as he was told, which was another new experience for Hassan: giving orders to a white man and seeing them obeyed without hesitation, without question.

He didn't understand these Americans, what they hoped to gain from helping Hezbollah embarrass their elected government, nor did he care. It was enough for him to know that he could trust these men to help him carry out his mission. After that...

He couldn't think beyond the mission. It was almost too much to believe, despite assistance from their unexpected allies, that the plan would still come off without what the Americans referred to as a hitch. His soldiers came prepared to die, and some of them, he thought, would truthfully be disappointed if they didn't have a chance to sacrifice their lives for the *jihad*.

The practice exercise would help them to survive, but none among them would deceive himself into believing it would be like this—so easy—when they moved against the enemy in earnest. There would be no harmless blanks when that day came; no dummy hand grenades or simulated plastic charges, sculpted out of clay.

"They're doing well, so far," Wallace Schroder said, leaning forward in his seat against the safety harness.

"It is still a game," Hassan replied.

He understood what all commanders know—or should know—in regard to war games. They were useful in their way; as practice, and to fire men's spirits on the eve of mortal combat. Even so, the players entered into such a contest in the knowledge that they would be called upon to suffer no real harm. There was a different rush entirely when a fight was joined for real and men began to bleed, began to die. Death motivated soldiers in a way that speeches never could, propelling some toward greatness, others into ignominious defeat.

"The time?" Hassan inquired.

"They're fifteen minutes into it," Schroder replied. "That's not bad."

"It will be dark when they attack," Hassan reminded his companion, "and the distance will be greater."

"We'll run through it all again tonight. Try out the goggles."

Special headgear had been purchased for the raiders, Nitefinder goggles that converted a pitch-black night into greenish dusk for the hunter equipped with the infrared spotters. There was nothing special to be learned about the goggles, but it would be helpful if Hassan's commandos grew accustomed to their weight, the eerie new perspective they imparted to the world.

Another edge, Hassan told himself, in the fight against superior numbers and fortifications. Their enemies would be familiar with the battleground from long exposure and repeated drills, possessed of gear that would include all manner of high-tech security devices. Hassan's men, in turn, had been forewarned by one of their American accomplices, but understanding risks and beating them were very different things. A man could be prepared to fight and still get beaten, if his flesh and spirit weren't strong enough.

At least Hassan felt confident on that score. Even though his men would be outnumbered and outgunned, no weakness of the spirit would be found among them. They had courage to spare, if only that were enough to win battles and wars.

But it wasn't.

Brave men died every day, some of them needlessly, in vain. If they had been empowered to resurrect all of the valiant freedom fighters he had known in recent years, Hassan would have possessed a standing army large enough to challenge the Israelis in the stolen territory they called home. It might have been a very different war, but that wasn't to be.

Instead, his war went on forever, countless skirmishes in place of grand, apocalyptic battles. There were days when Hassan despaired of ever seeing final victory.

No matter.

He would keep on fighting for his children yet unborn, and for their children, generations of his people who would have a chance at peace and freedom in their homeland only if a dedicated people's army kept the pressure on their enemies and never missed an opportunity to strike for justice.

War without end, in God's name.

"Team Three reporting in," the pilot said. "They lost one man, but got the job done."

That left four teams still to go, and all of them should be done soon, if they were still on schedule. And if not, they would be privileged to try again that night, with nothing but their injured feelings riding on the line.

Tomorrow or the next day, when they moved against their chosen adversaries, there would be no cushion or guaranteed safety, no margin of error. The bullets and explosives would be real, each step potentially the last. For some, that knowledge made the crucial difference, kicked their senses into high gear, as it were. No practice exercise could fully duplicate the tension or the heat of combat. Men who took the war games casually would fight like demons when the real thing came their way.

And they would have to do exactly that, this time around.

It wouldn't be enough to save their lives, of course—not all of them—but that was as expected. The Americans were fond of saying that you could not make an omelet without breaking eggs, and many eggs would be broken in the next day or two.

AHMED JAZMIL WENT through the doorway firing from the hip, a quick left and right with the silenced submachine gun, cartridge casings bouncing on the floor around his feet. He caught one of the young defenders just emerging from an anteroom immediately on his right and punched imaginary bullets through his chest.

The white man blinked and started to reach for the pistol on his hip. It took a second burst to stop him short, remind him of the rules, and then he let his shoulders slump a little with resignation and defeat.

Jazmil moved past him, instantly dismissed him from consideration. Assad and Duabi were behind him, almost crowding on his heels, their weapons covering his brisk advance. Jazmil felt the adrenaline pumping, short hairs bristling on his nape, the same excitement—nearly so, at least—of combat in the raw. He knew the bullets and grenades were dummies, but the next phase of the exercise—its culmination—would be all too real.

As if to punctuate the thought, a burst of automatic fire, not silenced, suddenly erupted from the far end of the corridor. Jazmil went down immediately, belly on the floor, and wriggled toward the doorway on his left. Had he been hit, in theory?

No.

Duabi leapt through the door behind him, Jazmil waiting for another heartbeat, looking for Assad. The unseen enemy loosed another burst. At last, he peeked outside and saw the final member of his team standing in the middle of the hallway.

"Got *you*, Abdul," a mocking voice called from the far end of the hallway. Assad nodded before he turned away, retreating out of sight.

One down, then, and Jazmil knew well enough that some of their strike force would die in the final attack. It was a given, understood, accepted as a fact of life in warfare. Soldiers die, and winners persevere.

"Be ready," he commanded Duabi. Almost before he finished speaking, Jazmil had replaced the submachine gun's magazine and palmed one of the dud grenades. He pulled the pin because he was supposed to, and because the small things counted in reality. Duabi was mimicking his actions—new mag, hand grenade, pin gone.

Duabi went first, a wild pitch through the doorway, whipping his right arm around with force enough to bruise it on the doorjamb. Gunfire stuttered briefly, then he heard one of the shooters yell, "Grenade!"

And there would never be a better time.

Jazmil broke from cover in a crouch, already moving down the hallway toward his startled enemies. Duabi ran close behind him, lobbing the second grenade in an overhand pitch that was dead on the target, dropping the metal egg in front of an open doorway, seeing it wobble to the left and out of sight.

Jazmil imagined the explosion, rushing forward with his shoulders hunched, as if to dodge flying shrapnel, keeping a firm grip on the submachine gun as he ran. Doors were open on both sides, with some of the defenders scowling at the two grenades as if the dummies had released some kind of rancid odor, several others rising from protective postures, moving back to greet the enemy with M-16s.

Too late.

The muffled submachine guns stuttered left and right, unloading the better part of two full magazines while the Americans stood there and took it. In other circumstances, they would all be stretched out dead or writhing on the floor, and Jazmil saw that in his mind's eye, too.

It made him smile, the thought of so much death among his enemies. He pictured blood, smeared on the floor, the walls, and nearly laughed out loud.

"What's so funny?" one of the dead men inquired resentfully.

Instead of answering, Jazmil took up his compact two-way radio and thumbed the button to transmit.

"Team Two," he told the air. "Mission accomplished. One man lost."

"Acknowledged," came the small voice from a distance. "Stay in place and wait for further orders."

"Understood."

He clipped the radio back on his belt, relaxed and slung the MP-5 SD-3, muzzle downward, from his shoulder. Turning his back on the Americans, he joined Duabi for the walk back to the door where they had entered.

It hadn't been a simple victory, despite the fact that it was bloodless on both sides. His team had managed to succeed, with one man out of three eliminated, but he still had no idea of what had happened with his comrades in the other penetration teams.

And this was daylight, Jazmil told himself. Less ground to cover, and—perhaps—a smaller, somewhat less determined force defending a facility without the various security devices they were given to expect. How would it be when they attacked in darkness, faced with motion sensors, fiber optics and closed-circuit television cameras, when blanks and dummy hand grenades gave way to live munitions in the hands of determined soldiers fighting for their lives?

A brief chill gripped Jazmil, then turned into a shiver of excitement. This could be the mission he was born to carry out, his destiny. The hand of God would be open to receive him if he gave his life in battle.

He had to sell it dearly, though, with no pointless suicidal gestures in the early stages of the fight. Death, in and of itself, was not his goal. He had a mission to carry out, and he was anxious to repeat the exercise once more, in darkness.

He would get his chance that very night.

**10**

*Washington, D.C.*

Brognola thought of a half dozen reasons why he should stay later at the office, but he finally discarded each of them in turn. He wasn't satisfied with progress on the current mission, but the problems were beyond his reach and personal control. If he was bound to worry, the big Fed decided, he might just as well be worrying at home.

He scanned his desk for any paperwork that absolutely couldn't wait, found nothing all that urgent and pushed his chair back with a weary sigh. Arms stretched above his head, he cracked his neck and shoulders, working out the kinks that came from sitting at a desk for hours on end.

It had been different in the good old days, when he was often in the field. He was heavier these days, and seldom found the time or energy to work out in a gym. Brognola wasn't fat, but he was creeping up on chunky, even with his wife's best efforts in the dietary realm. He nibbled on the job—a doughnut first thing in the morning with his coffee; something from the cafeteria at midmorning break; a little something more to help the afternoon along—and it was adding up.

He didn't wear a gun around the office, but he traveled armed outside. Despite his rank at Justice, there had been occasions in the recent past when this or that bad actor made attempts to take him out. It didn't happen every day, of course, but one time was enough to get you killed, if you were unprepared.

He reached inside the upper right-hand drawer of his desk, lifting out the Smith & Wesson Model 411 double-action automatic in its clip-on holster. The piece was chambered for the Smith & Wesson .40-caliber round—the classic 10 mm cartridge—and had lately been adopted as the standard side arm of the FBI. Handlers claimed that with proper loading, the .40-caliber weapon combined the stopping power of the old Colt .45 with penetration equal to a hot .357 Magnum load. Brognola wasn't sure about the details, but he knew the weapon was a certified man-stopper, with eleven rounds in the magazine and one more in the chamber.

Clipping on the weapon and the extra ammo pouch was a routine procedure, but it never failed to put Brognola on alert, raising his consciousness of danger to a higher level. In the office, even hanging out around the house, he had a chance to lose himself in mundane tasks, forget about the war that went on night and day, around the clock, throughout his country and around the world.

It didn't hurt to forget for a while, unless you lost your focus when it counted, let the enemy get in behind you, on your blind side. It was all a matter of perspective, standing watch.

He locked his desk and removed his jacket from the hanger behind the door, slipping it on. Another key locked the door behind him as he left his private office, yet another for the outer door to the reception area. The corridor was empty but for Andy, one of the custodians, who had begun to make his early rounds with mop and bucket.

The elevator door hissed open, and Brognola stepped inside. The big Fed had the car to himself as he pressed the button for the subterranean garage. There were no stops along the way, and within a minute he stepped out into the chilly cave of the garage. His footsteps echoed in the open space as he paced off the pools of light and shadow, flicking glances left and right from force of habit.

There was strict security at Justice, top to bottom, given the state of crime and terrorism in the land. The entrance to the underground garage was sealed by metal gates, with uniforms on guard around the clock and automatic weapons close at hand. The guards knew Hal Brognola at a glance, but they still checked his laminated ID card each morning, the same way sentries at a military base would ask to see the general's orders. It was SOP.

Brognola reached his car, unlocked the door and slid behind the steering wheel. He switched on the engine and took a moment to adjust the air conditioner, then backed out of the numbered space and followed the illuminated Exit signs suspended from the concrete rafters overhead. There was no ID check for parties leaving the garage, but one of the three guards on duty still took time to eyeball Brognola and nod before he keyed the gate.

The big Fed powered up the three-lane ramp and turned on his blinker, letting several cars roll past before he found a gap in traffic. Pulling onto Ninth Street, then rolling south toward Constitution Avenue, he lined up for the long run that would take him through the heart of Wonderland, across the Potomac on the Theodore Roosevelt Memorial Bridge and back home to Arlington.

It was a trip that Brognola made twice a day, five days a week, and sometimes six or seven. He had never run into a problem on the road, going or coming, but he kept a sharp eye on his rearview mirror, all the same. He had no reason to believe that anyone was trailing him, or had a reason to, but he could never be sure.

The first stoplight loomed ahead of him, and Brognola eased on the brake, his four-door Plymouth coasting to a halt behind a florist's van.

"Come on," he said to no one in particular, "let's roll."

"NOT YET," Eulon Trask said. "I want him moving, so we don't get hung up here."

"Okay."

"You ready back there?" Trask asked, turning to the men behind him.

"Ready," Roland Jakes replied, hands fiddling with the Ingram MAC-10 submachine gun in his lap.

George Larcom had an Uzi, but he saw no need to check and double-check it. "Anytime," he said.

Trask had a Tec-9 pistol with a 32-round magazine and five-inch shrouded barrel, earlier converted to selective fire by gunsmiths on retainer with the NRP. Between the three of them, Trask figured they could do the dog and wriggle out of any problem they encountered with the Feds or blue suits.

Easy.

Trask didn't know the target personally. Some big shot with Justice, he was told. Their mole had fingered him, explained a bit about his function in the government. It didn't mean a hill of beans to Trask, but when the word came down to take the joker out, he meant to do as he was told.

The drones in Washington were in for a surprise, and no mistake. It would have been a kick to hang around when he was done, to take a look at the expressions on their stupid faces when they got a taste of what was coming down the line.

A preview of coming attractions.

They had been cruising when the mark came out of the garage at Justice, Elliott griping on and on about the gas gauge after driving from Virginia, irritating Trask so bad he was about to snap, when everything fell into place. The mark was running late, but not *that* late. There was still ample daylight for a hit-and-run procedure, and the traffic had begun to thin a little with the hour, even though it never really cleared on Constitution Avenue from 6:00 a.m. to 9:00 p.m.

It was a muggy afternoon, and Trask would rather have used the air-conditioning than riding with the windows down, sweat soaking through his T-shirt, but they had to keep an open field of fire. So he would take a shower later, when he had the time, knock back a frosty beer or three while they compared notes on the hit.

Right here, right now, the heat would do just fine.

The drive-by yesterday had given them a feel for territory, but there had been no way to predict which way their mark would turn when he came out of the garage, what kind of driver he would be, in terms of speed, lane changes, jumping lights and so forth. As it was, they nearly lost him, passing him going in the opposite direction, and they had to whip around the block—up Ninth to Pennsylvania, west to Tenth, back down to Constitution—and they lost two blocks on the maneuver.

Back on Constitution Avenue, westbound, they were forced to make up time, blow through the yellow light across Eleventh Street, trying hard to close the gap. They had another mile or so to run before they hit the river and the bridge cut off their options. To the west of the Potomac, in Arlington, they had a whole new list of problems to contend with.

"I want to get it done before the bridge," Trask said.

"I'm working on it," Elliott shot back.

"Work harder, damn it!"

They came up through traffic in the block between Thirteenth and Fourteenth streets, with the National Museum of American History on their left, headquarters of the Interstate Commerce Commission on the right. Up ahead, to the southwest, the Washington Monument thrust skyward like a rocket on the launching pad—or a rude, insulting finger.

Traffic held them back, but Elliott was making progress, jumping one or two cars at a time, their target doing likewise when he saw an opening. He didn't seem to be aware of their approach yet, but why should he be? In all this traffic, it would take a psychic to work out that he was being followed.

Around two-thirds of all the cars that Trask could see were westbound, bailing out of Washington and heading for bedroom suburbs in Virginia. When the sun went down in D.C., Trask knew, the town belonged to cops, street gangs and the political high rollers who existed in an endless round of parties at the taxpayers' expense.

He wasn't clear on how this hit, specifically, would help to change all that, but he was trained to follow orders without question, trusting his superiors to deal with strategy and consequences. Trust was hard to come by these days, when the politicians used the military as a tool to keep themselves in office, but he would have trusted Colonel Schroder with his life, with the few small dreams that still remained intact.

The motorists around them didn't glance in their direction, paying no attention whatsoever to the four men in the dark blue Buick. That would change, Trask realized, the moment shooting started, but the first impulse of any witness to a killing was self-preservation. Duck and run. Forget about remembering descriptions for police, sketch artists, photo lineups. Watch your ass, and let the other guy do likewise.

Coming up on Fourteenth Street, and they were gaining nicely. At this rate, Trask decided, they should overtake their target by the time they got to Seventeenth, with room to spare. He kept a firm grip on the Tec-9 pistol, index finger curled around the trigger, waiting for the moment when his mark would be in range, a clear shot at the craggy profile.

Ski masks would have covered their identities, beyond all doubt, but Trask knew four masked men would have been all the more conspicuous on Pennsylvania Avenue. And in a town where every third or fourth vehicle came equipped with a car phone, an alert to the police would certainly have doomed them well before they had a chance to carry out their mission.

"Getting there," Elliott stated.

Trask wasn't blind. He knew how close they were, how far they had to go, but if talking to himself helped the driver, then he could live with it. A long block lay between their Buick and the Plymouth they were stalking, but the target's lead had been reduced by half, perhaps two-thirds of the original distance.

"Can you pass him on the left?"

"That's the plan," Elliott answered. "All I have to do is get around this idiot and we've got a chance."

The idiot in question was an elderly man whose idea of progress seemed to be hogging the fast lane at five or ten miles per hour below the posted speed limit. Blaring horns meant nothing to him—probably stone deaf, thought Trask—but he wasn't about to yield until the lane ran out.

"Old bastard," Elliott muttered, going for the break a moment later. Never mind the turning indicator, as he veered into the center lane and cut off a Mercedes-Benz, pulling level with the old man in a flash. The target was two car lengths ahead, and the old man on their left was driving slowly enough that Elliott had no trouble cutting back in front of him. He was about to shoot a finger at the driver when Trask reached out and pulled his hand down.

"Concentrate!" he snapped. "Don't give him any extra reasons to remember us."

"Okay, okay."

The Buick was accelerating smoothly, drawing closer to the target. Trask shifted in his seat to give himself a better angle.

Any second now...

IT WAS A FLUKE that Hal Brognola saw the guns. Somebody leaned on a horn behind him, and he checked the driver's mirror out of simple curiosity to find out who was raising hell. It seemed to be an old man in a Honda Prelude, barely tall enough to see across the dashboard, blaring at a dark blue Buick that had cut in front of him to make some time. He shot a quick glance at the Buick, windows down on his side, elbows showing front and back.

And guns.

He couldn't tell if there were two or three—it made no difference at the moment, either way. One bullet or a dozen, dead was dead.

Brognola hit the Plymouth's brakes and lurched forward with the force of the deceleration, leaning to his right and ducking out of sight across the seat. Things started to happen from that point on, in rapid-fire.

The car behind Brognola's touched his bumper with sufficient force to push the Plymouth forward several feet against resistance from the brakes. At the same time, converging streams of automatic fire blew out Brognola's window on the driver's side and showered him with broken glass. The windshield blew a heartbeat later, two bullets striking the dashboard.

In a flash, momentum took the Buick past his vehicle, and the big Fed was quick to take advantage of the lull in firing. Traffic had begun to clog around him and behind the Plymouth, drivers gaping at the spectacle and trying to avoid involvement in the drive-by shooting. Brognola sat up and spied a gap in traffic to his right, veering over so that several vehicles lay between himself and his assailants.

Shit! The lights were red at Seventeenth Street, just ahead, and Brognola could see no way of rushing things unless he drove up on the sidewalk, or across the rolling lawn of the Elipse, immediately on his right. He drew the Smith & Wesson from its holster, flicked off the safety and placed the weapon on the seat beside him. Glancing to his left, beyond a Volvo with a frightened-looking woman at the wheel, he was in time to see the Buick gunners angling for another shot.

Brognola ducked again as bullets splattered off the Volvo's hood and reached out for the Plymouth, rattling all around him. Up ahead, the lights went green in time for the Justice man to glimpse the change as he dropped out of sight and traffic started rolling forward.

Go!

It was a dicey proposition, driving blind, and as the Plymouth started rolling, gathering momentum, he was forced to risk another peek across the dashboard. It was chaos in the intersection, drivers swerving to avoid the gunmen in the Buick, while the hit car tried to leave its lane and pull in closer to Brognola.

Bearing down on the accelerator, Brognola raced forward, feeling an impact as some vehicle scraped broadside against his Plymouth. Any doubts he might have had about which vehicle had struck him vanished when the automatic weapons opened up at point-blank range, blew out the windows on the other side and started ripping gashes in the seat above him.

Reaching upward with the Smith & Wesson in his left hand, Brognola fired two quick shots across the windowsill, secure in the belief that he wouldn't place any innocents at risk. It seemed to work, the contact broken as the Buick veered away to gain some distance, giving the big Fed the chance to pull ahead.

He had to see the road, and that meant offering his enemies a target. There were no good options as he switched hands with the automatic, gripped the Plymouth's wheel and bolted upright. He was entering the intersection now, the Buick hanging steady on his left and drifting back to meet him. Brognola saw angry faces snarling at him over guns and cranked off two more shots, one round chipping paint from the Buick's fender.

Then he was through the intersection, winding up the engine, as his adversaries opened fire again. Brognola steeled his nerves to keep from ducking, hunched across the steering wheel and cleared the box at Seventeenth Street, running for his life.

Virginia Avenue branched off Constitution on the right, and Brognola veered in that direction, hearing brakes squeal as he cut across the right-hand lane. He hoped the snarl would keep his enemies from following, but he felt far from confident.

Approaching the Department of Interior headquarters, he checked his rearview mirror just in time to see the Buick make the turnoff. There appeared to be some damage on the driver's side, an ugly scrape, but they were making decent speed and gaining ground.

He had a hard choice coming up. At Twenty-third Street, he could hold his present course and drive until Virginia Avenue ran out at the Potomac's Rock River tributary, or he could try a new direction. Heading north one block would bring him to the campus of George Washington University, two more beyond that to reach Washington Circle. If he turned south, it was a long five blocks to the Lincoln Memorial and a shot at Arlington Memorial Drive across the river, assuming he could make it.

Choices.

In the actual event, he made a screeching left-hand turn on Twenty-third, working the brake and accelerator in tandem, nearly colliding with a city bus as he blew through the intersection with yellow winking into red. The Buick didn't hesitate, charging through the red and clipping a motorcyclist on the fly.

Brognola wove through traffic like a madman, with the State Department flashing past him on his left. The gunners in the Buick had begun to fire at the big Fed once more, but they were having trouble with their accuracy. He did what he could to keep his head down, but he had to watch the road if he was going to survive.

He caught a blessed green light coming up on Constitution Avenue and made a beeline for the circle that enclosed the Lincoln Memorial. Behind him, the Buick kept pace, much of the racket from its guns blown away in the slipstream of momentum, bullets bouncing off the trunk and roof when they got lucky.

Should he keep right on around the circle, or take any one of several roads that branched away?

A lucky bullet stole his choice when he was halfway through the loop, his left rear tire exploding, rubber flapping on the blacktop. Brognola released his pistol, needing both hands as he fought the skid, and even then he couldn't keep the Plymouth on the road. He lost it near the western end of the Reflecting Pool and hopped the curb, bailing out as the motor stalled.

He saw the Buick coming, two guns poking out of the driver's side and firing well before they had a solid fix. Brognola kept his own return fire measured, as precise as possible, without the kind of wild-ass firing so familiar from the offerings of Hollywood. He scored at least one hit, but on the driver's door, low down.

They swept past, not stopping as he had expected, and Brognola made a point of squinting at the license plate. He noted a partial number, but it should be enough, together with the general description and the bullet holes.

The big Fed took advantage of the moment to reload his pistol, snapping in a second magazine. He had his sights lined up, the Smith & Wesson steady in a firm two-handed grip, just when the Buick should have made another pass...but it didn't return.

He heard the sirens now, saw flashing lights approaching from Constitution Avenue and from Twenty-third. The Buick still had several options for escape, but Brognola wasn't in a position to give chase.

Forget it.

He was still alive, unscathed.

Now he could start to think about the payback game.

**11**

*Silesia, Maryland*

The stolen Buick, scarred with bullet holes, was found in Alexandria, Virginia, ninety minutes after Hal Brognola supplied investigators with the partial license number. Two hours later federal agents called upon the lawful owner, the Reverend Hubert Elroy Jackson, at his home in Fredericksburg. The car had been reported stolen shortly after noon the previous day, and there was no good reason to suspect the sixty-year-old Pentecostal minister of any link to the attempted murder.

They caught a break on fingerprints; two latents on the outside of the driver's door matched through the FBI to military service records for one Robert Beamish Elliott, age twenty-five. His file with the Marine Corps yielded one arrest for being drunk in quarters midway through his four-year hitch, but he had still received an honorable discharge from the Corps. A cross-reference to the FBI's Security Division showed that Elliott was listed as an early member of the National Redemption Party, photographed in uniform at rallies and reported as a frequent visitor to Camp Redemption in Idaho.

So far, so good.

ID was one thing, but point investigators to their suspect's current whereabouts. For that, the FBI began to check a list of drops, safehouses and the like, within a hundred-mile radius of Washington, D.C. They came up with four addresses, three of them apparently abandoned. Number four, outside Silesia, Maryland, had lights on and a pair of cars outside when G-men checked at 12:05 a.m.

They were prepared to field a Bureau SWAT team when the word came down from Justice to withdraw, forget about it. Someone else would pick it up from there.

When someone else arrived at 1:15 a.m., he made a drive-by of the house and spotted one light showing toward the back. Both cars were still out front, with no sentries visible from Bolan's angle of approach. He made a creeping circuit of the block to check for spotters, came up empty and secured his wheels a half block north of his intended target in the carport of a vacant house that sported a For Sale sign in the yard.

In seconds flat he ditched his sport coat and stripped off his slacks, to show the jet black skinsuit underneath, with the Beretta 93-R in a shoulder rig. He buckled on a web belt, with the Desert Eagle .44 Magnum on his hip, spare magazines for both pistols slotted into Velcro pouches circling his waist. His Uzi submachine gun had a silencer attached that added three pounds to the weapon's total weight without sacrificing close-range accuracy or stopping power.

He passed beside the empty house, cut through the backyard to an alley lined with trash cans and proceeded to his left, counting houses until he reached the one he sought. The fence was solidly constructed out of two-by-fours, no evident alarms or sensors. The warrior tested it for noise, made sure that it would take his weight and scrambled over in a flash.

He landed in a crouch on brittle grass that crunched beneath his feet. There was no dog in the yard, no lookout, no alarm as Bolan rose and drifted toward the house. From where he stood, the light was to his right, around the corner, spilling from what the warrior took to be a bedroom window.

He had no idea who was in the house, how many men or guns he would be facing when he made his way inside. There had been no time for a title check or lingering surveillance on the building. He had needed to move before the hit team or their allies had a chance to scatter. It was a judgment call, but he would have to play the rest of it by ear once he made contact with the enemy. If there were noncombatants on the premises, then he would do his best to spare them.

The back door to the house was locked. He peered in through a window set into the top half of the door and beheld an empty kitchen. He knelt before the door and went to work with slender picks, the tumblers falling into place in seconds flat. There was a safety chain in place, as well, but Bolan came prepared, a pair of lightweight cutters from a pocket of his skinsuit shearing through the links to make his way inside.

He left the door ajar behind him as a ready exit hatch, in case the probe went south. The kitchen smelled of beans and coffee, with an undertone of stale tobacco. Bolan stood and listened to the house, picking up a muffled sound of voices backed by music. Television? Radio? He moved in that direction, with the Uzi braced against his hip.

THE DAY HAD GONE TO HELL, and there was nothing Eulon Trask could do to make it right. Their target had escaped in D.C., and the only thing he had to show for the attempted hit was a persistent headache, brought about by Colonel Schroder screaming at him on the telephone.

So fuck it.

He could either try again or let it go. Of course, the mark would have his guard up now, and it would take a suicide battalion to ensure success, if that would even do the trick. His orders were to let it go, hide out the next few days until the main event went down and it was time to come on strong. Each soldier would be needed then, but in the meantime he was perfectly content to stand outside the line of fire.

The house in Maryland was nothing special, one of twenty-five or thirty places scattered around the country where beleaguered soldiers or the NRP could hide out in emergencies. It had been purchased with donations from the faithful, and from all appearances was operated as a rental property, with dummy owners on the books for purposes of title registration and taxation. Maintenance was handled, more or less, by front men for the party, and the neighbors had no cause to complain about the way the lawn was mowed, the siding painted, this or that.

But was it safe?

He thought about the raid on Camp Redemption, wondering how *that* went down, and wondered whether any safehouse really lived up to its name these days. Their mission, after all, was to assault and devastate the leading safehouse of them all, in such a way that its controllers, the November criminals, would be revealed for who and what they were.

It was a lethal game that two could play, and the result could still go either way.

Trask thought about the days ahead, the Arab team that was rehearsing to obliterate the target. Colonel Schroder knew there was a chance that they would fail, but that was beside the point. It was the effort—and the headlines that would follow when some friendly contacts in the press began to do their thing—that Schroder and the NRP were looking forward to.

It was the break they had been looking for since Schroder organized the party and began to drill his troops.

Trask hoped that they would have to hole up at the house only another day or two. He was already feeling claustrophobic, but you grew accustomed to the feeling—sharing quarters, giving up your privacy—when you were in the service. It would all be worth it, he conceded, when the victory was won.

Until that time, though, he would just as soon not share a house with Bobby Elliott, whose nervous mannerisms drove Trask up a wall. He hated Bobby's griping, and the way he chewed his fingernails like some punk kid about to face a heavy test in calculus. He was an ex-Marine, for God's sake, and he still acted like a rookie, wet behind the ears.

It was coming up on 1:30 a.m. when Trask decided he should try to get some sleep. He didn't know if it would work, but he was sick of listening to news spots on the radio about their failure in D.C. There was no news, anyway, beyond restatement of the same old facts he had been hearing for the past six hours or so: one Harold Brognola, out of Justice, narrowly surviving an attack by unknown gunmen as he left his office, with no leads or suspects yet identified.

Or were they holding back on that? Trask wondered if the FBI and local police were stonewalling the media to give themselves a little elbow room. Were cruisers on their way right now to throw a ring around the safehouse—minus the lights and all until the noose was snug around Trask's neck?

Slow down, he told himself. Relax. The feebs had nothing, or they would have shown up with their guns and warrants hours ago. Still, Trask was glad to have the Tec-9 pistol at his side as he lay down to catch his forty winks. He cocked it, put the safety on and reached out to kill the bedside lamp.

Trask had his eyes closed, focusing on sleep and blanking out his mind, when someone in the hallway shouted, "Holy shit!" The next sound, right on top of it, could easily have been somebody coughing, maybe dropping things or dragging furniture across a bare wood floor, but it was none of the above.

A silencer!

Trask bolted upright, grabbing for his weapon, flicking off the safety as he crossed the darkened bedroom to grope for the doorknob. Someone was in the house. Christ, what now?

He put the question out of mind and concentrated on survival, one hand on the doorknob, wondering what he should do. The shout from Bobby had aroused his other men. Trask heard them shouting questions. If they could clear it up...

No way.

He was the leader of the team, and it was his job to command.

He turned the knob and inched the door back far enough to check the hall outside.

BOLAN'S RULE OF THUMB was to expect the unexpected, try to scope the angles in advance and plan ahead, with countermeasures for a wide range of contingencies. It helped, of course, if you had floor plans and a head count on your enemies—and he had neither. He was on unfamiliar ground, no clear fix on the enemy, beyond the fact that they could fit in two cars...maybe.

Never mind.

He was proceeding down a darkened hallway, toward the sound of what he now took for a radio, when he detected seepage of pale light beneath a closer door, ahead and to his left. The rush of water through a toilet, seconds later, solved the mystery, and he was waiting when the door swung open, lighting up a broad wedge of the corridor and framing Bolan in the sudden glare.

The man who stepped into the hall was Robert Elliott, a perfect match for service ID photos faxed from Washington. He wore a T-shirt and a sagging pair of Jockey shorts. He hesitated on the threshold, reaching underneath the waistband of his shorts to scratch himself.

Even with the itch, though, he was wide awake, and he saw Bolan in a flash, took in the Uzi, blacksuit, camou paint on hands and face. It added up to trouble, and he chose the only course of action suited to his awkward situation.

"Holy shit!"

The Uzi stuttered, three or four 9 mm parabellum rounds ripping through the target's chest and slamming him backward against the doorjamb. Gravity took over and pulled him down into a seated posture.

Another door came open farther down the hall, and Bolan swiveled toward the sound in time to see a head bob out, then duck back again. Surprise was out the window, and if the second man was armed—

Whatever doubts he might have harbored on that score were instantly wiped out, as muzzle-flashes started winking at him from the doorway, bullets chewing up the wall a few feet to his left. It was a semiautomatic weapon, and even when he didn't aim, the guy was coming close enough to score a lucky hit if he kept on.

The bathroom beckoned, and the warrior dodged in that direction, leaping across the dead man's outstretched leg and slapping the light switch as he crossed the threshold. Darkness made them even and prevented him from being blinded by the light behind him when he tried to bring the Uzi into play.

At least two men were firing at him now, the bullets chewing plasterboard and chipping splinters from the wooden doorjamb. Bolan hunkered down and waited for a momentary lull. He had no fragmentation grenades, since he hadn't been sure if there would be civilians in the house, but now he took a flash-bang stun grenade from his web belt and pulled the safety pin, holding the spoon in place while he waited for a chance to make the pitch.

As if in answer to a silent prayer, both shooters took a break—reloading? Bolan wondered—and he saw his opportunity. A hasty glance around the doorjamb was followed by a sidearm pitch, and Bolan saw the grenade bounce once before he ducked back under cover, cupping both ears with his hands.

If he was accurate, the stun grenade should detonate between the doorways, left and right, from which defensive fire was emanating at the moment. He didn't expect the same results he would have gotten if the bomb had fallen into one room or the other, but if nothing else, at least the flash-bang ought to give him something in the nature of an edge.

He counted seconds in his mind and got to "four" when the explosion rocked him, shock waves rippling through the walls. His eyes were closed against the flash, with two walls in the way, but anyone exposed directly to the blinding glare would need a moment to regain his eyesight—not to mention his recovery from the concussion of the blast. It wouldn't kill—unless, perhaps, the bomb went off immediately in a target's face—but it was specially designed to stun and incapacitate a man or men on the receiving end.

He moved immediately, charging from the bathroom with his Uzi primed and ready. On his right, the bedroom door where he had seen a man peek out was closed now, no apparent threat to Bolan at the moment. In the absence of a challenge, he didn't have the time to check it out.

He came in through a swirl of smoke and cordite fumes, hearing groans from the open door immediately on his left. He turned in that direction and found a gunner stretched out on his back, with one hand clasped across his eyes, the other raising a MAC-10 submachine gun. Bolan shot him in the chest, then turned back toward the other sniper's nest.

There, the shooter had been quick enough to dodge the main force of the blast, but he was still a bit disoriented as he came back firing short bursts from a mini-Uzi. The Executioner dropped to a fighting crouch, with bullets swarming overhead, and answered with a spray of parabellum rounds. His target seemed to stumble, twisting as he fell, and he was dead before he hit the carpet in a boneless sprawl.

Three down, and none of them could answer Bolan's questions. That left one, behind him, and he had to take the guy alive, grill him, hoping he would spill some information about the Hezbollah commandos—where they were, the nature of their mission in the States.

Determined not to fail, he turned and walked back toward the silent bedroom door.

EULON TRASK HAD DECIDED to run. The trick was getting out. His bedroom had a single door, which opened on the hall, where, by the sound of it, his enemy was mopping up the other members of his team. There was no decent place to hide, once he ruled out the closet and the bed as certain death traps. The window was his only option.

Trask crossed the room in six long strides, threw back the draperies and ducked, expecting danger from outside. When nothing happened in the next few seconds, he stood cautiously and started checking out the window as a possible escape hatch.

One side opened with a hand crank, ample room for him to scramble through if he removed the screen. Thoughts racing, he began to crank the window open, cursing as the handle balked from disuse. Finally he had it open far enough to clear his body, but the screen remained. It wasn't one of those that was simply wedged into place outside the window glass: this screen was soundly fastened to the windowframe itself, with three screws on a side.

Removing it the normal way meant standing in the flower bed with a Phillips screwdriver, removing all the screws and lifting out the screen. Instead, Trask punched his fist directly through the center of the fine wire mesh, grabbed hold of one large flap and ripped it backward, tossing it aside. Another rip and Trask was confident that he could wriggle through the window, even if it proved to be uncomfortable.

He exited headfirst, the Tec-9 in his right hand for protection, and the pull of gravity took over when he lost his balance on the windowsill. Trask landed with a thump in the planter, then scrambled clear, running toward the street and driveway, where the cars were parked.

There was a moment's panic as he cleared the flower bed, remembering the car keys, but he had been resting in his jeans—a personal concession to security—and the keys for both were in his pocket.

Suddenly, in front of him, stood a wooden gate he had forgotten all about. Trask stopped in time to keep from running into it face first, but he had no key for the padlock that secured its hasp. Disgusted, knowing that his enemy could come for him at any moment, Trask set the Tec-9's safety, stuffed the weapon into his pants and started to climb. Sharp pain told him when a splinter pierced his left big toe, and for a moment, at the apex, he nearly lost his weapon. He snagged it in the gap between two boards, but then he cleared the hurdle, tumbling onto hands and knees.

The cars were right there, waiting for him, less than fifty feet away. Trask hesitated, even so, still waiting for the other shoe to drop. He found it unbelievable that one man would be sent against them. A gunman waiting in the shadows beyond the cars could nail him when he made his move. Or would they have men waiting *in* the cars?

Forget it. He could sit and wait for someone to come tapping on his shoulder, maybe shoot him in the back, or he could seize the moment, try to save himself.

Go, damn it!

Trask made sure he had the car keys in his right hand, the Tec-9 in his left, before he broke from cover. He threw himself behind the wheel of the Cutlass and groped for the ignition. He found it, gave the key a twist and felt the engine come to life. If there was anybody watching, waiting for him, they would certainly start shooting now, before he cleared the driveway.

Nothing.

Trask slammed the shift into reverse, released the parking brake and powered out of there. He didn't watch his mirror, veered a bit off course and bounced across a corner of the curb with force enough to blur his vision, snap his teeth together.

Watch it!

He was in the street now, shifting into drive, his mind racing. Where to go? Should he reach out to Colonel Schroder with a plea for help? A warning?

Or was it possible that *Schroder* sent the gunman to punish them for the snafu in Washington? Trask hadn't recognized the face, but he had glimpsed the shooter only for an instant in the semidarkness. He didn't know every member of the NRP, of course, and yet—

No way.

His mind wouldn't accept the possibility, because it canceled hope, and hope, right now, was what he needed most of all.

He was a mile away and running clear before he thought about the photographs.

**12**

*Silver Spring, Maryland*

General Arthur Coltrane lived alone. A lifelong bachelor whose life was focused on service of his country, he had little need for human warmth or contact. Sometimes, when he had a special itch to scratch, he dealt with a Bethesda escort agency that guaranteed discretion for a price. Aside from that, and certain social functions at the Pentagon, he cherished privacy and kept to a small, select circle of friends. It was no surprise, therefore, that Coltrane was in bed alone when his telephone rang at 2:40 a.m.

He reached it on the second ring. Proximity and years of practice made it easy.

"Yes?"

"I'm sorry, General," said Wallace Schroder's worried voice. "We've a problem here."

"You have that other number handy?" Coltrane asked.

"Yes, sir."

"All right, then. Give me fifteen minutes."

Dressing in a hurry was a talent every soldier learned in boot camp, and it served him now. He switched on a lamp, and dressed in denim jeans, a sweatshirt, leather moccasins. The buzz cut spared him any need to comb his hair and primp before a mirror. Grabbing car keys off the dresser, he was in the closed garage four minutes after hanging up the telephone, and ten more seconds put him in the driver's seat.

He keyed the automatic opener and waited while the door retracted on its roller, then backed into the driveway. Six minutes from the house, in normal daytime traffic, was an Exxon station with a public telephone in back. The station closed at 10:00 p.m. on weeknights, and the clean-up crew was long gone when the general arrived. He parked adjacent to the phone booth, cracked his door and waited for the telephone to ring.

The call came through at 2:16, a minute late by Coltrane's dashboard clock. No problem. Coltrane stepped into the booth and picked up as the third ring was beginning. He said nothing, waiting for the caller to identify himself.

"It's me." The same voice, no mistaking it.

"Your line's secure?" Coltrane asked.

"Yes, sir."

"Go ahead."

"You heard we missed in Washington, I guess," Schroder said, sounding nervous as he spoke.

"I did. It was disturbing."

"Yes, sir. I agree. We put the team to bed until this all blows over."

"Very wise."

"The problem is, sir, someone hit them at the safehouse about an hour ago."

"Survivors?"

"One. That makes three more in the bag."

"Who was responsible?" Coltrane queried.

"I wish I knew. The bastard didn't stick around."

"It wasn't an official effort, then?"

"Not on the record, anyway. The cops are calling it 'persons unknown.'"

"The casualties are traceable?" Coltrane asked.

"To the party? I imagine so. The FBI has files, whatever."

"Have they been in touch?"

"Not yet. I mean, they tried to call about the thing out west, you know, but I'm still on vacation when they ask."

"A few more days won't hurt, then," Coltrane said.

"I wouldn't think so."

"Then I don't see any problem."

"Well..."

"What is it, Wallace?"

"There were photographs," Schroder replied, almost whispering.

"Explain yourself."

"I'm still not clear on how it happened, sir, but some of the surveillance photographs got left behind."

"Surveillance photos of the *target?*"

"Yes, sir."

"When you say that they were 'left behind,' exactly what is that supposed to mean?"

"My Number Two was with the team in Washington. He had a couple of the photos with him, sir. When they got hit tonight—this morning—he got out. It was a scramble, what I hear, and by the time he thought about the pictures, he was five or six miles down the road."

Coltrane said nothing for a moment, felt the earth tilt on its axis, out of line and back again. He felt as if the ground might open up and swallow him alive. Their preparations, months of planning, all of it flushed down the toilet, just because some stupid—

He caught himself and swallowed hard, made certain that he could control his voice before he spoke. "This is very disturbing news," he said between clenched teeth.

"I understand, sir."

"All our plans are now at risk."

"It might not be that bad."

"Excuse me? Are you taking medication, Wallace? Do you understand what you are saying?"

"Sir . . . yes, sir . . . I mean, we don't know if the cops will recognize what they're about."

"You're guessing now."

"A couple snapshots, sir. It could be anyplace. Where would they start to look?"

The general answered with a question of his own. "And what if the police don't have them, Wallace?"

"Come again, sir?"

"Persons unknown, you said. What if the shooter walked off with your photos? What then?"

"I don't follow you, sir."

"So I gather. I'm asking you what we can do if some 'person unknown' has the photos and works out coordinates."

"How could he do that?" Schroder asked.

"You may recall yesterday—was it just yesterday, Wallace?—I asked about your trouble out in Idaho, if someone from the target could have been involved."

"Yes, sir. My answer is still the same. I don't see how—"

"You don't see how a shooter could have tracked your team from Washington back to their safehouse, either, do you?"

"Sir—"

"There seems to be a whole wide range of things that you don't see."

"I don't believe there's any danger—"

"How much longer?" the general asked.

"Sir?"

"How long before our friends are ready to proceed?"

"It's Thursday now," he said. "Tomorrow, Saturday at the outside."

"Let's pray they have the time. Do you keep in touch with the Almighty, Wallace?"

"When I can, sir."

"Very well," the general said. "Tomorrow, then, or Saturday at the outside."

He was about to cradle the receiver, when he thought of one more thing to say.

"I hope you realize, my friend, that if this blows up in your face, you're on your own."

"Yes, sir."

"I hope so, Wallace. I sincerely hope so."

*Laurel, Maryland*

IT WAS A FLUKE that Bolan even found the photographs. The final gunner had slipped out ahead of him, the open window and its shredded screen mute testimony to the avenue of his escape. As the warrior stuck his head outside, he heard a screech of rubber from the street and knew that he had missed his chance.

Three down, and one away.

Once more, there would be no chance to interrogate his enemies and try to find out what was going on, their tie-in to the Hezbollah commandos. He was running dangerously short of time, with the unmuffled gunfire from his adversaries and the flash-bang, but he took a moment, found the bedroom light switch and flicked it on.

The place was sparsely furnished, with a rumpled bed and dime-store chest of drawers, a denim jacket draped across a straight-backed chair and nothing in the closet. Bolan was about to check the drawers when he noticed a manila envelope atop the dresser, weighted down with a long magazine for some kind of machine pistol.

He pushed the clip aside and picked up the envelope. It was light, nothing much to the contents, and Bolan peeled the flap back, tilting out a set of glossy eight-by-tens. There were five photographs in all, and he paged through them one by one, seeing a bird's-eye view of some facility, a rural setting, no clear landmarks in the photos to identify the setting at a glance. It didn't look like satellite photography, perhaps a spy plane or the civilian equivalent.

At first he didn't recognize the setting. It was wrong somehow—an unfamiliar angle, maybe, or a simple glitch between the eyes and brain. Then, recognition struck him like a roundhouse punch between the eyes. He blinked twice, stuffed the photos back inside their envelope and tucked it underneath his belt.

How could it be?

There was no time to think about that now. He put the house of death behind him, walked back to his car and started driving, almost in a daze. It took him something like a mile to put his thoughts in order, and he kept on driving, north to Laurel, looking for a telephone.

He had to get in touch with Brognola at once.

The K mart store was closed, but it had telephones outside, three open booths lined up against the wall, left of the exit. Bolan parked his rental at the yellow curb, ignoring signs that warned him he was risking a citation or a tow-away by stopping in a fire lane. In the circumstances, he would risk it.

The warrior left the car, shrugged on his sport coat to conceal the 93-R in its shoulder rig. He chose a telephone, fed coins into the slot and tapped out eleven digits from his memory.

Brognola picked up on the first ring, as if he were sitting by the telephone. And, Bolan thought, he almost certainly had been.

"Hello?"

"It's Striker. Open line."

"All taken care of, then?"

"One miss," he said. "I picked up something you should see, though."

"Yeah? What's that?"

"Surveillance photos," Bolan told him. "Aerials."

"Of what, pray tell?"

"The Farm."

For all of twenty seconds, Bolan could have sworn the line was dead. Brognola might have hung up on him, but he didn't hear a dial tone. Finally, when his old friend spoke again, the sound seemed to come from somewhere on the dark side of the moon.

"You're sure about that?"

"No mistake."

"Well, shit."

"You know what this means," Bolan said.

"A whole list comes to mind," Brognola answered, "and I don't like any of the choices."

"There's a leak."

"Maybe not."

"I'm open to alternative suggestions."

Brognola was silent for another ten or fifteen seconds. Finally he grumbled, "Hell, you might be right."

"No maybe," Bolan told him fiercely. "Someone needs to run the list."

"I can't believe it's anybody on the team," Brognola said.

"You could be right," the Executioner replied.

"Who, then?"

"That's what I'm working on. I had a thought."

"You want to clue me in, or should I check my Ouija board?"

"I'll need your help," Bolan said.

"Oh?"

"I want a meeting with the Man," he said. "ASAP."

*Falmouth, Virginia*

THE TRICK, when General Coltrane chewed you out, was to refrain from brooding, concentrate on any measures you could take to rectify the situation in a hurry. Wallace Schroder knew why he was on the hot seat—it had been his man who dropped the ball, big time—and he wasn't about to shirk responsibility. When they were past the crisis, if they made it, Eulon Trask would have a major problem on his hands, but in the meantime...

What?

They weren't screwed yet, as far as Schroder could determine. Granted, he would have said anything to get the general off his back, but there was still no evidence that the police had found, much less interpreted, the aerial surveillance photos.

Trask told him they were in an envelope, left in his bedroom at the safehouse. It figured that someone had to find them, then—the shooter or the cops. He almost hoped it *was* the cops. The blue suits could be counted on to fumble, stall and screw things up. The Feds were hardly an improvement, though they played around with more advanced technology and sometimes got it right despite themselves.

What worried Schroder most was the alternative that General Coltrane kept suggesting, pushing it as if he had secret inside knowledge that he wouldn't share. Suppose the target was responsible for Schroder's recent problems, figured out what he was up to and took steps to counteract his plan. What then?

In that case, Schroder told himself, already scowling, they were screwed.

He didn't mind about the Arabs. They were never meant to walk away from this, in any case. They were beyond expendable—a living sacrifice, in fact. If they were being set up for a slaughter, that was fine, as long as they got far enough and raised sufficient hell to blow the target's cover.

Nothing had been left to chance so far. They had a few stray allies in the media—a couple of reporters on the West Coast, one in Birmingham, another in New York—who were on tap to push the story when it broke. Each would receive a set of photographs—the same damned aerial surveillance snapshots that were giving Schroder fits—once the assault was under way. It would be their job to discover how it all turned out and spread the news around the world.

The point, as Schroder understood the plan, was to expose their target for the first time to the light of public scrutiny, and thus embarrass the November criminals on two fronts: first, for lying to the people for years on end and running covert killer operations that defied the law, existing treaties and the spirit of the Constitution; secondly, for being so incompetent that Arabs from the Middle East could scope out the target and strike a heavy blow with no apparent difficulty, even if they died in the attempt.

It stood to raise a mighty shitstorm for the White House. Never mind that the subversive program had been instituted by a predecessor. This was the man who liked to call himself the "Ethics President," yet he had made no effort to dismantle the unlawful program in his first three years of service. When the newsies started digging, they would doubtless turn up cases where the President had fielded members of the secret team to push his own agenda.

It was perfect, if they didn't screw things up.

A warning to the enemy meant new security precautions, stiffer odds against the hit team breaking through and making any kind of inroads at the target site. Division of the strike force into three- and four-man squads should logically prevent the home team from annihilating all of them at once, improve their chances of inflicting damage on the hardsite.

Once the story broke, it would be time for Schroder and his people to lie low, avoid the Feds and anybody else who was dispatched to run them down. The overt side of things—a well-financed PR machine—was waiting in the wings to challenge Congress and the White House, push for an impeachment vote, or, failing that, to keep the story rolling right on through election time.

It was a story that had smear potential well beyond the scope of Watergate and Iran-Contra. No one had been killed in those great scandals, and the chief executive in each case had apparently stopped short of authorizing felonies before the fact. This time, there would be corpses in abundance, and with a bit of journalistic spadework, the Oval Office would be directly implicated all the way. A President who had maligned, downplayed and undercut the lawful military would be publicly exposed as an assassin once removed, who issued murder contracts on his enemies around the world.

From there, it would be no great trick to field a slate of new, untainted hopefuls for the House and Senate, nominate a real-life hero for the nation's highest office.

Someone like the general.

All he had to do, Schroder thought, was to pull off the first phase without an absolute disaster for their side. He didn't even need a victory, as long as he could get his players in the game.

So why, he asked himself, was he so scared?

## Arlington, Virginia

HAL BROGNOLA had considered checking into a hotel for several days, until the smoke cleared and he found out what was going on, but in the end he had decided not to run and hide. A team of federal agents was assigned to watch his home, and the big Fed kept several loaded guns on hand. If anyone came looking for him at the house, he was prepared to send them back in body bags.

The call from Striker was another problem altogether. Brognola began to see an outline of the enemy's design, though much of it was still obscure. The Farm had been attacked before, and he couldn't rule out the possibility of yet another raid, but he would have to guess at means and motive.

Would Wallace Schroder's National Redemption Party throw in with Hezbollah, a group the party openly despised, to carry out this kind of operation? What would they achieve by joining forces with the enemy? And more to the point, how had they learned of Stony Man's existence?

Striker clearly had some notions on that score, and Hal Brognola was concerned about the implications of his war-

rior's new request. A meeting with the Man was not un-
heard of, granted—it had happened two or three times
before, though never with the present White House occu-
pant—but it required a very special set of circumstances.
There were certain risks involved, not least of which, in
Brognola's opinion, was the danger posed for all concerned
by Bolan's mounting rage.

The big guy had been holding something back, no doubt
about it. He was outraged at the prospect of a raid on Stony
Man, no doubt remembering the time that a traitor in the
ranks had cost him dearly. The raiders had killed April
Rose, Barbara Price's predecessor, and Andrzej Konzaki,
Stony Man's first weapons smith, as well as crippling Aaron
Kurtzman with a bullet in the spine. If Bolan smelled another rat, Brognola wouldn't want to be the man who stood
between the soldier and his target.

The problem was that only certain people in the country
knew about the Farm. There was the live-in staff, of course,
including handpicked military personnel in the security and
maintenance divisions who were sworn to secrecy forever-
more. Outside the Farm itself, there were the frontline warriors: Bolan and Grimaldi, Able Team and Phoenix Force.
In San Diego, Bolan's brother, Johnny Gray, knew certain
details of the project, though he hadn't actually seen or vis-
ited the Farm. Around the capital, while Brognola main-
tained secure connections with a shopping list of military
services and law-enforcement agencies, full knowledge of
the cover project was restricted to Brognola, Leo Turrin—
also known as Leonard Justice—and the President of the
United States.

If there had been a leak—and there was no denying it,
with the surveillance photographs in hand—then who had
done the leaking?

The Justice man ran the list of trusted staffers through his
mind: Aaron Kurtzman, Barbara Price, John Kissinger,
Huntington Wethers, Akira Tokaido, Carmen Delahunt. It
was impossible for him to picture any one of them as selling out the common cause. Likewise for Leo and the men of
Able Team and Phoenix Force. Support-team members
came and went, of course, as tours of duty were completed,
leaving several dozen individuals at large on any given day
who could have pointed fingers at the Farm, described the

layout, even if they had no working knowledge of the missions that originated there. Potential staffers were subjected to a battery of psychological examinations prior to their assignment, cautioned once again in exit interviews, upon departure, to make sure they understood the legal risks involved in talking out of turn. Still, human nature being what it was, the only ironclad guarantee of silence would have been annihilation, and Brognola wouldn't make that drastic step a matter of routine.

And then there was the Man.

Each chief executive from Stony Man's creation to the present day had ratified the secret bargain, dealing with Brognola one-on-one. Vice presidents and cabinet members were excluded from the pact, until such time—and it had never happened yet—that death or incapacitation left the Oval Office vacant in a dire emergency.

Now, Bolan seemed to have his sights fixed on the President, and Brognola had known him long enough to realize that nothing short of Doomsday would prevent his punishing a sellout who betrayed the cause and called up painful memories of April Rose.

In that case, Brognola had cause to wonder if the President himself would stand a chance against the Executioner.

Brognola, for his part, had no good reason to believe the Man was part of any plot against his secret team, but he would check it out, along with any other possibility, no matter how farfetched it seemed. And he would start with a phone call to Kurtzman at the Farm.

There was a different angle that Brognola wanted to examine, and the Bear's computer files would help him run it down. With any luck at all, he might have something to report when he joined Bolan and the President in Wonderland the following morning.

Brognola was looking forward to that meeting with a sense of dread, but he wouldn't have missed it for the world.

**13**

*Washington, D.C.*

Some cities never sleep. Las Vegas offers action to compulsive gamblers around the clock. New York combines commerce and culture with a thriving underworld of crime. Los Angeles keeps up a steady beat for would-be superstars. In Washington, the business of domestic government and foreign policy demands full-time attention from the men and women pledged to keep the ship of state on course at any cost.

Two hours remained before the sun was due to rise, and Bolan still had traffic to contend with as he crossed the Arlington Memorial Bridge, eastbound across the Potomac. He took his time and observed the posted limit, knowing it would be a waste of time and energy to show up early at the chosen rendezvous.

Brognola's call had fixed the meet, and Bolan knew how much his friend had risked to honor that unusual request. It would have taken a compelling argument to roust the President from bed at 4:30 a.m. A crisis, right, and it was fair to say the present situation qualified.

If the impending threat to Stony Man was genuine, a crisis was exactly what they faced.

The Farm was on alert by now, a hasty message from Brognola being all it took to put the site on Defcon 1. The guards were ever watchful, but a scramble brought out the heavy weapons and canceled any leaves. While penetration of the Farm without an invitation was supposed to be impossible at any time, he knew that there were different levels of preparedness, some more rigorous than others. A substantial threat did more to put a hard force on alert than any hundred drills and exercises.

Yet experience taught Bolan that there were no fool-proof plans, no fortress that was totally impervious to infiltration or assault. The first attack on Stony Man had been a revelation, teaching vital lessons to the home team, but the warrior knew there were ways and means of circumventing even the strongest defenses. An air drop, perhaps, or—

Bolan caught himself, abandoning the fruitless train of thought, and concentrated on his driving. Southbound on Ohio Drive, with the Potomac River on his right, a one-way street until he found the loop for West Basin Drive and began to reverse his direction. Now he had the Tidal Basin on his starboard flank, no tourists prowling at this hour of the morning. West Potomac Park lay dead ahead, and Bolan started looking for the turnoff that would take him to the public parking lot.

He knew it was a gamble, asking for a face-off with the Man. The grandeur of the Oval Office, in and of itself, would be enough to put most people off the plan entirely, but the Executioner was made of sterner stuff. Once he had recognized a threat, the only course of action that remained was to remove and neutralize that threat by any means available.

His mind had run the same list of potential suspects as Brognola, though his list had necessarily included Hal, as well. It was a passing thought, at worst, and Bolan never seriously counted the big Fed as a potential traitor. Even so, there had been leaks at Justice in the past, and nothing could be overlooked when valiant lives were riding on the line.

And Bolan's thoughts kept on returning to the President.

It wasn't wholly logical, he realized, but politicians were a breed apart. They lived and breathed for power, recognition and prestige. The very best of motives could be twisted and subverted over time, until a man who started out with honorable public service on his mind became a grotesque caricature of his former self, committed solely to the pursuit of wealth and influence. And then, he thought, there were the politicians who wouldn't recognize an honorable notion if it slithered up one leg and bit them on the ass.

He had no fixed agenda for his meeting with the President. There were specific questions he was bound to ask, but where it went from there depended on the answers he received, and whether Bolan felt he could accept those answers as the unadulterated truth.

The first time Bolan had attended a meeting with a President he had been a fugitive, with numerous indictments pending and a steep price on his head from both sides of the law. He had approached that meet with reluctance, even apprehension, but it worked out for the best: a pardon from the White House and a new life overall, including the creation of Brognola's secret hardsite in the Blue Ridge Mountains of Virginia.

Driving, Bolan thought about another visit with the Man, a day of mourning following the first assault on Stony Man, when he was looking for a traitor, nursing mortal hatred in his heart. It had been close, that time, but once again the warrior and the President were in accord. The turncoats had been rooted out and punished in the classic Bolan style.

They wouldn't be alone this time, he understood. Brognola was supposed to be on hand, and the warrior knew there would be Secret Service agents standing by. At least he didn't have to guard against the federal agents turning on him, trying to arrest or kill him at the meeting site.

Or did he?

If the President had turned on Stony Man, then he would be capable of any treachery. Conversely, if the leak had come from someone lower down the White House ladder—from an aide or cabinet-level officer, perhaps—then someone else could have prepared the Secret Service bodyguard to act on special orders, spring a trap without the Man's cooperation or consent. It wouldn't matter, after he was dead, who planned the trap, or whether they were reprimanded after the fact.

He would remain on full alert, then, and he wasn't giving up his guns to anyone, in spite of rank.

The meeting was scheduled to start in three minutes. Bolan knew the President's reputation for cutting it close on schedules and deadlines, and he wondered whether he'd show up at all.

The easy thing, if Bolan's worst scenario played out, would be to send a limo full of gunmen, leave the Man at home, where he was safe. Steps could be taken to ensure Brognola's silence, anything from not-so-subtle blackmail to a lethal "accident." A covert cleanup at the Farm could be accomplished, Bolan calculated, with the same efficiency that had prevailed through its construction and concealment from the world at large.

So watch it.

He could see the sprawl of West Potomac Park ahead of him, his headlights barely pushing back the shadows there. He saw the entrance to the parking lot ahead, and he decided there was no point in stalling. He could wait there, sitting in the car, as well as someplace else. The ambush—if there *was* an ambush coming—would proceed in any case.

He pulled in, off the one-way road, and started scouting for a place to park. No shortage, with the lot deserted, and he chose a middle point, where he could watch the road and the shadows.

The warrior killed the lights and engine, slipped the 93-R from its armpit sheath and settled back to wait.


"WE'RE ALMOST THERE, sir."

When the forward shotgun rider spoke, Brognola nearly jumped. It was ridiculous, but there was nothing he could do about the nerves. He rode beside the President, two feet of space between them in the back seat of the armor-plated limousine that could withstand repeated hits from anything below the caliber of field artillery and keep on rolling with a minimum of damage to the passengers inside.

As it happened, Brognola wasn't worried about his personal safety. With or without the stylish tank, he had no fear of Bolan and only slight misgivings about the presidential bodyguards. The Man had promised him there would be no surprises at the meeting, but Brognola's mind couldn't help picturing worst-case scenarios: a cordon thrown around the park; Striker pledging to resist, without plugging a badge, while the hunters had no such compunctions; a blaze of automatic fire, with tracers streaming through the night.

It wouldn't go that way, of course—not even if the Man had treachery in mind. The stalkers wouldn't be in uniform, and they wouldn't be loading tracers—nothing to attract attention to their little hunting expedition. Silencers could be employed, if they were finicky, to keep the party private.

The call from Bolan for a meeting was unusual, but it hadn't been threatening. The Secret Service agents had no reason to suppose that they were dealing with a rogue who might attempt to harm the President. If Bolan's evident suspicions were correct, though, and the source of treachery lay somewhere in or near the White House, it was always possible that someone—high or low—would try to end it here.

The information Brognola had gleaned from Stony Man, some thirty minutes before the meeting with the President, appeared to make that grim scenario unlikely. Not impossible, he couldn't take it that far, but he had a far more plausible scenario in mind. There had been no way to connect with Bolan in advance, head off the meeting, but he hoped he could defuse the situation, take some measure of the heat off, even now.

But first he needed time to tell his story, make sure Bolan understood.

The Man had listened to him on the short drive over from the White House, Secret Service agents riding on the jump seats, facing the big Fed and staring out the window, playing deaf and dumb. They did a lot of that, on the protection detail, and while Brognola was theoretically required to trust them, he did everything within his power to keep the details sketchy—leaving out the names, for instance—in the hope that he could fill the details in with Bolan present, when they had the limo to themselves.

That would depend on several things, of course. He had to keep his fingers crossed that there was no trap waiting when the Executioner arrived, since that would ruin everything, being the final breach of trust. Beyond that hurdle, he would have to bide his time, observe the necessary protocol and try to get a word in edgewise.

Simple, right...provided no one on the home team had an itchy trigger finger, and the principals both kept their cool. It seemed unthinkable that Bolan would make any move against the Man, and yet...

The first time raiders hit the Farm, on the directions of a traitor, they had murdered Bolan's lady love and jeopardized the whole Phoenix program, potentially dozens—or hundreds—of lives. The Executioner's vengeance in that case had been swift, remorseless, final. No survivors. If he saw another similar threat on the horizon, there was no doubt in Brognola's mind that Bolan would exert himself to the limit, using any means available, to head the problem off.

And if he thought the threat originated from the Oval Office...then what?

Bolan's personal, unwritten code forbade him using lethal force against a lawman—city, county, state or federal. In the warrior's eyes, they were "soldiers of the same side," regardless of an individual officer's personality or private corruption. No human endeavor was immune to human failings, and the headlines carried daily tales of officers involved in bribery, drug running, sex offenses, even murder. Regardless, Bolan's flag of truce was broad enough to cover one and all, but it didn't extend to other public servants, such as politicians.

He had dropped the hammer more than once on so-called statesmen, foreign and domestic, when he caught them with their fingers in the till—or dripping with the blood of innocents. If Bolan's amnesty on dirty cops appeared quixotic or illogical to some of his associates, at least they knew that it didn't extend to venal winners of the periodic popularity contests known as free elections. He had never moved against an office-holder at the presidential level, granted, but if Bolan had good reason to believe the chief executive was selling out his people and his oath of office, there was nothing to prevent a showdown that would stand the country on its ear—nothing and no one, perhaps, except for Hal Brognola and his news from Stony Man.

"Somebody waiting," said the Secret Service driver as they pulled into the parking lot. Brognola saw the dark sedan, glanced back in time to see their tail car—five more agents, armed for bear—stop short to block the only exit from the lot. The limo kept on rolling, all eyes pinned on Bolan's car, until they stopped a dozen paces short, with the sedan framed in their headlights.

The Executioner stepped out of the car immediately, both hands empty, hanging easy at his sides. Three agents cleared the limousine, almost in lockstep, while the driver kept his seat, prepared to power out of there at the first sign of a threat to his exalted passenger.

Brognola kept his fingers crossed and offered up a silent prayer for peace. He didn't need a lot of time to get his point across, but if it fell apart before he even had a chance to speak, then it was hopeless.

In another moment he would have his answer, one way or another.

Any second now.

IT WAS A SHORT WALK—thirty-five or forty feet from one car to the other—but it could be all the time and space he had, if someone crouching in the shadows had an itchy trigger finger. Bolan fought the urge to duck and cover, knowing any reckless moves at this stage of the game were tantamount to suicide. Three agents stood by the limo, with a carload in reserve, and Bolan knew before he took his first step from the rental car that he wouldn't fire on them, no matter what they had in mind for him.

Case closed.

It was a quirk that went back to the first day of his one-man war against the Mafia, in Massachusetts, and he hadn't deviated from the simple rule in any subsequent campaign. He never would, and if that meant his life was over here and now, so be it.

Someone else would carry on in Bolan's place. If nothing else, at least the crew at Stony Man would be forewarned of danger coming their way, given some chance to defend themselves.

They didn't frisk him at the limo, even knowing he was armed. So far, so good, and Bolan stepped into the spacious vehicle, picked out a jump seat opposite the Man. He nodded curtly to Brognola and registered the driver shifting in his seat, behind him, knowing full well that the first aggressive move he made would be the signal for a Glaser safety slug to detonate inside his brain.

Okay, so everybody understood the rules.

With no one in the car to introduce him, as was done at public gatherings, the President began to speak without preamble, going for position in their verbal one-on-one.

"I'm glad we have this chance to meet," he said. "I know you've spoken personally to a couple of my predecessors, but there's normally a distance kept between my office and your team."

"That's how it was supposed to play, sir," Bolan answered.

"Granted, but I don't like losing touch. You've served this country well beyond the call, and I'm aware of that. It's understood. If there's a problem, some threat to the program, tell me what you need, and we can work it out."

"I hope so," Bolan said, reserving judgment.

"There's the matter of a leak, I understand," the President went on, "that's put your base at risk."

"Affirmative." His voice and eyes were both as hard as tempered steel.

"Before we talk about the details, there's something you should hear."

"I'm listening."

The President nodded at Brognola, and Bolan waited while his friend cleared his throat. "Bear ran a trace while we were setting up the meet. You know how we keep track of former personnel."

"Okay."

It was standard practice at the Farm to run spot checks on former staffers when they were discharged from the service. Nothing heavy or invasive, but it only made good sense to keep in touch and learn if one-time personnel with vital

secrets locked inside their brains had gone astray somehow—a sidestep into criminal activity, perhaps, or even
fraternizing with potential enemies.

"You're not acquainted with the guards," Brognola said,
continuing. "No reason why you should be. Some time back
we had a sergeant from the Special Forces, Joseph Lewis
Gardner, on the grounds crew. Nothing out of line, as far as
we can tell, while he was on the site. He did his job, rotated
out and took his discharge after six years in the uniform."

"So, what's the problem?" Bolan asked.

"In February 1993, he joined the National Redemption
Party in Seattle, moved down to their camp in Idaho. It
raised a flag when we found out about it through the Bureau, but we had no reason, then, to view the NRP as active opposition."

"And this sergeant—Gardner, was it?"

"Right." Brognola's voice and the expression on his face
were solemn, even grim.

"What kind of access did he have around the Farm?"

"He worked outside," Brognola said. "Came in the
house from time to time, of course, and there's no telling
what he might have picked up, talking to the other staff. For
sure, he could provide the opposition with a layout of the
grounds, a partial floor plan of the house and detailed
briefing on security precautions."

Bolan let his mind assimilate the information. It was
something they had long feared at the Farm: a staffer, past
or present, who would sell out the operation for money,
ideology, whatever. Short of having staffers executed when
their tours of duty ended, there was little Price and Kurtzman could do about the risk. They kept an eye on former
guards, sporadically, but Stony Man didn't possess the
mandate, funds or personnel to cover every ex-employee for
the remainder of his or her life. The military screened all
Stony personnel, politically and mentally, before they got
the job, but people changed, and some knew how to beat the
box when they were tested on the polygraph.

If Brognola's report was accurate, he would have to re-evaluate his early hunch that someone in or near the White House was responsible for blowing Stony Man. An instant flood of mixed emotions nearly overpowered him—relief, confusion, disappointment, anger—and a stubborn helping of suspicion.

"You said this Gardner hangs out at the camp in Idaho?" Bolan asked.

"Used to," Brognola amended, with a frown for Bolan and a hasty sidelong glance in the direction of the President. "They had a little problem out there recently. Some men were killed, but Gardner's definitely not among them. Squeezing one of the survivors, Bureau agents learned that he moved on about a month ago. They say he went 'back East,' whatever that means."

"Previous addresses?"

"Working on it," Brognola said. "Nothing yet, but I'm still hopeful."

Bolan knew what that meant. It was fifty-fifty that his quarry would escape completely, or he would be hunted down too late for Bolan and the Stony team to benefit from any knowledge. That called for some alternative responses, and the Executioner's mind was racing even as he spoke.

"No other leads on NRP's connection to Hezbollah?" he asked.

"Another goose egg. If I had to guess, I'd say they want a little distance from the operation, someone they can point to as an enemy of the United States. That way, they agitate the population, maybe bag some converts in the process."

Bolan saw a glimmer at the tunnel's distant mouth. "There could be more to it than that," he said.

"Such as?"

"Exposure," Bolan said. "Who is it Schroder hates the most?"

"The government," Brognola replied without a trace of hesitation.

"Right. And blowing Stony Man would be a great embarrassment to the so-called November criminals." As Bolan spoke the words, he caught a grimace from the President. "Exposure of the Farm means a congressional investigation, at the very least. There could be changes in the wind."

He didn't have to spell it out. The President saw where his train of thought was headed and scowled. No matter that the present chief executive wasn't responsible for setting up the Phoenix program; he had kept the Farm on line and taken full advantage of its services—in frank defiance of prevailing laws that ranged from violations of neutrality through arson, kidnapping and multiple premeditated homicides. They were high crimes and misdemeanors, definitely, with sufficient ammunition for the grandfather of all impeachment trials.

"I'd obviously hate to see this hit the media," he said, eyes shifting from Brognola to the Executioner and back again. "I have my selfish reasons, granted, but exposure also means the end of Stony Man and everyone associated with the project. If I go down, it means surrendering the office. Go back home and sell my memoirs, somewhere in the low eight figures. This makes Watergate look like a Boy Scout jamboree, okay. But what about your people on the ground?"

They got the point, of course. The Nuremberg defense would never wash, and they had known it going in. For Bolan and Grimaldi, Able Team and Phoenix Force, it would mean hiding out for life or taking on an endless string of trials in the United States and several dozen "friendly" nations. It was entirely possible that some or all of them would be condemned to die; if not, the lot of them—with their support troops—would be facing life without parole in maximum security, and that, in itself, would be a death sentence. Bolan and his comrades had too many mortal enemies out there for them to last long in a cage.

"I'd better go," the warrior said at last, to no one in particular. "I've got a lot of catching up to do."

"Stay frosty, hey?" Brognola said. "And stay in touch. A few more hours and we'll know for sure if we've got anything on Gardner."

"Right." With a last nod to the President, he left the limousine. "Good morning, sir."

He hesitated when the President stuck out his hand, reached back to grasp it and found the presidential handshake firm and dry.

"Good luck. God bless you."

"Thank you, sir."

And he was thinking, as he closed the limo door behind him, that he could use the help right now.

## 14

*Baltimore, Maryland*

"I wish we could have pulled this gig last night," Grimaldi muttered, driving west on Eager Street to Hornwood, turning north from there. "We're looking at a ton of witnesses if this unravels."

Bolan recognized the problem, but he saw no options. It had barely been an hour since Brognola called the scramble, fifteen minutes to collect their gear and head out through morning traffic.

"Let's just get it done," he said.

The target stood in close proximity to Johnson Square, a park five minutes north of the state penitentiary at Madison and Greenmount. The location was ironic, when he thought about it, but he wrote it off as geographical coincidence. The lockup posed no threat to Bolan's plan. In fact, if they were swift and smooth enough, there should be no alarm to rouse the neighborhood.

He wasn't sure where Brognola's tip had come from—someone on the inside of the NRP, presumably—but he was less concerned about the source than its reliability. The big Fed seemed to think it was a solid lead, and that was good enough for Bolan, most particularly since it was the only lead he had.

"Next to the corner house," Grimaldi said, a stiff nod to his left. The number painted on the curb matched Brognola's directions to the hideout. "Who owns this again?"

"Somebody from the NRP," Bolan replied. He hadn't pressed Brognola for a name, as long as one Joe Gardner was on the premises.

"What kind of backup does he have?"

"No information. We should assume the worst."

As Bolan spoke, he reached between his feet, opened his gym bag and lifted out an Uzi with a folding stock and silencer attached. He snapped a magazine in place, cocked the weapon and set the safety, making sure the military sling was clear.

"How do you want to play it?" Grimaldi asked, finishing an easy circuit of the block.

"I'll go in through the back," Bolan said. "You stake out the front, in case he blows that way."

"You want me in the car?"

"Unless it starts to fall apart. I'd rather have the wheels available than one more body in the house."

"Your call. I'll drop you by the alley, then come back around in front. Two minutes, tops."

"Sounds right."

Grimaldi pulled up close beside the alley's mouth and waited while the Executioner stepped out. Before the car had reached the corner, Bolan was already moving toward his destination, passing by the corner house and halting at the second. He faced chain-link fencing, six feet tall, with twists of wire like slender spikes along the top. Instead of climbing over, he spent a moment looking out for sentries, dogs, security devices. There was nothing but a padlock on the gate, and the warrior scrambled over the fence in lieu of taking time to pick the lock.

The draperies were drawn on every window he could see, and while that didn't rule out spotters watching his approach, he saw no evidence of furtive motion that would indicate he had been seen. If anyone was bailing out the front, Grimaldi would be waiting for them, and the racket would alert him when it happened.

The Executioner moved along the south side of the yard, cut across to crouch below the windows, then reached the back door unopposed. This time, for stealth's sake, he picked the lock and eased his way inside. A washer-dryer combination took up half the narrow entryway, immediately on his right, with cabinets overhead. From there, he moved into the pantry, with a smallish kitchen on his right, then down a corridor that branched to a living room on one side, bath and bedrooms on the long end of the L.

No sign of anyone so far, and Bolan waited, listening, his senses reaching for a clue to the location of the stranger he was seeking. The first noise, when it came, was from the direction of the bedrooms. It was nothing he could put his finger on, but it was all he had, so far.

He turned in that direction, leading with the silenced Uzi, pacing off the corridor.

JOE GARDNER HAD BEGUN to think that he was getting paranoid. Since yesterday he couldn't seem to get a grip on what was happening around him. It had all been crystal clear in the beginning, simple when he thought about it, knowing all he had to do was pass along some information, bank his money and stand by while others took the heavy risks. It wasn't as if they were expecting him to lead a penetration or anything, so he could just relax and take it easy, right?

Dead wrong.

The first hit, on the Arab strike team in Virginia, had been nothing but a warm-up for the blitz on Camp Redemption in Idaho. Nobody from the NRP had favored him with details, but the television network news and CNN made up the difference, beaming estimated body counts and scenes of wreckage live, across the country, to his safehouse.

"Safehouse." Shit.

If Schroder's people couldn't hold the compound proper, with their months of training, automatic weapons and explosives, how was he supposed to feel secure? A sitting duck could always fly away, at least, but Gardner had his orders to stay exactly where he was until he got the word to move.

Okay.

He was a soldier, had been since he graduated high school, and he was accustomed to receiving orders. This was different, though. Despite his membership in Schroder's NRP, a personal belief that they should overthrow the present government and start from scratch, experience had taught him to look out for number one. He wasn't in the

self-deception business, and he understood that each new
setback jeopardized the main event.

This deal in D.C., for instance.

Someone, either from the party or the Arab strike team,
had gone after Mr. Big in Washington, and they had screwed
up. And, thought Gardner, if they couldn't stop one man,
what did that say about their chances for success on D day?

He had done his part already, with the briefings and coordinates, the maps and sketches. He wouldn't presume to
tell the frontline soldiers how to do their job. If they blew it,
Gardner would be disappointed, certainly, but he wasn't
prepared to go down with the rest.

Not yet.

Ideology was one thing but survival took priority in
Gardner's book, and if he had an option of surviving rich
or poor, then it was no real choice at all. Given any kind of
chance, he would take the money and run.

He was packing, in fact, just in case, when his sixth sense
kicked in . . . or was it a noise, from the rear of the house?

Gardner stood rock steady, counting ninety seconds in his
mind, without hearing another sound—if there had even
*been* a sound. The open suitcase on his bed was half filled
with the meager clothing from his closet and a plastic zip-
per bag that held his shaving gear and toiletries. He hadn't
emptied the chest of drawers yet, but it wouldn't take five
minutes to complete his packing.

But first he felt a need to check things out.

The pistol on his hip, secure in its Bianchi AccuMold
holster, was the Heckler & Koch P-7 M-10, the 10-round
semiautomatic chambered in .40 caliber, with a squeeze-
cocking lever that prevented accidental discharge, while
permitting a shooter to draw, cock and fire the weapon in
one fluid motion.

That was fast-draw time, though, in the heat of battle. At
the moment, Gardner took it easy, slipping the pistol from
its high-ride sheath and moving in the direction of the bedroom door. He hesitated on the threshold, inches short of
stepping out into the hall. Once more, he strained his ears
to listen, anything at all to swing the balance, one way or
another.

He took a deep breath and held it for a moment, slowly releasing the air through his nostrils.

Silence.

Gardner stepped into the hallway, swiveled toward the living room and kitchen, freezing when he was suddenly confronted by a black-clad stranger standing at the far end of the hall. His startled eyes zoomed into focus on the Uzi in the intruder's hands.

Reaction came a heartbeat later, and Gardner had to pride himself on the recovery. Before a conscious thought could formulate, he was in motion, crouching, dodging back in the direction of the open doorway, snapping up the H&K P-7 M-10 for a quick shot on the fly.

Before the automatic bucked in Gardner's fist, the Uzi stuttered, spewing bullets through the fat tub of its silencer and gouging divots in the wall. His own shot didn't seem to score, as far as he could tell, before a parabellum slug ripped through his shoulder and slammed him against the door-jamb, the floor rushing up to meet his face.

In spite of all the training, Gardner dropped his side arm, had a vague impression of it bouncing on the carpet, then he lost a moment, while the pain and shock took over, shutting down his mind. When he came back in focus seconds later, he was lying on his back, the black-clad stranger looming over him. The muzzle of the Uzi, aimed directly at his face, looked like a storm drain from Gardner's position on the floor.

"Who are you?" the traitor managed to ask, hating that it came out in a whisper.

"I'm the guy who's taking you away from all this," Bolan replied. "We need to have a little talk."

GRIMALDI DIDN'T CARE for sitting in the car, wide open, waiting while the hit went down a few yards distant, shielded from his view by walls, doors, curtains. Anything could happen in the house, and he would be oblivious to all of it unless a bullet or a body came out through the front.

He had the radio, of course, but it was silent at the moment, useless if his friend ran out of luck and stopped a lethal round, or suffered any other injury that would prevent his calling out for help.

The timing made Grimaldi nervous on a set like this. He felt conspicuous, a stranger parked outside in broad daylight, with his car engine idling. The dashboard clock said Bolan should have been inside the house two minutes, give or take a second, and—

The shot was barely audible, a muffled *pop* from the direction of the house. Grimaldi doubted if the neighbors would have heard a thing.

It wasn't Bolan's Uzi, with the silencer attached. His adversary, then—or, maybe, one of several in the house. He was about to make a judgment call, decide if he should go in through the front and blow the standing plan, when suddenly the walkie-talkie on the seat beside him whispered with a burst of static.

"Ready?" Bolan asked him.

"Anytime you are," Grimaldi answered.

"In the alley. Out."

Grimaldi put the car in gear, pulled out and made his way around the block until he saw the alley's mouth ahead. He turned into the alley, creeping along behind the corner house to reach his destination.

Bolan met him at the chain-link fence, the gate already standing open. Gardner matched his Army photograph, as far as Grimaldi could tell. His head sagged forward, with his chin against his chest, one arm thrown over Bolan's shoulders, while the other dangled at his side, blood soaking through the sleeve and shoulder of his denim shirt.

Grimaldi set the parking brake and turned in his seat to reach the back door's inside handle. Bolan showed his human cargo all the courtesy he would have shown a sack of laundry, shoving Gardner in the car, before he scrambled in and slammed the door behind him.

"Go!"

The stash they had selected was a vacant warehouse north of central Baltimore, off Highway 83, near Druid Hill Park. Ten minutes put them in the shadow of the loading dock, with Gardner moaning all the way. He offered no resistance to the move when Grimaldi switched off the engine, came around and helped drag him out.

The guy was unresisting as they carted him around the west side of the warehouse, pausing for a moment there, while Bolan used his key to open up a metal door. Inside, the place was cool and dark, lights flaring at the touch of a wall-mounted switch. With the door locked snug behind them, they proceeded to a smallish office space, where furnishings consisted of a single straight-backed wooden chair.

Their captive seemed completely out of it as Bolan dumped him in the chair and went to work securing his arms and legs.

"Better check the car," the Executioner said.

"Right."

The car was fine, of course, but Bolan was giving his friend an out. Grimaldi took it, knowing that it would be crass of him to spurn the gesture. Bolan had a job to do, and he would do it, whatever it took. Jack, for his part, knew enough to give the big guy breathing room when it was needed.

So he went to check the car, and he would wait there by the loading dock while Bolan did his thing. When it was over, one way or another, they would have the information they required. Grimaldi had no doubts on that score.

It was crisis time, and they were looking at a deadline—still unknown, but no doubt looming closer by the moment. Stony Man and all their friends were hanging in the balance, because a traitor had decided loyalty mattered less than personal revenge, greed, satisfaction—whatever the motive.

Before he finished with Joe Gardner, the Executioner would have all the answers he required, and they could go to work.

BOLAN BROUGHT THE GUY around with smelling salts and slaps designed to set his cheeks on fire without inflicting any major damage, nothing that would tip him back into unconsciousness. Bolan studied that face and tried to remember. They hadn't been introduced, but had he seen the guy before during visits to the Farm? A driver, maybe, taking

Bolan from the airstrip to the house? Had they rubbed shoulders in the mess hall, walking down a corridor? Would he have glimpsed Joe Gardner on patrol around the property?

Dark eyes were focused on him now, with just the right amount of trepidation. Gardner was a one-time Green Beret, which meant he had survived preemptive training for interrogations, but he had been some years out of uniform, and he had never faced the real thing in his life, before today.

"Where am I?" the captive asked.

"Up shit creek without a paddle," Bolan told him honestly. "It's time we had that talk."

"I'm bleeding."

"That proves you're still alive," the warrior countered.

"What do you want?"

"I'll ask the questions. Do you know me?"

He could almost see wheels turning in the captive's mind, alert to any question that would yield an opening, a chance to save himself. It was a time for long shots, when he had no other options left.

"Nobody introduced us," Gardner said. "I've seen you, once or twice."

"And where was that?"

Another fleeting hesitation. Should he lie, or try to bluff it out? He had to have seen the answer in his captor's eyes.

"Around the Farm."

"You took an oath," Bolan pointed out.

Gardner nodded. "Right."

"And broke it."

This time, Gardner tried to shrug, but handcuffs and the sharp pain of his wound defeated him. "The way I see it," he replied, "this country sold *me* out. The years in service, all for what? So we can kiss up to the Russians and the Red Chinese? Don't tell me communism's dead. I see it every time I watch the news or catch a new press conference from the White House. Screw the little man who served his country. Pile those benefits on Cubans, Haitians, faggots—"

His head rocked with the force of Bolan's open-handed blow, blood leaking from the corner of his mouth.

"Cut the rhetoric!" Bolan warned him. "Neither one of us has time to play those word games."

"Jesus, man!"

The Beretta 93-R seemed to come from nowhere, holding level on Gardner's face. Bolan thumbed the hammer back and let him hear it.

"Time for twenty questions," the warrior said. "The first time I suspect you're lying to me, you can kiss your ass goodbye."

"You can't do this," Gardner protested.

"Look around you. It's done. I'll give you time to think about it, though. Five seconds."

He counted down the numbers in his mind until the time ran out.

"First question," Bolan said. "Where can I find the strike team?"

"It's need-to-know. Once they got the background information, I was frozen out."

"They'd want a dress rehearsal."

"I suppose." The prisoner was thinking fast now, calculating whether he could save himself.

"I'm running out of patience. You're running out of time."

"I swear to God, I don't know where they are. These guys don't trust anybody, okay?"

"It's fine with me," Bolan said, sighting the Beretta, "but it doesn't do you any good."

"Hold on a sec, for Christ's sake! I was told they wanted someplace near the target, similar terrain, you know."

The Blue Ridge Mountains? Bolan frowned. Why not?

"How long have they been working on this?"

"Eight, nine months, I figure." Gardner's face was grim. "We talked about it earlier than that, but I was never sure if anybody took it seriously till they started dealing with the rags."

"And they were chosen for publicity?"

"What else? You think the party *likes* these fuckers? They're expendable. If they get wasted at the Farm, okay. If not, somebody meets them after, and they get a big surprise."

The Hezbollah commandos made no difference now. He reckoned they were dead men, either way. The first concern for Bolan was the NRP, its leadership and sponsors. Men of violence and divided loyalties who possessed the secrets of the Farm and wouldn't hesitate to move against it later, if the present scheme fell through.

"I need to know who's paying," Bolan said.

"What do you mean?"

"The party's run by Wallace Schroder, but he's not the money man. Who pays the tab? Who pulls the strings?"

"Nobody ever filled me in on that, I swear. I always talked to Eulon Trask. He's Schroder's number two—on this gig, anyway."

He filed the name away for access through the Stony Man computers. It was time to roll, and Bolan only had one question left.

"I'm curious," he said to Gardner. "How much did they pay you?"

"What?" The captive seemed confused.

"What was your asking price? How much do souls go for these days?"

"A quarter million," Gardner told him. "Half up front, half on delivery. It sounded fair to me."

"Okay, that's all." He rose and moved to stand behind the straight-back chair.

The captive saw a gleam of hope. "You'll let me go?"

"Did I say that? You'll do your time."

"Aw, man—"

The Executioner rapped the butt of the Beretta against the man's temple. If Gardner didn't bleed to death first, someone from Justice would pick him up when Grimaldi eventually made the call. All considered, it was more than the traitor deserved.

The Stony Man pilot was waiting for him on the loading dock. "So, what's the word?" he asked.

"We're looking for a target in the mountains," Bolan told him, "not too far from Stony Man."

"Uh-oh."

"You got that right."

Uh-oh, and then some.

Time was running short. In fact, the Executioner was painfully aware, they might have none at all.

## 15

*Blue Ridge Mountains*

"You know damned well we can't abort. It's not an option."

Wallace Schroder's voice was calm, pitched well below the scream of rage that would have been appropriate, all things considered. Standing at attention, close enough for him to reach across the military-surplus desk and slap that stupid face, stood Eulon Trask, the author of his misery, whose idiotic negligence put everything at mortal risk.

"Just a suggestion, sir." There was a tremor in the stupid bastard's voice that almost brought a smile to Schroder's lips. Almost.

"If I want your advice, I'll ask for it."

"Yes, sir."

"It's your fault that we have this problem, Eulon. No one else's. Is that clear?"

"Yes, sir."

"You might as well have rented billboards on the highway to announce our plan."

"Sir, I—"

"Shut up! You've done enough, without a fling at insubordination. Are we clear on that?"

"Yes, sir." Trask showed a little more humility, but not enough to take the edge off Schroder's pent-up fury.

"We're proceeding with the plan because we have no viable alternative. The only way to rein in our cohorts, at this point, would be to annihilate the team. That's wasteful, and it smacks of panic. Having come this far, we should at least attempt to get our money's worth, don't you agree?"

"Yes, sir."

"The only way that I can see to do that, Eulon, is to give the plan a goose. How close to ready are they?"

"Two rehearsals, one at night. I don't know that a third would make much difference, sir. They've got the layout fresh in mind, and they're enthusiastic. What I hear, you won't get any arguments about an early jump-off."

"Fine. We might just salvage something from this screwup yet." Before Trask could relax, though, Schroder added, "Just to help the odds along, I think we ought to have a man on board the team, don't you?"

Trask hesitated half a beat too long, then said, "Yes, sir. Sounds like a good idea."

"You're volunteering, then?"

"Yes, sir . . . unless you think the presence of Americans would jeopardize security."

"You plan on getting captured, Eulon?"

"No, sir."

"I don't see a problem, then. Do you?"

"No, sir."

"Coordinate with Hassan. You'll go tonight."

"Yes, sir."

"Dismissed."

It felt good, reaming Eulon out for his mistakes, the minor pleasure of command recalling Schroder's mind to days of active service, when he wore his country's uniform with pride. Before the rot set in—or, more precisely, in the days before he was aware of the corruption, nothing short of treason, that pervaded Washington. The White House, Congress, the Supreme Court—all of it, in fact, was controlled by sellouts who put personal ambition first, above their love of country and their pride of race.

There was a new day coming, though, and Schroder's National Redemption Party would be instrumental in that change. He was in no position to take credit for the plan, not yet, but history would vindicate his methods once the noble end had been achieved.

He had a flash of déjà vu just then. Where had he heard those words before?

Ends justify the means. Well, sometimes, anyway. In Vietnam they had been overrun by bleeding hearts who wouldn't let the military do its job. God knows you couldn't zap a terrorist in those days without someone snapping pictures for the media and printing lies about the "baby killers" who were slaughtering "innocent women and children."

Bullshit.

Schroder knew that war was hell; it was designed that way, to separate the wheat and chaff. The strong survived, and while that didn't always mean the good guys came out on top, still, history had ways and means of balancing the books. It took a while for Hitler and the Japanese to meet with their comeuppance, even longer for the Communists in Russia, but the wheel kept turning, and the folks who managed to hang on, surviving through adversity, would one day be on top again.

Sometimes, of course, it helped if you could give the wheel a shove. Instead of standing on the sidelines, waiting for a traitorous regime to fall apart or push the people to a point where they rebelled in fury and disgust, a savvy warrior had the chance to light a fuse from time to time. Stay clear and watch it blow, then pick the pieces up as best he could and start from scratch.

It wasn't as if they had a lot to lose in terms of civilized society. The major cities were reduced to urban-jungle status, ruled by greedy, grasping politicians, terrorized by psychopaths and street gangs, with the nation's moral fiber undermined by drugs, pornography, interracial marriages, you name it.

It was Sodom and Gomorrah for the 1990s, and the Lord had given up on punishment—or maybe he was tied up with more pressing matters on the far side of the universe. Whatever, when it came to solving problems of morale and morals, humankind would have to stand alone. The mob would need a leader, though, and he, in turn, would need an army to defend him and enforce his will.

No problem.

Mopping up was Wallace Schroder's specialty, and he enjoyed his work. Soon, now, and he would have another chance to do what he did best.

And God help anyone who tried to stop him.

## Stony Man Farm

THE WARNING OF A RAID directed at the Farm hit Aaron Kurtzman like a swift punch to the solar plexus, bringing up bitter, painful memories that he had tried to leave behind.

He could remember walking like a normal man—or running, if he felt the urge, wind in his face, blood pumping with the pleasant effort of exertion. Never quite the social animal, he still got in a dance from time to time in those days, and the legs came into play when he had the pleasure of bringing a young woman to his bed.

A bullet to the spine had changed all that. He still had no clear fix on whether it had been an aimed shot or a stray, would never know for sure, and it no longer preyed on Kurtzman's mind. A soldier took his chances, even in the rear lines of defense, and it was no good crying over spilled blood.

This time, though, they had a slim lead on the opposition. Still no word on when the raid was coming down, but any warning was a bonus, in the circumstances. He had canceled leaves, called in a dozen reinforcements, and the Farm was now on full alert. A casual observer wouldn't see the difference, but the hardsite—never easy for an infiltrator, at the most relaxed of times—was battened down for war.

A quick computer check had verified that all the sensors and surveillance cameras were fully operational, no glitches in the system that would let nightcrawlers slip in unobserved. The net included motion sensors, infrared detector beams and fiber-optic gear concealed at various strategic points on the perimeter and grounds. The airstrip was secure, its dummy mobile home in place to block the runway, two men standing by the radar, a bank of miniguns and Stingers that would bring down any aircraft trying to approach the Farm. Beyond that, the visible "farmhands"

were loaded for bear, wearing Kevlar body armor underneath their denim work clothes, traveling in pairs and keeping automatic weapons out of sight but close to hand. The
reinforcements were on standby in the air-conditioned barn,
with full combat gear and two-man, four-wheeled ATVs for
rapid transport to the point of contact, if and when the
Hezbollah commandos made their move.

The downside was a total ignorance of where and when
their enemy would strike, together with a head count on the
hit team. Kurtzman reckoned the assault force would be
relatively small, two dozen men or less. It would be difficult—though not impossible, by any means—for Arab terrorists to field a larger force on U.S. soil. The numbers game
was only part of it, however. A committed terrorist, prepared to sacrifice himself for God and the cause, was capable of wreaking havoc well beyond the scope of men who
cared about survival. There was no surrender for a kamikaze warrior, only victory or death.

For the fanatics, all too often, victory *was* death.

If it came down, there would be no holds barred, no
quarter asked or offered on the killing ground. The farmhouse should be relatively safe, but Kurtzman took no
chances. Wedged between his left thigh and the armrest of
his chair, he kept a Glock 21 semiautomatic pistol, the .45-
caliber version, with thirteen rounds in the magazine and
one up the spout. Four extra magazines were distributed in
Kurtzman's pockets, readily available at need.

His odds of seeing action were remote at best, but he
would be prepared for trouble if it came. And he wouldn't
be faulted, in the words of one Clint Eastwood movie char-
acter, "for lack of shooting back."

He thought of April and Andrzej, their first fatalities at
Stony Man, and knew he could have been another. Just another inch or two, and Kurtzman would have gone out in a
body bag instead of on a stretcher.

Luck.

You either had it or your didn't. There were some who
said a soldier made his own, and maybe they were right, in
terms of preparation, training and the like, but there was
still an element of chance to every battle. The most cau-

tious fighting man could twist an ankle, miss a crucial shot or overlook a sniper in the distance. Smart guys bought the farm, the same as dummies, and they all wound up together in the end.

But when they came for Kurtzman this time—if they came—he would be ready, waiting. He was all done giving things away.

Whatever Kurtzman's adversaries wanted from him this time, they would have to take by force.

## The Pentagon

THE ONE THING General Arthur Coltrane never learned to like about his chosen craft was waiting. On the battlefield, experience had taught him, those who snooze are apt to lose their lives. The general's reputation had been built on raw aggression, rooting out the enemy and chasing him until he dropped or turned to fight and die.

It galled him now to be so close and know that some pathetic bungler in the ranks might ruin everything. An extra set of photographs, for God's sake, left behind where anyone could find them. In the field, he would have countered such an act of negligence by moving up the schedule, pushing right ahead before his enemies could take advantage of the error. Crush them in their huts and trenches, grind them into dog chow with artillery and small-arms fire. It was a different game in covert operations, though, especially when those operations had been planned and carried out in flagrant violation of the law.

He was working without a net this time, no expectation of support from his superiors if anything went wrong. A court-martial would be the least of Coltrane's problems if the word got out. Security was paramount, not only to prevent his serving prison time, but to ensure that phase two of his plan went off without a hitch.

The power brokers would be reeling when the story broke: guerrilla forays and assassinations sponsored by the government, concealed from Congress and the people. Dozens, maybe hundreds, of illegal executions carried out on orders from the White House, some of them on U.S. soil.

He smiled to think of it, that cocky left-wing bastard in the Oval Office, squirming in the spotlight of a scandal.

The nation would be rocked to its foundation, ready for a savior when the smoke cleared, and who better to fulfill that role than one who had devoted decades to the service of his country under fire? It meant resigning his commission to pursue civilian office, but for Coltrane it was just a case of shifting gears. He had done everything within his power, as a military officer, to save the country from impending ruin. It was time he tried another angle of attack.

It made him furious to think that Schroder had suggested canceling the raid. One of his soldiers stumbled, made a crucial error, and the colonel was prepared to scrub their plans as if the time and energy invested were for nothing. Idiot! It was a miracle that he had ever risen to command, with nerves so frail.

Coltrane removed a whiskey bottle from his desk and poured himself a double shot, replacing the bottle and closing the drawer before he drank the fiery amber liquid. It was the one drink he allowed himself before he finished supper in the mess. Restraint and discipline were everything.

That was a lesson Coltrane's fellow countrymen would have to learn, once he was settled in the White House. Education would be part of his campaign, of course, but you could only say so much and still hope for the sheep to put an *x* beside your name the second Tuesday in November. He would have to fudge a little, tiptoe cautiously around some issues, but the central message would be there for everyone to see and understand: America was on the skids, no welcome end in sight, and it could all fall down unless the people used their right—and their responsibility—to turn that self-destructive course around.

By voting for a man of action and integrity, damn right.

It would be something of a new experience, persuading men and women to accept him, rather than commanding their obedience and snapping orders that were never disobeyed. There would be momentary stumbling blocks—the courts and Congress, for example—but he reckoned that some changes would be made once he was finally inaugurated and the people saw what he could do. Amendments to the Constitution were like any other part of the elective process, a popularity contest, wooing support from the great unwashed masses. It was bound to be rocky at first, but once his countrymen had seen what he could do, the way he started turning things around, they would support him all the way.

And there would always be the NRP to help him out with special problems, clearing out the deadwood when he couldn't do the job with recalls or impeachment.

One way or another, he *would* do the job. And if he somehow got rich in the bargain, well, who ever said a patriot shouldn't live well?

George Washington had set the standard back in revolutionary times, when he accepted the appointment as commander of the new American militia. Wise man that he was, the father of his country had spurned a salary, requesting only that he be reimbursed for expenses when the job was done.

And what a job it was.

Before the redcoats finally gave up the ghost at Yorktown, General George had logged "expenses" to the tune of some $200,000—better than five million dollars in today's inflated currency. All that, and he had likewise earned the adulation of his countrymen. He could have been the President for life, but it was easier to step down after two terms and retire to his plantation in Virginia, where the slaves were busy picking cotton for the champion of liberty.

Not bad.

Not bad at all.

Coltrane had no plantation, but he had his age to think about. Two terms should be enough, if he was able to handpick his own successor, someone who would carry on the work, but he would make some changes, all the same. Repeal that pesky Twenty-second Amendment for starters, the one that restricted a President's service to two terms in office. After that, well . . .

Coltrane caught himself. Before he started reinventing government, issuing terse executive orders, he had to get himself elected. And before he could do that, he needed

Schroder's people and the Arabs to perform their parts on schedule.

Soon, now.

It was getting closer by the moment. He could almost smell the gunsmoke.

## Stony Man Farm

THE WAITING put his nerves on edge, but Bolan had no choice. The only option he could think of was a joke: start cruising Skyline Drive from Front Royal down to Waynesboro and back again, with detours onto every side road he could find, an aimless search for enemies who might not even have their base camp in the Blue Ridge Mountains.

*Close* was relative, he knew. If they were seeking similar terrain, they could be somewhere in the Appalachians, fifteen miles due west, the Alleghenies just beyond, or in the Iron Range, fifty miles southwest. That still left West Virginia, Maryland, North Carolina—all within an easy drive of Stony Man, when they were ready to proceed.

The best move, he had finally agreed with Hal and Jack, was for him to remain at Stony Man in a defensive posture, while Brognola pulled some strings and tried to get a fix on the elusive enemy. If the big Fed could pull it off, then Bolan would be ready to go on a moment's notice, carrying the war to his enemy's doorstep.

He sipped a tepid cup of coffee, sat and thought about the other times when he had waited for a scramble, knowing death was waiting for him at the target site. Like Kurtzman, downstairs in the War Room, Bolan also thought about the last time raiders had invaded Stony Man. On that occasion they had caught him by surprise, cut down the woman he had loved and come damned close to scuttling the project altogether.

Not this time.

If he could find them in advance, rain cleansing fire upon them in their own backyard, so much the better, but he wasn't counting on a lucky break. The worst scenario, a full-blown raid against the Farm, would find him ready, waiting for them, night or day.

Whatever else the raiders were expecting, had prepared for, they wouldn't be counting on a showdown with the Executioner. He understood their mind-set, realized that gunmen with Hezbollah were ready—even anxious—for a shot at holy martyrdom in God's name, but they were human beings underneath the rhetoric and posturing, still subject to the fears that deviled other men. If he could strike them hard enough and fast enough, he had a fair shot at demoralizing them, defeating them in detail.

Anyway, it sounded good in theory.

He had come close to asking Barbara Price to leave the Farm, sit this one out, but he had stopped himself in time to keep from adding insult to the pressure she was feeling. Barbara was a trained professional, damned good at what she did, and sending her away—assuming Bolan had that power—would have weakened their defenses, in addition to her wounded feelings and the damage Bolan would have done to their relationship. He understood—or thought he did, at any rate—her need to be accepted as a valued, equal member of the team, and she had proved herself in that capacity a thousand times. As for the risk that came along with playing in the majors, she would simply have to take her chances with the rest.

Bolan turned his thoughts to the dangers they faced from even a successful defense of the Farm. A certain amount of noise and pyrotechnics was acceptable, but if the shooting match got out of hand, outside authorities would certainly become involved. A fix from Washington could do the trick, but only if it came in time to scotch publicity. One leak to television or the tabloids, and the "people's right to know" would scuttle Stony Man and thus achieve the raiders' goal. For all he knew, considering the climate of the times, the project might be canceled, in lieu of relocation to a new secure facility.

Above all else, he could not let that happen. There was too much sweat and blood invested in the Farm for Bolan to accept defeat with anything approximating grace.

The Hezbollah commandos, when they came, would be expecting trouble.

Bolan meant to take it one step further, and deliver them to hell on earth.

He was about to pour himself another cup of coffee, when he heard a static whisper from the intercom, resolving into Aaron Kurtzman's voice.

"I need you in the War Room, Striker, Barbara, Jack. We've got our fix."

**16**

*Blue Ridge Mountains*

"I hope they've got the right place spotted," Grimaldi said.

Bolan hoped so, too, but he wasn't about to voice the doubt aloud. No superstitious soldier, he still saw no point in tempting fate.

"They got the fix," he said, his own voice sounding louder in his earphones than the Cobra gunship's rotors whipping circles overhead.

The quickest way to scan the mountains, Hal Brognola had decided, was a military overflight from Quantico. The Douglas EA-3B Skywarrior reconnaissance aircraft had completed three passes in just under twenty minutes, cruising at 610 miles per hour, using all its tricks from an altitude of ten thousand feet. The video and still shots picked out ranger stations, campgrounds, scenic turnouts, rest stops, bridle trails, the base at Stony Man—and something else.

Due north, eleven miles from Stony Man, there was another, smaller spread. The buildings had a temporary feel about them, but the layout was familiar—too familiar, though constructed on a smaller scale—and infrared receivers on the Douglas scout plane said the base was occupied. There were two dozen men, or thereabouts, with six or seven vehicles.

The rest was paperwork and phone calls, running title searches, scavenging the public record through computer linkups. An eighty-year-old farmer by the name of Ernie Voyles had sold the property the previous year, retired to Florida and bought himself a piece of sunshine by the sea.

The purchaser was down in black-and-white as Thomas Loudermilk, a legal mouthpiece for assorted right-wing groups, including Schroder's National Redemption Party.

Bingo.

There was maybe one chance in a million that the NRP facility had no connection to the coming raid on Stony Man, but Bolan had no faith in such coincidence. He was prepared to treat the compound's occupants as hostile in the absence of persuasive evidence that they were innocent, lay waste to their facility, and kill anything that moved.

But he was also seeking information.

Nagging at the back of Bolan's mind was the suspicion that there had to be more to Schroder's plot than simply blitzing Stony Man. What was he hoping to accomplish, on the eve of an election year, besides embarrassing the government and—

Bolan stopped himself right there.

Embarrassing the government. "November criminals." If Schroder had the means of undermining one regime, what would prevent him from selecting an alternative?

Slow down!

The mission had priorities, and number one was wiping out the hit team. When that job was done, the pressing danger neutralized, there would be time enough to look for Schroder, take him off somewhere and squeeze him until he sang in stereo. Before he finished with the would-be savior of America, Mack Bolan meant to know him inside out.

"Coming up," Grimaldi said. "I still think we should hit them from the air and get it over with."

"We're doing both," Bolan replied. "Too much opportunity for breakaways, if we're restricted to a bird's-eye view. Besides, there might be someone on the ground I need to talk to."

"Do you think he'd let you get a word in edgewise?"

"Never know until you try."

"How much time do you need?" Grimaldi asked.

"I'll call you when I'm in position. We don't have a lot of time to make the drop."

That much was obvious. Dusk would fall across the great mountains like a giant's shadow, peaks and crags contributing obstructions to the sinking sun. Gullies flushed with light one moment would be pitch-dark the next, transformed into obstacle courses, complete with fallen logs and thorny creepers, smooth stones slimed with algae in the creekbeds, slick enough to drop a careless hiker on his buttocks. Aside from natural obstacles, his enemies had owned the tract long enough to lay in some impressive traps, if they were so inclined, and he would have to watch his step, beginning when he hit the ground.

"One klick," Grimaldi told him, with true regret in his voice.

"I'm ready."

They wouldn't touch down, and Bolan had the harness buckle on almost before he finished speaking. It was easy, with the quick-release straps that would open at his touch, once he was on the deck below. Of course, if anybody saw him coming down, he made an easy target, dangling underneath the chopper like a spider hanging on a strand of silk.

The winch whined overhead, and Bolan made the drop in seconds flat, as if rappeling down a cliff or wall. On contact, the warrior hastily released the clips that held his harness fast and stepped clear of the rigging, watched it wriggle out of reach as Grimaldi began to climb, the Cobra rising until it disappeared above the treetops.

They were still in radio communication, but he didn't test the linkup at the moment, fearing any sentries in the forest might coincidentally be tuned in to the frequency. They ran a risk already, with the chopper's noise and visibility. There was no point in pushing it with chatter on the radio until the fat was in the fire.

Soon, now.

He checked the compass, verified his heading and struck off into the deep, dark woods.

THE TENSION wasn't thick enough to cut with power tools, perhaps, but you could feel it all the same. Schroder hadn't warned the Arabs that they were swiftly running out of time, but he knew they were on edge. It didn't seem to matter if they planned to sacrifice themselves or not; the human element was never absolutely vanquished, even with devoted kamikaze warriors who, ostensibly, had nothing left to lose.

He watched them wandering around the camp in twos and threes, discussing God knew what in muted tones. Did they have families back home? Were there little kamikazes waiting for a chance to crash and burn?

Did anybody really give a shit?

From Schroder's point of view, it was a major irritant that he was forced to join them at the compound, oversee the final preparations for their strike, but there had been no viable alternative. With Coltrane on the warpath, there was no way he could leave the job to Eulon Trask alone. It simply made good sense for him to supervise the final preparations, wave the Hezbollah commandos off as they departed on their final mission.

The flip side of his job was making sure that none of them survived. He had to trust them, once they reached the target, confident that each would save a bullet or grenade to kill himself before he let himself be captured by the enemy. If some were able to escape, though, it would be a different story. There were contact points arranged, with pickup times, and members of the NRP had been assigned to watch the drops and pay off the "fortunate" survivors in lead.

If it came down to that, there would be loose ends dangling, federal agents wondering who finished off the hitters, but by that time, those in charge of the covert facility would be so busy covering their asses, they would have no time for chasing shadows. There would be a shitstorm in D.C. when news of Stony Man leaked out, and Schroder's contacts in the gutter press were standing by to make sure it got maximum exposure when the guns went off. They didn't know the story yet, of course, but they were primed to roll with anything that crossed their desks and push it as if the Second Coming was at hand.

The single hitch, potentially, was Eulon Trask. Despite his first impulse toward punishment, it came to Schroder now, with time to let his anger cool, that it would be a stupid blunder to send Trask in among the Arabs. With his luck, Trask would be the first man killed, and fingerprints would

link him to the NRP before you had a chance to slap a wild
sow's ass and holler soo-eee.

No.

If he decided Trask had to go—and, frankly, he was still
inclined in that direction—Schroder could arrange a private accident to do the job. A man like Trask wouldn't be
missed by anyone of consequence if he should disappear
some evening, down a mine shaft in Nevada or as gator bait
in some Louisiana bayou. There were endless opportunities
for toxic-waste disposal in the great United States.

And they would soon be getting even greater, once the
people—with a little nudging from the National Redemption Party—rose up to dispose of the November criminals.
The day was coming, sooner than he would have let himself
believe.

And what would happen then?

They had to think about the old man's presidential race—
no hint of scandal or affiliation with the NRP until the votes
were in and he was settled in the White House. After that it
wouldn't matter. They could flaunt their colors for the
world to see.

Red, white and blue. Damn right!

He caught a glimpse of Trask approaching from the far
side of the camp and waited for his tarnished number two
to close the gap. It pained him, but he smiled at the hapless
screwup.

"All ready, Eulon?"

"Nearly, sir. They're packing up. I've got my own gear
squared away."

"About that, Eulon... I've been thinking." Schroder saw
the frown on Trask's face, stuck somewhere in the void between faint hope and stolid resignation.

"Yes, sir?"

"I've been thinking it would be a waste of talent, having
you go with our friends tonight. I need you here to help coordinate the cleanup. Just in case, you understand?"

"Yes, sir! Of course, sir." Trask tried not to look or
sound relieved, but he almost wilted where he stood.
"Whatever you say, sir. I'm totally at your disposal."

"Understood. Now, if you wouldn't mind—"

The rapid-fire explosions rocked him on his heels, sent shock waves rippling through the camp like thunderbolts from heaven. Spinning to his left, the NRP commander was in time to see the motor pool go up in smoke and flame, the vehicles detonating one after another, like a string of giant firecrackers.

He gaped at Trask, found the soldier gaping back at him. Blind fury gripped him, staining everything he saw a brilliant crimson.

"Don't just stand there, asshole!" Schroder bellowed. "Go and find out what the fuck is happening!"

TARIK HASSAN WAS SITTING in his barracks, huddled over bird's-eye recon photos with Musa Kmeid, when it began. He had no warning, no way to prepare himself. One moment, they were speaking quietly, Musa suggesting an alternative approach to what was clearly the command post of their target. Then, as if a giant fist had struck the clapboard house, the roof fell in.

No, that wasn't precisely true. It merely seemed that way, with the concussion of the blast.

In fact, the windows shattered, violently imploding, spraying shards of glass around the room like bullets. Several struck Hassan as he dived for the floor, but he ignored their sting, the warmth of fresh blood running on his flank and shoulder. Nothing broken, yet. As long as he could fight, or run away, he wasn't wholly at the mercy of his enemies.

Kmeid was bleeding from an ugly gash above one eye, when next Hassan could see him through the swirling pall of dust and acrid smoke. He recognized the smell of burning oil and gasoline, remembering that they were situated near the motor pool.

He crawled toward the cot, where his weapons were stashed. Fumbling with the pistol belt, he got it on without sitting up to expose himself, gritting his teeth as secondary blasts from the motor pool told him the vehicles were burning, their fuel tanks detonating from the heat. He clutched the MP-5 SD-3 submachine gun to his chest and prayed, hoping it would be enough to see him through.

They had somehow been traced. That much was obvious before he ever took a peek outside. It was impossible to brand the motor pool's destruction as an accident, spontaneous combustion or a careless soldier smoking near the barrels of surplus gasoline. Such things might happen in the movies or imaginative fiction, but real life was something else. When you were three short hours from embarking on the most important battle of your life, such an event could only mean one thing.

The enemy had tracked them down, and an attack was under way.

"Up! Quickly!" he shouted to Kmeid. "Prepare yourself!"

In fact, his second in command was already prepared, the Colt Commando carbine ready in his hands. Kmeid's young face wasn't exactly pale—his natural complexion balked at that—but he looked worried, even stunned, like the survivor of a head-on auto crash.

Hassan moved toward the doorway on hands and knees, his head down, alert to sounds of automatic weapons firing in the camp. A stray round came in through the nearest window, no glass left to stop it, and he heard it strike the wall behind him, several feet above his head. Kmeid flinched at the noise but held his ground, presenting the gunners outside with a fair view of his head and shoulders, until Hassan grabbed his arm and dragged him down to the floor.

"What's happening, Tarik?"

In lieu of answering the foolish question, he wormed closer to the door, reached up to grasp the knob and opened it a crack. At first the drifting smoke obscured his view, but then he made out figures dashing here and there, as if without direction, dodging slugs and shrapnel, stopping now and then to fire at unseen targets.

His men were fighting for their lives.

The raid was off, that much he understood without the concept being put in words. Without the vehicles, afoot on unfamiliar ground, they would be lucky to survive, much less escape to fight again another day.

So be it. If destruction was their lot, Hassan and his commandos were prepared to sell their lives at such a price that it would be a Pyrrhic victory for their opponents.

If he couldn't wreak havoc on the special target they had chosen, at least he could stand like a man and a warrior of God, trading shots with his enemies until one or the other of them lay sprawled in the dust.

It felt strange, now, at the last minutes, to contemplate death as a relative certainty. Despite all his training, the raids he had led in the past, Hassan had reached a point where he allowed himself to think primarily of others in the role of human sacrifices to *jihad*. He had been relatively safe for some years, and the time had come for him to show that he still had a warrior's mettle, nerve enough to place his body on the firing line.

He drew the door back wide enough to slip outside, not crawling like an animal, however. With new energy, he scrambled to his feet, reached down to grab his companion and drag him upright. They had to set an example for the others, give their very best, and never mind the cost.

Tarik Hassan stepped outside to meet his destiny.

IT HAD BEEN RELATIVELY simple, going in. He met one lookout on the south side of the property and dropped him with a silenced round from the Beretta 93-R. A quick glimpse of the dead man's face told the warrior he was one of the Redemption Party's rank and file, a young man in his twenties. How long out of service to his country?

Never mind.

Some choices were irrevocable, once you crossed the line, a silent vote of confidence for one side or the other, good or evil, and it almost seemed inconsequential at the time, until the tab came due.

He kept on moving and put the dead man out of mind. The guy had lots of company, and none of them had any relevance for Bolan at the moment. Closing on the camp, with scattered buildings now in view, he had to say the place didn't look much like Stony Man. They had reduced the scale, of course, compelled to work with what they had, but if he thought about it for a moment, squinted just the right way, maybe it was close enough.

Too close.

He didn't bother counting heads, with full dark coming on. It would have been a waste of time, and Grimaldi was waiting for him, no doubt champing at the bit.

So, first things first.

He meant to isolate his enemies, deprive them of mobility, whichever way it went from there. The motor pool, well eastward of the simulated target buildings, was his first stop as he circled the perimeter. Shaped charges from his OD satchel were fastened to the undersides of four vehicles, leaving three to blow with the concussion. The timers were synchronized to go as one, with ninety seconds' lead time for the Executioner to find another vantage point.

From wiring up the motor pool, Bolan moved to find a place behind a structure vaguely reminiscent of the barn at Stony Man. Its placement in relation to the house was wrong, some thirty paces off, but they had limited space to work with. The exterior seemed accurate enough, but you could pick that up from aerial photography or Joseph Gardner's personal description. He was curious about the floor plans—how much did they really know?—but there would be no time to check it out. If Bolan's plan went off on schedule, and he hadn't missed the strike team proper, their accumulated knowledge would be useless.

Bolan's Colt Commando carbine had been fitted with a 37 mm M-203 launcher underneath the barrel and a 90-round drum magazine to get things rolling. Spare grenades and magazines for the Commando crossed his chest in camou bandoliers, while his web belt and shoulder sling held surplus ammo pouches for the .44 Magnum Desert Eagle and the Beretta in its armpit rig. The blade of Bolan's fighting knife was seven inches long, jet black and double-edged; it had a wicked knuckle-duster grip and solid pommel, sharpened to a point for cracking skulls.

He crouched in shadow, with nightfall coming on, and waited for the string of planted charges to erupt. There was no need to check his watch, as he could hear the numbers running in his head. Relentless. They had no concern whatever for the lives and dreams of men.

The charges went together, right on schedule, and he watched the vehicles go up as if by magic, God's hand reaching down to nudge them with a fiery finger of destruction. Secondary blasts from ruptured fuel tanks followed almost simultaneously. For a heartbeat, Bolan thought about the risk of forest fire, but there had been a fair amount of rain the past two weeks, and he would have to take the chance in any case.

The string of rapid-fire explosions had the same effect on the Executioner's enemies as the detonation of a starting pistol would have on a group of athletes standing ready on their marks. At once, the compound was alive with khaki uniforms and men in varied stages of undress, but all of them were armed, each looking for a target.

Bolan gave them one, a flitting shadow, firing from the hip. He chose his marks, milking short precision bursts of 5.56 mm tumblers from his carbine, dropping runners in their tracks. The gunfire only added to their sense of overall confusion, to the point that soon he had at least a dozen of them firing wildly back and forth across the forest compound, some of them at one another.

Chaos.

When a soldier was outnumbered and outgunned, confusion in the hostile ranks could be his greatest ally, anything to shake up the bastards and keep them guessing, head off any kind of organized defense.

The M-203 launcher belched a high-explosive round into the middle of the killing ground, its smoky blast obliterating one young runner, staggering two others so that they were easy prey for Bolan's probing rifle fire. He kept on moving, shunning the temptation that would make him stationary, a sitting target for his enemies.

And it was time to call the cavalry.

He raised a hand to key the microphone he wore and spoke four words.

"Let's do it, Wings."

## 17

Grimaldi got the word and instantly acknowledged. "Roger that!"

The Cobra was a lethal lady, instantly responsive to his knowing touch. The Stony Man pilot took her north at treetop level, with the new T53-70X engine and the Bell 412 rotor working overtime, pushing the gunship toward her maximum speed of 150 miles per hour with the short wings fully loaded.

This wasn't the same ship Grimaldi had used in Idaho, and he had brand-new toys to play with. In the forward turret, a 7.62 mm M-28 minigun shared space with a 40 mm M-129 grenade launcher, giving the pilot the choice of whether he would rock and roll or shake and bake. Each stubby wing was tipped with a quad launcher for the deadly Hellfire missiles, laser guided from the chopper's nose, each rocket capable of taking out a heavy tank. Between the Hellfires and the Cobra's landing strut, to starboard, was a 20 mm Gatling gun, the larger brother of the minigun, with armor-piercing rounds and a cyclic rate of six thousand rounds per minute. On the port side, rounding out the package, was an M-157 launching pod with seven 2.57-inch rockets nestled in their separate tubes, all armed and ready for the kill.

How much ungodly havoc could he wreak with that list of selected goodies?

There was only one way to find out.

The recon photos had detected nothing in the way of antiaircraft batteries, but you could never be too sure. A similar report would doubtless have been filed for Stony Man, but they had everything from runway obstacles to ack-

ack guns and Stingers waiting, carefully concealed, if anybody came too close without an invitation.

Fine.

Grimaldi didn't plan on landing to discuss the price of figs and land mines with the Hezbollah commandos. He would be content to scourge them from the air, but even that could be a fatal error if the targets were prepared. One SAM would bring him down in flames, and even small-arms could do the trick if they got lucky.

Screw it!

The pilot's best friend on earth was down there, fighting for his life, the lives of nearly everyone they both held dear. A certain risk came with the territory, and Grimaldi didn't feel like shirking now, when he was this close to the goal, with so much riding on the play.

Another moment, and he didn't need his instruments to find the hostile camp. A cloud of smoke was rising from the compound, tattered by the breeze at treetop level, better than a beacon when it came to homing in. They would be scrambling on the ground, like ants disrupted when a football struck their nest, and he could take advantage of the moment, use the lapse against them with a vengeance.

Perfect.

Nosing through the smoke, he came in for a strafing run. So many running targets down below, he didn't bother counting. He squeezed the trigger, milking short bursts from the minigun and 20 mm Gatling, plus a pair of 40 mm high-explosive rounds to punctuate the greeting. He was past them, banking for a second run, before they fully understood that this attack was coming at them from the ground *and* from the air.

It would have been ideal if there were speakers mounted underneath the gunship, some way he could taunt them, insult heaped on top of injury. On second thought, it was a childish notion, and would clearly have demeaned his enemies, along with Jack himself.

There is a certain dignity involved in dying for a cause, however wretched it might be, however brutish its proponents. True believers, from Masada to the killing ground of Waco, Texas, are invested with the stature that accrues to saints and lunatics. They might be despised for their deeds, reviled for their cruelty, denounced as insane . . . but underneath the condemnation, there is still a grudging sense of wonder at the kind of faith that leads to human sacrifice.

Grimaldi gave his targets that, if nothing else. He didn't hate them, in the sense that he would hate a man who raped his sister, but he knew they had to die. With true believers, there was no room for negotiation, nothing in the way of middle ground. You either knuckled under, gave them what they wanted, or you took them out.

Like now.

THE FIRST THING Eulon Trask could think of was to try to save the motor pool, round up a fire brigade and stop the flames from spreading any further. Several seconds gaping at the damage told him that the vehicles were hopeless, but he had the camp to think about.

And somewhere in the middle of it all, before the shooting started, Trask tried to work out what was happening.

They were on foot, for damn sure. Every piece of rolling stock they had, except for two light trail bikes, had been lined up in the motor pool, and it was gone now. Shot to hell. It took about five seconds for the thought to register that this could hardly be an accident, and by the time that notion put down roots, Trask knew they were in trouble.

Everything beyond that point was stream of consciousness, a blur of thought synapses sparking, mental switches being thrown on automatic. Someone had to have tracked them down, and if the pricks were here, it meant they had been working from the recon photos Trask had inadvertently abandoned at the safehouse.

Jesus H., that made the whole thing *his* fault, and he didn't have a clue on how to put it right. One thing he knew, for sure: before you tried to solve a problem, it was mandatory that you understand exactly what was going on. In this case, he would have to make at least a general ID on the attackers, try to guess their number and organize a suitable resistance.

All in something like one minute flat.

And even that, he knew, might be too late.

The shooting started then, with short bursts from his right, no silencer. Did that mean it was one of the attackers, or an Arab who had removed the customized suppressor from his weapon? Either way, it was more racket in the forest, maybe echoing as far as Skyline Drive, with smoke to bring the forest rangers running, if they didn't get the fire out PDQ.

Forget about it.

How was he supposed to organize a firefighting detachment, when his troops were too disorganized to physically defend themselves? *His* troops? That was a laugh. The Arabs took their orders from Tarik Hassan or not at all, and at the moment they were running aimlessly around the compound, seeking cover, stopping here and there to fire at shadows in among the trees.

Trask had his pistol drawn and cocked, for all the good that it would do, when suddenly he heard a brand-new racket coming at him from the south. He recognized the sound at once, a frigging helicopter, and he wondered if it was the rangers, here already, or a new disaster bearing down upon him.

The good news was, he didn't have to wait a long time for his answer. Seconds after Trask heard the rotors whipping air, the Cobra came in view, already firing on the soldiers in the camp. He threw himself to one side of the glide path, saw the bullets raising spurts of dust, while high-explosive rounds went off like minithunderclaps, every thirty yards or so. Before he hit the deck, facedown, he had a glimpse of soldiers jerking, stumbling, falling.

An aerial attack—and hadn't someone told him that a chopper toasted his amigos out in Idaho? Damned right. Which spelled conspiracy, but what was that worth in the present circumstances? Did it help him, knowing two assaults were almost certainly related, when he might not live to share the news with anyone who mattered?

Trask was freaking, recognizing the symptoms, and made every effort to control himself. It didn't matter, at the moment, what had happened to his friends in Idaho. Those boys were dead, and there was nothing Trask could do to bring them back. The best that he could hope for was to

keep from joining them within the next few minutes, maybe
do a little something that would go toward evening the
score.

But first he needed cover. After that, he had to find himself a target, someone on the other side, a flesh-and-blood
example of the enemy, to let him know what he was up
against.

The pistol felt inadequate for starters, and he pushed off
from his prone position, sprinting toward the makeshift armory. Not many weapons remained, with the Arabs all
equipped and sentries on patrol, but there should still be
several automatic weapons, possibly a rifle he could use for
the duration.

Anything.

He felt pathetic, small and helpless, like an insect in those
old TV commercials where a can of bug spray sporting arms
like Arnold Schwarzenegger sent the ants and roaches
scrambling for their lives. Of course, they never made it,
dropping in a cloud of noxious fumes before they had a
chance to reach their hidey-holes.

Still, that was television. This was life and death.

He reached the armory, avoiding contact with the gunship on its second pass, and shouldered through the door.
It was unlocked, at least. Small favors. Squinting in the
gloom, he saw two Uzis and a Smith & Wesson SMG before his eyes picked out an M-16 A-1. He had to root around
for magazines and load the rifle, but he got it done, stuffed
extras in his pockets and cocked the weapon as he back-
tracked toward the door.

Trask cleared the threshold running like a college quar-
terback with nothing but the Heisman Trophy on his mind
and open ground in front of him. He covered all of fifteen
feet before the armory exploded and the stunning impact
drove him forward, sprawling on his face.

THE COBRA GUNSHIP swooped low on its second pass, and
Bolan took advantage of the bloody chaos reigning in its
wake. He broke from cover, circling around the barnlike
structure, closing on his enemies.

He saw a number of them down, scattered in the smoke and dust that trailed Grimaldi's strafing runs. The minigun bored tidy holes, but there was blood and mutilated flesh where 20 mm armor-piercing rounds met human bodies, treating them to the respect a fireman's ax might show for balsa wood and tissue paper.

It took a moment, even with him standing in the open, for the Hezbollah commandos to identify Mack Bolan as an enemy. He reckoned that their time spent in the camp was relatively short, with most of Schroder's personnel deliberately kept at arm's length for security. One white man might resemble any other to these strangers in a strange land—except that this particular white man came complete with warpaint on his face and carried weapons they wouldn't have seen around the camp.

A couple of them pointed at him, and when he shot those two, the fat was in the fire. From that point on, the bullets started coming at him from all angles, Bolan ducking, dodging, firing back and breaking for the nearest building that appeared to offer sanctuary.

Only when he hit the doorstep did he realize that he was running to a model of the farmhouse where his friends were stationed, just a few miles south, at Stony Man. The door surrendered to a flying kick, no evidence that it was locked, and Bolan ducked immediately to his left. The wall was no great shield against incoming rounds, but the warrior found a flea-market sofa and tipped it over, sheltering behind it as he shoved it closer to the nearest window.

There was a world of difference, Bolan knew, between a haven and a trap. When *safe* turned into *cornered,* it was time to seek a change of scene. His enemies didn't have his measure yet, but several men were firing at the farmhouse, peppering the broad facade with bullets, ripping up the door and windowframes. How long before they got around to using hand grenades, incendiaries?

Bolan didn't plan to wait around and see.

Unlike the house at Stony Man, this one had been constructed on a shotgun pattern, featuring an exit at the rear, in line with the front door. He didn't know if they were covering the exit yet, but if they weren't, a few more moments would correct the oversight.

Which meant that the warrior had no time to waste.

He thumbed another high-explosive round into the M-203's launcher, checked his angle and prepared to make his move. It had to go like clockwork or the effort would be worse than useless. Listening to Jack Grimaldi strafe the camp outside, he knew it was imperative that he get out before a rocket or a burst of cannon fire ripped through the mock-up of the farmhouse.

Bolan came up firing short bursts from the automatic carbine. He glimpsed movement through the shattered window, one guy stumbling, going down. The Executioner triggered the grenade without a target clear in mind, a little more confusion for the enemy to deal with, and he was already moving by the time it detonated in the outer yard. Ignoring screams and curses, most of them in Arabic, he turned and bolted for the back door of the farmhouse, realizing in a flash how little it resembled Stony Man HQ. The rough facade was close, but they were either guessing on the floor plan or they didn't have the time to flesh it out.

In either case, he hoped that negligence would be another stumbling block, in case enough determined raiders managed to escape the killing pen and tried to carry out their task.

The back door opened inward. Bolan hesitated for a moment, then grabbed the knob and twisted, jerked it open, leading with the carbine as he cleared the doorstep. Two young guns—one Hezbollah, one NRP—were just arriving, looking startled, and he stitched them with a zigzag burst that dropped them onto grass.

So much for quiet exits.

He was reaching for another HE round to load the launcher, give the shooters out in front a little something to delay their rush, when he looked up and saw Grimaldi's Cobra swooping down on target from the north. A puff of smoke from starboard, and a rocket hurtled toward its mark, bright flames stretched out behind it in the velvet dusk.

Bolan ran.

There was no fancy terminology to cover it. The Executioner was running for his life, before the Hellfire missile found its target and delivered on the promise of its name. A heartbeat later, when the shock wave caught him in mid-strike, he gripped his carbine tightly in both hands, determined not to lose it when he fell. A gust of superheated wind pushed Bolan forward, stole his balance, but he saved it with a shoulder roll that would have cost him points in judo class. It did the trick, though, and he wound up in a fighting crouch, head down, eyes closed against the cloud of smoke and dust that suddenly enveloped him. Debris from the explosion was predominately plywood, shattered two-by-fours and splinters of the cheap furniture. He raised an arm to shield his head and powered out of there before the larger pieces started raining down.

He still had work to do and ample targets before he could declare the strike a victory.

And information.

More than anything, he had to know who was responsible for the idea of an attack on Stony Man.

TARIK HASSAN DID WHAT he could to rally his disorderly commandos—those who still survived, at least. He had already seen at least a dozen of them dead or gravely wounded, representing more than half his fighting force. The helicopter swooping overhead was dropping more of them with every pass.

The best Hassan could hope for was survival, possibly with soldiers to assist him in his flight. Musa Kmeid was still beside him, bleeding freely from a shrapnel graze, but collecting others was a problem in the circumstances.

On his first attempt, Hassan had tried to beckon young Hamil Ismah, but the Hezbollah assassin had a dazed expression on his face, as if his eyes had stared into the pits of hell and seen himself already there, chained up and writhing in the flames. He didn't answer to his name, but wandered off across the compound, trailing his assault rifle behind him by the sling, so that its muzzle dragged along the ground.

Hassan had better luck the second time. He hailed Mohammed Duabi, gratified when the man responded to his voice and turned to jog in his direction, perfectly alert and in control. When Duabi had closed the gap to thirty feet, though, he was cut down. The Cobra gunship came in low and fast, its cannon thrumming like a great bass fiddle, and Hassan watched his man disintegrate, the 20 mm armor-piercing bullets tearing the terrorist apart.

Hassan hid beside the mess hall, stretched out on the ground with Kmeid at his side. Ahmed Jazmil had passed them moments earlier, with several men strung out behind him, seemingly intent on some objective, but Hassan didn't call out to them. He was afraid that one or all of them might fire on him, or that he might somehow give himself away to unseen enemies.

In short, he was afraid.

It was humiliating, most especially to a liberation warrior weaned on suffering and sacrifice, the value of a suicidal gesture, but he couldn't bring himself to die for nothing. Glancing swiftly to his left, he looked for a reproach in his comrade's eyes, but found nothing but relief.

Ironically he was repulsed by Musa's cowardice, a knee-jerk attitude that clashed immediately with his own survival instinct. Rather than waste precious time attempting to define and reconcile the contradictory emotions, he ignored them, focused on the killing ground in front of him and kept on looking for a handy exit.

Forest surrounded them, but escaping to the woods meant fleeing overland on foot, through miles and miles of unfamiliar wilderness. Hassan didn't possess a map or compass, and while he was capable of navigating empty-handed, there remained the questions of pursuit, his adversaries and the countless pitfalls that awaited him outside the camp.

Unless he traced the access road, and thereby placed himself at even greater risk, it could be days before he found another house or settlement. And when he did, what then? Would the police be waiting for him? Vigilantes roused by the reports on radio and television? One thing he had learned about Americans was that they loved their guns and often kept them loaded, close at hand. Especially in the

Southern states and rural areas, a prowler ran the risk of being shot before he had a chance to plead for food and water. Propaganda films and CNN assured him that it happened all the time.

Of course, the yokels weren't accustomed to receiving Palestinian guerrilla fighters on their doorsteps, but he couldn't trust his life to luck. The prospect of an endless chase through wilderness and urban combat zones, with countless skirmishes along the way, dismayed Hassan. Assuming he could reach a major town or city, what was he supposed to do for money, transportation, field support? The National Redemption Party was his backup network in the States, and its commanders were among the targets penned up in the present shooting gallery.

The problem in his mind was like a hoop snake, rolling downhill toward a cliff, while it devoured itself, beginning at the tail. If there was a solution, it eluded him.

With sudden anger, he dismissed the tangled problem from his mind. The only men who had to worry were survivors. Even worry was a sweet alternative to death, and he had wits enough to solve the riddle, given time. Escape came first. Evade the enemy, seek out a temporary haven and take stock of their supplies, the options readily available.

If they went hungry for the next few days, so be it. Palestinians were long accustomed to the taste of want and shriveled bellies. With their silenced weapons, they could hunt when it was safe enough, their enemies dispersed.

The enemy.

Who was it, and how many did they face? He looked in vain for blue serge uniforms or jackets blazoned with the FBI initials. The swift and deadly raid didn't impress him as a normal law-enforcement tactic in the States. Americans were big on warrants, bullhorns, giving adversaries ten or fifteen chances to surrender.

This was something else.

But if he meant to sort it out, take any kind of countermeasures or exact revenge, he had to save himself.

"This way!" he told Kmeid, and started crawling toward the nearest line of trees.

**18**

The shots that nearly took Bolan's head off came from his left. He saw the gunman from the corner of his eyes, a moving form that stopped too suddenly and froze, the rifle braced and aiming. Instinct made him duck and dive before he verified the man's intent, and the split-second difference saved his life. He heard the bullets snap and sizzle overhead, too close for comfort, but it only counted if they scored.

He swung the Colt Commando toward his adversary, triggering a short burst as he fell. The tumblers raked his adversary's legs and groin, a less than perfect setup, but it did the job. He watched the young man topple over backward, grimacing in pain, still pumping bullets from the M-16 as he went down. A second burst from Bolan's carbine finished it and left his would-be killer stretched out on the ground, a broken mannequin.

How many down? He didn't know and had no time to speculate. Without a head count on his enemy, any estimate of casualties would be a waste, in any case. It only mattered that he stop the Hezbollah strike team, prevent them moving on to Stony Man, and that he find out—somehow—who had hatched the plan.

Joseph Gardner's knowledge was the seed, he realized, and there was fertile soil in Schroder's National Redemption Party, but the target and the method of attack were both a bit obscure for Schroder's taste, when there were countless long-haired liberals, blacks and Jews to serve as targets. Raiding Stony Man, exposing the clandestine operation, was a step toward something else, a larger plan still hidden from his view.

He needed someone from the top ranks of the NRP to set him straight and point him toward the mastermind in charge of the conspiracy. And if he meant to find that person here, this evening, he had to get it done before Grimaldi's Cobra laid the camp to waste.

But first he had to keep himself alive.

As if in answer to his silent thoughts, a burst of automatic fire ripped up the ground a foot from Bolan's elbow, on his right. He snapped his head in that direction, with the carbine following, and caught a Hezbollah guerrilla lining up his second burst. The Colt Commando stuttered, a half dozen rounds exploding from its muzzle, staggering the Arab, dropping him before he had a chance to fire again.

Before his target hit the ground, the Executioner was already up and running, straight line, never mind the fancy footwork, as he focused on his goal. The mess hall lay some thirty yards ahead of him, and he would have a bit of temporary cover if he made it there without being tagged by a rocket from Grimaldi's chopper.

Somehow he made it, bursting through the double doors and sliding underneath a long communal dining table, one of two that occupied the center of the room. He put his shoulder to it, flipped the table over on its side to form a shield of sorts between himself and those outside, the open doors no barricade between them. On his left, a butane-powered stove stood close beside a sink that operated from a hand pump, drawing water from a well somewhere below.

He focused on the chunky butane tank and had a sudden inspiration, worming from his vantage point directly opposite the door, until he lay behind the stove. A couple of the camp's defenders had him spotted now, or, rather, they had seen him duck inside the mess hall, pumping wild rounds through the walls and windows, no thought spared for accuracy at the moment.

Working swiftly, Bolan took a fragmentation grenade and wedged it between the stove and butane tank, removed the pin and held his breath until he satisfied himself the safety spoon was firmly braced. Using nylon fishing line extracted from a cargo pocket of his camouflage fatigues, he prepared a noose that looped around the neck of the grenade, without the spoon, its loose end trailing free.

Things got a trifle delicate from there. He made his way across the wooden floor, with bullets snapping overhead. Reaching the open doorway, he huddled on the left side and found a nail that he could loosen with the tip of his stiletto. One twist with the fishing line around the nail, and Bolan worked it back and forth between his fingers, making sure the nail would offer no sincere resistance to a sudden yank.

That done, he tossed the spool of line across the yawning doorway, following in a rush that set his adversaries firing like a bunch of drunken hunters at a turkey shoot. They missed, without exception, but a couple of their rounds were close enough to make him flinch as he was working on a second nail, the nylon line stretched taut across the doorway at ankle height.

He bolted back behind the capsized table, praying that a lucky bullet wouldn't snip the line and ruin everything before somebody sprung his trap. Behind him, bullet-punctured windows opened on nearby woods, but he would have to wait.

What was a trap without the bait?

"WE'VE GOT HIM cornered, Eulon!"

Rob Shearson's face was sweaty and tomato red from dodging bullets, missiles, you name it. He was breathing hard, and Trask decided to forgive the breach of military courtesy, if only he could figure out exactly what in holy hell was going on.

"Say what?"

The helicopter made another strafing run, but they were covered by the shadows of the onetime motor pool, all smoking, stinking wreckage now.

"We've got him cornered in the mess hall!"

"Who, for Christ's sake?"

Shearson blinked. "The bastard who's been shooting up the camp!"

Trask stabbed an index finger at the Cobra helicopter, swirling out of rifle range due east, immediately doubling back. "You call that cornered, Rob?"

"Not the helicopter, Eulon. Some guy on foot!"

"What fucking guy?"

"I don't know who he is! Come see him for yourself!"

Trask had a list of things that he would have preferred to do just then, and all of them included running, hiding, seeking shelter from the gunship that was ravaging the camp around him. He was just about to say as much, some doctored variation on the theme, when something in the other man's eyes or attitude convinced him to exert himself, display the dignity that was supposed to come with rank.

Some rank. Some dignity.

"Okay, let's go."

At that, they almost bought it on the short jog to the mess hall, reeling as a pair of skinny rockets struck the nearest barracks on their right and it disintegrated, flinging lumber, jagged shards and splinters in all directions. Trask felt needles lancing at his jaw and neck, reached up and found a clump of splinters embedded in his flesh. He ignored the pain and hurried on.

Three others waited for them at the mess hall, trying not to look conspicuous, keeping an escape hatch open for the Cobra's next close run. The front doors of the mess hall stood wide open, showing Trask a slice of darkness now that dusk had fallen. If he strained his eyes, he thought there was a hint of furtive movement, well back from the entryway.

"I can't see shit in there," he said to no one in particular.

"He's in there," Shearson said again.

As if to prove the point, a stream of automatic fire burst from the open doorway, making Trask duck to save himself, at least two bullets smacking Shearson in the chest and shoulder. Down he went without a whimper, stretched out on the ground.

"Who *is* that guy?" Trask demanded.

"Some kind of pro," the nearest living soldier told him, squeezing off three quick rounds from his M-16 A-1 in the direction of the mess hall's open doors.

There was at least a fifty-fifty chance, in Trask's estimation, that the helicopter would come back and wipe the mess hall off the map and solve the problem that way. Maybe, or it just might not. In any case, the glory lay in taking care of it himself, performing as he had been trained when he was still in the official uniform. If he could nail this guy and find out who he was, what this was all about . . .

Then what?

In fact, Trask didn't have a clue, but it was something concrete he could try, at least, instead of hiding like a frightened child and cringing as the Cobra stalked him from the air.

"Let's take him."

"Huh?" The nearest gunner plainly thought his ears were playing tricks on him. "Take who?"

"We flank the doorway, box him in," Trask said. "It shouldn't be that hard."

"Tell that to Rob."

Trask spun to face him like a rabid badger, with his weapon cocked and locked. "You wanna give me shit, boy? It's an order, and desertion under fire's a capital offense, so make your choice!"

"Let's do it," the young man said after fleeting hesitation, while his sidekick frowned and nodded.

Better.

"I'll break to the left," Trask said, "and you two take the right. We get that far, it shouldn't be too hard to pin him down. I'm first in through the door."

There was a chance that they would let him start, then shoot him in the back or simply run away, but Trask was stoked with confidence. The past few days, it seemed he had been ducking, dodging, hiding, mostly fucking up, and now he had a chance to make it right. A start, at least. If necessary, he would smoke these boys and do it on his own.

Trask made his break, swung wide around the mess hall doors and slid to safety with his back against the wall. A few yards to his right, the others also made it, safe and sound. He caught his breath, then he raised his right hand, fingers splayed. When both gunners were focused, he started counting down.

Five . . . four . . . three . . . two . . .

On *one,* he made his move around the corner, submachine gun spitting flame, brass spewing out of the ejection port. He had a glimpse of someone bailing through a window at the back, a shadow shape that might have been a man or his imagination. Swiveling to bring it under fire, he barely felt the trip wire as he hit it, registered the tension, there and gone, in his subconscious.

He knew he'd been suckered as the mess hall suddenly went up in flames around him. Walls and floor and everything were burning. *He* was burning, and the only thing that Eulon Trask could do about it was scream.

THEY NEVER MADE IT to the trees. Tarik Hassan was on his way, Musa Kmeid beside him, when the helicopter swooped down from the darkness, spraying bullets, ripping up the turf, transforming their escape hatch into one more lethal no-man's-land. Hassan ran back in the direction of the nearest structure that was still intact, as if he thought there would be shelter there. It was illusory, at best, but what else did he have in terms of options?

Nothing.

The MP-5 SD-3 submachine gun was a puny weapon when it came to dueling with a helicopter gunship, but Hassan went through the motions, squeezing off a few short bursts on the Cobra's next pass. He had no realistic hope of damaging his target, but at least the sense of doing something made him feel a bit less like a cornered, helpless animal.

Kmeid picked up on Hassan's action and his mood. The young man's M-16 A-1 was somewhat better suited for defense against attacking aircraft, and he knew it. Something in the moment drove Kmeid from cover, struggling to his feet and moving out into the open, with the rifle at his shoulder, pointed skyward. He was shouting at the helicopter, challenging the pilot to return, and he didn't have long to wait.

The Cobra came in from behind him, rotors throbbing loud enough to put him on alert. Hassan saw Kmeid turn to face his enemy, flame lancing from the muzzle of his weapon, cartridge casings littering the grass around his feet.

It was a sad, uneven contest, and it lasted only for a moment. Overhead, the helicopter seemed to shudder as its

20 mm cannon fired a stream of armor-piercing rounds. Hassan had seen the guns in action, with Israeli jets, and knew what they could do to buildings, armored vehicles, much less to human flesh. Kmeid was pulverized.

Hassan wasn't a man to panic. He had killed and witnessed killings, planted bombs and viewed the aftermath of blasts that scattered body parts like bits and pieces from a doll repair shop. Comrades had been slain before his eyes, and more than one—on being judged a traitor or a coward—had been executed by Hassan himself. In all that time, no other death had made him feel the nausea that possessed him now.

Determination brought him to his feet, the waves of dizziness receding as he turned and broke from cover, running for his life. Hassan had no idea where he was going, whether there was anyplace at all to hide. He simply realized that sitting still meant death, and he wasn't prepared to die that way. Not like Musa Kmeid.

In front of him, incredibly, Hassan saw a familiar face. The colonel, Schroder, had two soldiers with him, ducking in and out of shadows as they sought to dodge the roving helicopter. Moving on an interception course, Hassan met Schroder and his two companions near the south end of a barracks that had doubled as a target in their practice exercises. Schroder's face was streaked with dirt and soot, his aspect grim.

"So, what the hell do you want?" he demanded of Hassan.

"I wish to go with you," the Hezbollah commander told him.

"Screw that noise! I've lost the best part of my outfit, thanks to you. You're on your own."

Hassan blinked twice, amazed at the response. "But, what of all our plans?" he asked.

The sneering colonel raised his left hand, clenched into a fist, and rapped the knuckles lightly, twice, on Hassan's skull.

"Hello? Is anybody in there? Look around, for Christ's sake! We don't have a fucking plan. It's shot to hell, because of you."

Hassan felt anger pulsing through his veins. "I do not see—"

The warm touch of a weapon's muzzle underneath his chin was all it took to silence him.

"You don't see *what?*" Schroder asked, prodding with the gun. "My people lying dead, with your men right beside them? Fucking ashes, where the buildings used to be? That goddamned helicopter? Maybe you should get your eyes checked, pally, but you'll have to do it somewhere else. Now get the hell away from me, before I do the world a favor."

It was useless, talking to a lunatic. The man had obviously lost his mind. Hassan would have to save himself, and never mind the others. He could always find more soldiers, if and when he managed to regain his native soil.

He turned away from Schroder and his men, dismissed them from his mind as he struck off across the compound. He'd covered fifteen paces, twenty, when he heard the Cobra gunship coming back and knew that running wouldn't save him.

Standing fast, Hassan turned back to face the helicopter, saw the gunfire winking at him from its nose and from underneath one stubby wing. He tried to raise his submachine gun, but there was no time before the bullets reached him, shattering his world, his consciousness, a vast, white-hot kaleidoscope of colors bleeding swiftly into red, orange, purple, midnight black... and gone.

GRIMALDI COULDN'T TELL one target from another in the fire-lit slaughter pen below him, but he knew that he was scoring hits. A body count was immaterial, impossible with the reduction of his visibility from nightfall and the drifting pall of smoke, but there were still some targets standing, and he still had heavy weapons left with which to take them out.

Three major buildings and a handful of sheds remained unscathed in the camp. Grimaldi had four Hellfires left, two on each wing, and three more slender rockets in the M-157 launching pod. He used one of the latter on a barnlike structure situated on the west side of the compound. A direct hit on the loft peeled back a jagged section of the roof and lit a fire inside, flames spreading rapidly from loft to rafters, roof and walls. In seconds flat the whole damned place was burning, bright enough to shed some light on other targets in the killing zone.

There was no sign of Bolan yet, but Grimaldi had faith enough to trust that his old friend would use the radio to warn of any strikes in his immediate vicinity. If he was down, disabled or worse, then the pilot was free to scourge the camp at will. Their first priority—agreed upon before they lifted off from Stony Man—was that the Hezbollah commandos and their NRP supporters had to be purged like vermin, forcibly prohibited from acting out their master plan or wreaking any further havoc in the States.

Scorched earth, damned right.

Grimaldi keyed his microphone, for Bolan's sake, and told the empty air, "I'm dumping everything I've got."

And did exactly that on one last sweep, unloading with the Hellfires, 2.75-inch rockets, 40 mm high-explosive rounds and armor-piercing bullets from the 20 mm cannon. Instinct made him hold back on the minigun, in case he needed just a little something for the mop-up, but the rest of his munitions were expended in a space of fifteen seconds, Wallace Schroder's camp transformed into a seething hell of smoke and leaping flames.

Could anything survive down there?

Grimaldi hoped so. One man, anyway. Please, Jesus. One extraordinary warrior, searching for an answer on the killing ground, among the dead.

He took the chopper up a thousand feet above the drifting pall of smoke and started watching for survivors. Anything that moved among the dead.

"I'M DUMPING EVERYTHING I've got!"

The small voice spoke in Bolan's ear as Grimaldi swung back around and made a final run at the camp. It gave him time to look for cover—barely—and he threw himself behind a jumbled pile of smoking lumber that had been a barracks only moments earlier. With luck, he thought, Grinaldi wouldn't waste munitions plastering the same mark wice.

A combat veteran knew the sounds of hell on earth. It nattered not if he was called to arms in Europe, the Pa-ific, South Korea, Vietnam or one of the sporadic brush-ire wars that flared around the world from 1954 to 1995. Technology changed—delivery systems, sighting mecha-isms, the destructive power of specific rounds and war-eads—but the end result was always smoke, flame and hunder, mutilated flesh and young men screaming out the inal, agonizing moments of their lives. Death smelled the ame in Bosnia, the Bekaa Valley... or the Blue Ridge Mountains of Virginia.

Bolan lay facedown and waited for the storm to pass him y, earth tremors rippling through the ground beneath him, while the rockets shrieked above, the shock waves of their mpact numbing the warrior's ears.

And when he raised his head again, the camp was gone.

Not totally, of course. The flaming rubble of its former uildings still remained, smoke blotting out the stars, but ny prior resemblance to a place of human habitation had een swept away. The bodies he could see were torn and nangled, twisted into awkward postures, like the broken laythings of a muddy giant. More of them were hidden by he wreckage, or obliterated by the flames and rapid-fire xplosions that had torn the camp apart.

He rose on trembling legs and scanned the smoky killing round. It seemed impossible that anyone or anything could ave lived through Jack Grimaldi's holocaust, but there was urching movement off to his right. A survivor. The war-ior ducked and moved in that direction, homing in on the hadow that had first attracted his attention.

A stranger opened up when he was forty yards away and losing, no clear shot, but with an automatic weapon you an always keep your fingers crossed. In this case, Bolan's dversary had more nerve than luck. He missed by some-hing like a yard, the muzzle-flashes from his weapon help-ng Bolan spot the place where he had gone to ground.

They could have stalked each other through the night, xchanging shots, but Bolan chose to end it with a frag grenade. He chose a mark deliberately away from his intended target, some yards to the right, and lobbed it overhand, ducking back as the lethal egg dropped out of sight. The detonation, when it came, was like a wet firecracker in the wake of an artillery barrage, but it was all he needed.

Bolan heard his adversary moaning and moved in cautiously, aware that it could be a trap. He still had no idea whom he was facing, or how badly—if at all—his enemy was wounded.

The Executioner held the Colt Commando steady, with twenty rounds or so remaining in the big drum magazine. Reloading would have added only ten rounds to the weapon, and he let it go. If twenty couldn't do it, with his side arms for a backup, he was screwed.

The shadow man was stretched out on a patch of sooty, bloodstained grass, his head and shoulders propped against the wreckage of a small outbuilding, heedless of the fire that smoldered several feet away. One arm was wedged behind his back. His khaki pants were stained with crimson, torn by shrapnel, and he seemed to have no weapon within his reach. Still, Bolan took it easy, closing the gap.

"You wanna tell me who the hell you are?" Wallace Schroder asked.

"What's the difference?" Bolan asked.

"I'd like to know who fucked me up, okay."

"Who's not important. I can tell you how and why."

"Same difference. Shoot—no pun intended."

"You were out of touch," Bolan said, "working overtime to resurrect the good old days that never were. It gave you blind spots."

"Jesus, a philosopher."

"No, just a soldier."

"I'm a soldier, too."

"You were, before ambition and the bitterness took over."

"Anyway, looks like I blew it."

"You can still save something, if you want to."

"Yeah? What's that?"

"Your honor."

"What good's honor to a dead man?" Schroder asked.

"It might be all he's got."

"And you prescribe confession for the soul?"

"It couldn't hurt," Bolan replied.

"Oh, you'd be surprised."

"I don't believe you set this up yourself. You spent too many years in uniform, opposing groups like Hezbollah, to sell out your country."

"I'm not the sellout, mister! You need to take a look at Washington."

"I've been there," Bolan told him. "We have regular elections, if the people think the government's off track. We don't need Arab terrorists to help determine policy."

"All's fair, you know. Sometimes you take what you can get."

"That's why I'm here," the Executioner replied. "I need a name."

"That's it?"

"That's it."

"Okay, for all the good that it will do you." Schroder spoke the name, his eyes alert to any visible reaction from his nemesis. "Too bad you'll never have a chance to use it."

There was still some energy behind the move, despite Schroder's wounds, but Bolan saw it coming. Lurching forward, the colonel brought the arm out from behind his back, blunt fingers wrapped around an autoloading pistol. There was no finesse about the move, but it was still effective to a point.

The Colt Commando stuttered, a half dozen tumblers jolting Schroder backward, spreading scarlet blossoms on his chest. Another heartbeat, and he lost the side arm, lifeless fingers giving up their grip.

The warrior keyed the microphone and turned to seek out the chopper. "It's pickup time," he told Grimaldi. "We've got one more job to do."

**19**

*Silver Spring, Maryland*

The sixth sense of a veteran soldier couldn't be defined in psychiatric terms or measured by an EEG. It didn't show up in textbooks on anatomy, psychology or the "soft sciences," philosophy and such. The vast majority of human beings would deny that such a sense existed.

But they would be wrong.

A die-hard cynic, Arthur Coltrane had no faith in ESP, clairvoyance, spirit mediums or any of the other New Age charlatans who billed themselves as "sensitives," but he had seen the sixth sense working. It had saved his life on more than one occasion, and he had no reason to reject it now.

Too bad, since it was telling him that he was in deep trouble.

The feeling came from nowhere, like a cold draft down his collar, and he knew beyond a shadow of a doubt that Schroder and his team had screwed things up, somehow. The details didn't matter. For the moment, all he had to know was that their ship had sprung a leak the size of all outdoors, and he would have to sink or swim.

It was a trifle premature, perhaps, for Coltrane to predict disaster. There was nothing on TV or radio about a fumble on the one-yard line, but that meant nothing. The Feds were often clumsy, but they got it right from time to time, including blackouts in the media when there was bloody work remaining to be done.

What kind of work?

A little mopping up, perhaps.

Of course, the sixth sense wasn't always accurate, and even if it was, a snafu with the Arab team didn't automatically place Coltrane in jeopardy. There were layers of insulation built into his clandestine alliance with Wally Schroder and the NRP, a system of mutual protection that had served them both, so far.

Still he could almost smell the trouble coming, like a whiff of ozone in the air that lingered after lightning struck. The smell of failure lingered in his nostrils as the general took his suitcase from the closet and prepared to pack. Beside his suitcase, on the bed, was the Colt Model 1911A1 .45-caliber automatic that he stubbornly preferred, for tradition's sake, to the newer Beretta side arms that were standard in the U.S. military.

He had killed four men with this pistol. Two in Korea, one in Vietnam and one—a coked-out burglar brandishing a switchblade—in the very bedroom where he stood, five years earlier. It was coincidence and nothing more, he told himself, that none of them were white men. Soldiers didn't choose their enemies; they simply executed the maneuvers they were taught.

Coltrane considered all that he was giving up by running out: his rank, of course, and his reputation and the pension he would draw if he took time to file retirement papers. None of it seemed real just now, when he was focused on exposure and disgrace, the brief remainder of his life in federal prison.

No.

His rank and reputation would be stripped away, regardless, once the link with Schroder was established. The pension didn't matter. He had money in the Cayman Islands, well beyond the reach of Uncle Sam and the blood-sucking leeches of the IRS. A new identity was waiting for him, fabricated over time with all the necessary documents and records. Years of planning made it possible for him to disappear and be reborn as someone else within an hour's time.

The house was something he would miss, but there were other houses, and he knew that it would pass. There was no place in Arthur Coltrane's world for sentiment. From this day forward, every step he took had to hinge on logic, strategy, an instinct for self-preservation.

Just like always.

He had no family to speak of, no one who would miss him when he left. An older brother had been killed at Tinian in World War II. His younger sister, married and childless, lived in Philadelphia. They spoke by telephone at Christmas and on respective birthdays, but they hadn't seen each other for a decade. It never entered Coltrane's mind to wonder if his sole surviving relative would miss him, maybe shed a tear when he was gone.

The news, when it began to break, would dry up any tears.

He wondered if the Army would attempt to cover up the scandal. Twenty years earlier, or even ten, it would have been an automatic reflex: shred the paperwork and swear the witnesses to silence in the interest of the service. These days, though, the damned investigative journalists nosed into everything. Security and confidentiality had no more meaning in the modern world than trust or chastity.

All things considered, Coltrane felt a measure of relief that he was finally getting out.

His plan had been ambitious to a fault, and therein lay the problem. For a moment, as fleeting as it was, he had allowed his sense of duty and a gleam of hope to override the cynicism that was part of every military lifer's personal philosophy. He knew about the scheming lies and underhanded deals that passed for politics in the United States, the campaign promises that were abandoned.

It had been foolish for the general to believe that he could change a system that had managed to survive, with all its faults intact, for better than two hundred years. In all that time, the great "reforms" had always been a form of catering to this or that "oppressed" minority, relaxing standards to accommodate the least successful and least admirable members of society. He had to have been insane to think that he could ever win election to the White House, or, achieving that, make any lasting, beneficial changes in a system that rewarded sloth, corruption, decadence, while punishing initiative and honesty.

Coltrane had learned his lesson, though. If you can't beat 'em, leave 'em. Wally Schroder should be smart enough and tough enough to keep his mouth shut, for a while, at least. And if he wasn't it would make no difference to the general, either way. By that time Coltrane would have vanished, and his new civilian alter ego would be sitting on a tropic island, where the constables spoke Pidgin English and there was no extradition treaty.

Perfect.

All he had to do was vanish, shed his old life like a reptile's castoff skin and start from scratch.

But first...

That nagging sense was back, a whiff of danger more immediate than the fretting over what might happen in the next few days. The short hairs on his nape were standing up, a cold chill working down his spine. He hesitated, felt the house around him, the open bedroom doorway at his back.

Could there be someone in the house?

It was preposterous, of course—the Feds would never move that quickly, much less quietly—but he couldn't shake off the feeling of another body occupying space that Coltrane had reserved for private use.

He stopped himself just short of reaching for the Colt and turned to face the bedroom doorway, where a black-clad stranger waited for him on the threshold. The stranger had an automatic of his own, complete with silencer attached.

No burglar, then. The garb and weapon ruled that out. Nor did he fit the mold for any local, state or federal law-enforcement agency that Coltrane knew of.

"Can I help you?" He was proud to hear no tremor in his voice, despite the shock.

The stranger said, "I wouldn't be surprised."

ONCE BOLAN HAD THE NAME and passed it on, the rest was relatively easy. There had been no question of arrest, indictment, prosecution, since the only evidence had died with Wallace Schroder, and a public hearing on the case would ultimately blow the very secrecy that they were trying to maintain for Stony Man.

That meant a covert touch, and there was only one way it could go.

Brognola called the Man at home, spelled out the problem and proposed solution. Scandals had pursued the present chief executive almost from his inauguration, like a pack of hungry dingos snapping at his heels. The last thing he desired was one more problem in the headlines, much less one that should have rightfully been shared by several of his living predecessors. The decision might have been a painful one, or simply awkward, but there was no viable alternative.

By 10:15 p.m., they had the target's address, with assurances from Brognola that any uniformed response to calls for help would be delayed by ten or fifteen minutes, minimum.

It was enough.

They flew from Stony Man to College Park, and Bolan left Grimaldi at the airport, drove the four-plus miles to Silver Spring and found his target. The warrior parked in darkness and made his way inside the modest home. It wasn't difficult. The general was preparing to evacuate, more focused on departure than perimeter security.

Had someone tipped him off?

It didn't matter.

He stood and watched the general packing for a moment, felt the change as Brognola sensed his presence and turned to face him.

"Can I help you?"

"I wouldn't be surprised."

The general frowned. "I don't suppose there's anything to talk about?"

"Not much."

"A deal, perhaps?"

"Too late."

"Of course."

"One question."

"Which is . . . ?"

"Why?"

"That's easy." Coltrane stood at ease, adopting the parade rest posture, even in his civvies. "I got sick and tired of watching traitors, criminals and worse subvert the country and the Constitution I was under orders to defend. I don't know if you ever served . . ."

"I did my tour," Bolan replied, waiting for the rest of it.

"Well, then, you should know what I mean. The bastards sold us out at Potsdam, in Korea, Cuba, Vietnam, in Lebanon, Somalia—Christ, you name it. Every time you turn around, there's a new concession to our enemies. They send us out to fight with one hand tied behind our backs. It's like we're not allowed to fight, unless the damned civilian government can guarantee a stalemate or defeat.

"And what the hell's been going on at home?" the general asked rhetorically. "In thirty years, our education system has declined to Third World status, and we're turning out a generation that can barely read or write. The money that we should be spending on our future goes to welfare scum who never heard of birth control and wouldn't understand it if they had. Our murder rate has more than doubled, while convictions have declined by thirty-five percent. If a policeman does his duty, we indict him for excessive force and throw his ass in jail. Our prisons have revolving doors, and we're stuck with a President who's more concerned with socializing medicine or putting faggots in a foxhole than he is in fighting crime or balancing the budget. You stand there, with all this going on, and ask me why I think we need a change."

"Your motive's not the problem," Bolan answered. "It's your method. How did you expect to save the Constitution by subverting it?"

"All's fair," Coltrane said, smiling for the first time since he noticed Bolan standing in the bedroom doorway. "We're confronted with a situation where the people of this country have been screwed, deceived and pillaged for the past half century. Most of them never take the time to cast a ballot. Those who do are so damned ignorant, corrupt or simply disillusioned with the process that they keep on reelecting thieves and traitors. Hell, man, these days a scandal dealing with adultery or embezzlement does more to get a candidate elected than to keep him out of office. Get your picture in the supermarket tabloids, and you're on your way."

"And you thought Schroder's merry men could change all that, by bringing in some Middle Eastern terrorists?"

"The rags were strictly for deniability," Coltrane explained. "Surely you can see that. What we needed was a double threat, external *and* internal. If the terrorists were able to expose pervasive criminal activity involving this administration, that would be a bonus."

"For the NRP?"

"A simple vehicle," Coltrane replied, dismissing Schroder's private army with a shrug. "All dedicated men, of course, though some of them placed zeal above stability. We need blunt instruments from time to time. Agreed?"

"I'd say that all depends on how they're used."

"And how have you been used?"

"Today I'm on the garbage detail," Bolan told him, "cleaning up a toxic spill."

The general nodded, shifting his position slightly, toward the big Colt automatic lying on the bed. It wasn't cocked, and that would slow him a bit, but if he had a live round in the chamber, it was no big deal. The move was casual, designed to seem unconscious, and there would have been no point in Bolan telling him to freeze.

So Bolan watched and waited, while his target seemed to pause, considering his options. You could almost hear his mind at work, the distance measured, odds and angles calculated. Bolan's nightsuit and the silenced weapon in his hand told Coltrane all he had to know about the future. Anything was worth a try, when you had nothing left to lose.

"You don't mind if I finish packing?" One more nod to the illusion.

"Be my guest."

When Coltrane made his move, it was professional, well executed, almost stylish. Twisting to his right, he reached for the Colt, his free arm bent to take the impact as he struck the mattress, bouncing through a tidy somersault.

Reacting swiftly, Bolan squeezed off two rounds while his target was in motion, dodging sideways as the Colt exploded from a range of fifteen feet. It was a close thing, even so, the bullet whistling past his face, but the warrior was rewarded with a splash of crimson on the bedspread and a gasp of pain from Coltrane, as the general dropped from sight behind the bed.

How badly was he wounded? Bolan had no fix on where the shots had struck his target, or if both had scored. He crouched, immobile, thankful that the hanging spread would stop Coltrane from aiming underneath the bed frame.

But it wouldn't stop his firing blind.

The second .45 slug struck the wall to Bolan's left, while number three passed through the open doorway, smacking plaster somewhere in the hall outside. Say five rounds left, if he had started with a fully loaded magazine plus one more up the spout. It was enough to do the job, if he got lucky, but—

It would have been the time to use a frag grenade, if Bolan had one, but he settled for a slim incendiary stick. It popped and sizzled as he tossed it toward the queen-size bed, not hard enough to clear the other side. Another moment, and the spread was blazing, smoking up the room, as Bolan edged back toward the door.

A wild shot from the general missed him by a yard, then silence fell once more, except for the insistent crackling of the flames. He waited for the fire to spread and flush his quarry, holding the Beretta 93-R in a firm two-handed grip.

When Coltrane burst from cover seconds later, he was firing like a madman, one arm raised to shield his face from leaping flames, the other blasting with his big Colt .45, no target clearly visible. It was an easy tag, but Bolan took his time and got it right, a 3-round burst to Coltrane's chest that stopped the general cold and dropped him sprawling, facedown on the floor.

It had been Bolan's plan to search the house for any evidence that might need cleaning up, but he would trust the fire to do that for him. It was time to go, before he had to test Brognola's personal influence with the Silver Spring police.

Outside, the night was cool and clean, as yet untainted by the smell of smoke. The Executioner was grateful for the respite as he walked back to his car and drove away.

The bright flames in his rearview mirror dwindled swiftly and were gone.

# EPILOGUE

*Washington, D.C.*

"It's finished, then?"

"As far as we can tell," Brognola replied.

The Man was frowning thoughtfully, eyes scanning the familiar scenery as they drove west on Constitution Avenue. Mack Bolan, on the jump seat opposite, sat waiting for the President to speak. It took another moment, but the Man came back and focused on his two companions in the limousine.

"I trust you have no further doubts about a leak from our end," he told Bolan.

"No, sir."

"It was a close thing," the President said. "I don't mind telling you, I've had to give the program second thoughts."

The comment hung between them like a gauzy curtain, thin enough for shadows to reveal themselves, while their identity remained obscure. There seemed to be no point in answering or challenging the statement. If the White House pulled support for Stony Man, there would be no debate in Congress or the media. No one outside a handful of selected individuals would ever know the difference.

And it wouldn't stop Bolan's war.

He might be forced to do without assistance from the government, but he had gone that route before and managed to survive. In one form or another, he was still committed to the struggle, like a one-man doomsday weapon. No executive decree could stop him, since the Man hadn't initiated Bolan's war. The present chief executive was merely passing through the hellgrounds.

Bolan lived there.

And in time, he knew, he would die there.

But it wouldn't be today.

"I thought about it long and hard," the President went on, "and while I still have some misgivings, I've decided that the program should remain in operation for the moment. Maybe you should take another look at the security review," he told Brognola, "and make sure we don't have any more Joseph Gardners waiting in the wings."

"We're on it, sir."

"Okay, then." He turned back to Bolan. "Can I drop you somewhere?"

"This is fine," the warrior said, nodding toward the Vietnam Memorial, just passing on his right.

A signal to the driver, and the limo pulled to the curb, a second vehicle carrying a half dozen Secret Service agents pulling up behind. The presidential hand was offered and accepted.

"I would like to thank you personally for a job well done. I trust we can avoid unfortunate misunderstandings in the future."

Bolan matched his steady gaze and said, "I hope so, too."

"Goodbye, then. And in case we don't cross paths again, good luck."

A man made his own luck, Bolan thought, and settled for a simple "Thank you, sir."

It was a full day since the "tragic, accidental death" of General Arthur Coltrane at his home in Silver Spring. The media was buying it, and there had been no coverage at all of the assault on Wallace Schroder's Blue Ridge Mountain stronghold. Stony Man was safe . . . for now.

And there were new campaigns, new enemies, already waiting for the Executioner.

Before he chose another target, though, he had some thoughts to share with those who never made it home. About the call of duty and the limits of a man's endurance, the ungodly price some fighting men are called upon to pay.

The friendly ghosts were waiting for him.

Bolan had a feeling they would understand.

**America steps into a nuclear
face-off between ancient foes**

# STONY MAN™ 18
## STINGER

America's finest tactical neutralization arm, Stony Man,
is the President's wild card in the deadly game of global
terrorism. Acting both within and beyond the law, these
dedicated combat and techno warriors operate on one
principle: that terrorists must pay for their crimes.

In September, don't miss
the exciting conclusion to

# D.A. HODGMAN

# STAKEOUT
# SQUAD

## THE COLOR
## OF BLOOD

The law is the first target in a tide of killings engulfing Miami
in the not-to-be-missed conclusion of this urban police
action series. Stakeout Squad becomes shock troops in a
desperate attempt to pull Miami back from hell, but here
even force of arms may not be enough to halt the hate and
bloodshed....

Don't miss THE COLOR OF BLOOD, the final installment of
STAKEOUT SQUAD!

Look for it in September, wherever Gold Eagle books are sold.